D1365073

A Real Basket Case
An Agatha Award Finalist for Best First Novel

"*A Real Basket Case* and its author are a welcome addition to the mystery genre."—*Crimespree Magazine*

"An enjoyable mystery… *A Real Basket Case* should not be missed."—Romance Reviews Today, RomRevToday.com

"A clever, charming debut novel. Quick-paced and well written with clear and comfortable prose, *A Real Basket Case* is a perfect afternoon read for cozy fans."—SpinetinglerMag.com

"A crackling good novel with the kind of twists and turns that make roller coaster rides so scary and so much fun!"—Margaret Coel, author of *The Drowning Man*

"Groundwater brings new meaning to the term menopausal in this flawlessly crafted mystery. Her gutsy, power surging heroine keeps the pressure on until the final chapter."—Kathy Brandt, author of *Swimming with the Dead*

"Beth Groundwater has put together the perfect mixture of humor, thrills, and mystery. A terrific debut!"—Christine Goff, author of the Birdwatcher's Mystery series

WICKED
EDDIES

BETH GROUNDWATER

WICKED EDDIES

MIDNIGHT INK
WOODBURY, MINNESOTA

First Edition
First Printing, 2012

Book design by Donna Burch
Cover design by Lisa Novak
Cover image © Radius Images/PunchStock.com
Editing by Connie Hill

Midnight Ink, an imprint of Llewellyn Worldwide Ltd.

Library of Congress Cataloging-in-Publication Data

Groundwater, Beth.
  Wicked eddies : a Rocky Mountain outdoor adventures mystery / Beth Ground-water. — 1st ed.
      p.   cm. — (Rocky Mountain outdoor adventures mystery; 2)
   ISBN 978-0-7387-2163-7 (alk. paper)
1. White-water canoeing—Fiction. 2. Colorado—Fiction. I. Title.
   PS3607.R677W53   2012
   813'.6—dc23   2011046859

Midnight Ink
Llewellyn Worldwide Ltd.
2143 Wooddale Drive
Woodbury, MN 55125-2989
www.midnightinkbooks.com

Printed in the United States of America

To Neil, with love.
I couldn't choose a better paddling partner with whom
to navigate the turbulent waters of the river of life.

ONE

To paraphrase a deceased patriot, I regret that I have only
one life to give to my fly-fishing.
—ROBERT TRAVER

A SHINY BLACK RAVEN shot a raucous caw toward the blue white-water raft that nudged its nose into the Arkansas River bank. Disturbed, the bird flapped its wide wings and swooped to another large peachleaf willow farther downstream, where it scolded the two interlopers in the raft.

Ignoring the Native American's keeper of secrets, Mandy Tanner stowed her bow paddle and stepped out onto the muddy bank. She planted a sandaled foot against an exposed sandbar willow root to keep from slipping, then pulled on the bow line to beach the raft.

The stern paddler, Steve Hadley, her boss and the chief river ranger of the Arkansas Headwaters Recreation Area, swept his paddle in the calm water of the eddy to give her an assist.

Mandy secured the bow line to a nearby wooden post sunk into the river's shoreline at the Vallie Bridge campground for just that purpose. Then she stretched and drank in the sight of the collegiate range of the Colorado Rockies to the east. The fourteen-thousand-foot-plus peaks of Mt. Harvard, Mt. Oxford, Mt. Yale, Mt. Princeton, and Mt. Columbia knifed into the clear blue sky. Mandy reluctantly dragged her gaze down to the muddy earth and held the raft still for her boss.

"This should be an easy clean-up," Steve said while he clambered out of the raft.

Since the campground was solely walk-in or boat-in access, it had only sixteen primitive tent campsites partly shaded by four large peachtree willows. Even the pit toilets were located at the day use area next to the road about a hundred yards away. Vallie Bridge was the least used of the six campgrounds maintained by the AHRA.

"So you only assign yourself the easy ones?" Mandy flashed a teasing grin at Steve.

Of course, as Steve's partner on this end-of-the summer trash pickup excursion, she benefited from the light assignment, too. Usually she got the worst grunt work and shifts, this being her first season as a river ranger. That meant a lot of sweaty tree and brush removal and busy weekend river patrols dealing with clueless, and often inebriated, tourists.

"Seniority has its privileges." Steve unzipped his personal floatation device, shucked it, and tossed it into the raft. The short sleeves of his dark green ranger shirt exposed well-tanned and muscled arms.

2

Heat waves shimmered off the parched ground. Mandy followed Steve's lead, removing her PFD and lifting her blonde ponytail off her damp neck. An early September Monday in Chaffee County, this one was showing signs of being a record-breaking scorcher. While Steve took a long pull on his water bottle, Mandy shielded her eyes from the sun's glare and scanned the Vallie Bridge campground. All of the tent sites looked deserted.

With the annoyed raven now quiet, the only sound was the hot wind soughing through the nearby willow trees, bringing with it the scent of baking dry vegetation, and something else …

Mandy wrinkled her nose. "Something smells rank."

Bent over the raft unlashing a dry bag of supplies, Steve stopped, sat back on his haunches, and sniffed. "Probably a dead animal." He pulled a shovel out from under one of the raft's inflated gunnels and tossed it by Mandy's feet. "You can have the pleasure of burying it."

"Gee, thanks."

"Hey, I already pulled latrine duty."

Mandy nodded. Steve was right. He'd buried the dog and human waste they'd found at the last stop. Some people were truly animals.

The two of them had worked their way down the river from the Rincon Campground, cleaning up ad-hoc, undeveloped campsites along the shores. All AHRA campers were supposed to carry out their trash, and campers outside of developed camping areas were required to use a portable toilet and fire pan. But not all of them followed the rules. Thus the need for periodic clean-ups along the river.

Mandy helped Steve unload their supplies, including work gloves, heavy-duty trash bags, and their lunches stowed in waterproof containers. After pulling on her gloves and shouldering the shovel, she set off toward the dead animal odor. It seemed to be coming from the back of the campground.

Steve headed upstream with a trash bag slung over his arm.

Pausing at the first campsite, Mandy stuffed some slimy baked bean cans and an empty marshmallow bag in her green garbage bag. At the next site, she picked up cigarette butts and beer bottles crawling with ants.

Why do those two types of trash always seem to go together? She shook off the disgusted thought and sniffed again. The smell of death was more distinct, overpowering the fresh fishy tang of river water.

Mandy swiped sweat off her forehead, drank a swig from her water bottle, and took off again. Her river sandals crunched across sand, gravel, and sparse grass tufts. When she neared the willow tree in front of the fence separating the campground from private land, she saw a large lump on the ground. It lay in a depression on the far side of the tree, partially obscured by the wide, black-ridged trunk and some baby willows sprouting from the roots. The lump was dark and light blue, colors of cloth.

A sleeping bag? With a person on top? Maybe someone was sleeping off a late night of drinking.

Her suspicion was confirmed when she spied a couple of plastic six-pack rings by the nearest campfire ring. Mandy stooped to pick up the rings and stow them in her bag. The death smell was stronger now, coming in nauseating waves as the hot wind shook the willow's limbs and rustled the leaves. She heard a low hum of

4

buzzing flies. One flew past her nose, startling her. She scanned the area, but couldn't spot an animal carcass.

That person on the sleeping bag must really be dead to the world if he can't smell this. She hollered, "Hello? Ranger here. Sorry to disturb you."

Nothing. No movement from the bag.

The hairs rose on the back of Mandy's neck. Something was wrong here.

She ducked under a low-hanging branch and stepped into the welcome shade. Her eyes adjusted to the dimmed lighting while she rounded the trunk, approaching the sleeping bag from the foot. With her next step, observations flooded her senses.

The person was large and lying on his back, wearing blue jeans and socks. A rotund stomach strained against a blue-checked shirt.

A stick or something poked into the air near the head.

The death stench grew overpowering.

A dark stain spread out on the ground. *Blood?*

Mandy's heart thudded. Her ears buzzed along with the angry cloud of flies which, disturbed by her approach, rose.

She looked down at the face, now no longer obscured by flies. A middle-aged man's face, it was bloated and gray, distorted, the lips open in a silent scream.

At the neck, an angry red gash crawled with maggots. Embedded in the gash was the blade of a small camping hatchet, the handle pointing straight at Mandy.

She staggered back, dropped her shovel, tripped over a rock, thudded on her rump. Tearing her gaze from the horror, she turned her head and heaved up her breakfast.

———

Sitting with her back against a willow tree and her knees drawn up before her, Mandy stared out over the water, hoping to release the grisly image burned on her retinas. She tried to force her thoughts to flow with the calming movement of the water sparkling in the sunlight. The river's story was that life goes on, regardless. Death, however, still stalked her mind.

Footsteps approached and someone cleared his throat beside her. She looked up.

Steve leaned down to rest a hand on her shoulder, his brow furrowed. "Feeling better?"

Mandy nodded, even though it wasn't true.

He squatted and joined her in contemplating the river. The last hour flashed through her synapses. After her stomach had stopped contracting, she'd hollered Steve's name over and over while she scrambled away on all fours, putting distance between herself and the dead man.

When Steve came running, she'd warned him before he saw the body, so he could steel himself. Then he radioed headquarters, which dispatched calls to the fire department for an ambulance, the county coroner, and the Chaffee County Sheriff's Office. Mandy and Steve had waited for the caravan to drive, with lights flashing, across the County Road 45 bridge to the day use area parking lot, then up the hundred-yard gravel walking path to the campground. The vehicle occupants got out, to a cacophony of slamming doors, and pulled out a stretcher and forensic equipment.

Detective Victor Quintana had quickly gone to work, directing evidence collection and telling Mandy and Steve to stay put. By now, it was well past lunchtime, but Mandy hadn't the stomach to eat the PBJ sandwich baking in the World War II relic waterproof ammo box that served as her lunchbox.

She'd noticed Steve hadn't touched his lunch either.

Quintana crunched up and lowered his stocky, middle-aged frame onto a downed log across from Mandy and Steve. Sweat circles bloomed under the armpits of his dark blue uniform. He swiped a handkerchief across his swarthy brow, then stowed it in his pants pocket.

Stroking his black mustache, he peered at her. "Second death in your first season. Might be a record, Mandy."

"At least this one was already dead when I found him." Mandy winced. "Sorry, that came out bad."

"I know what you mean," Quintana said with a nod. He took out a pen and his trusty notebook and opened it to a blank page. "Walk me through the discovery, starting with getting out of the raft." He waved his hand toward their raft, still bobbing next to the river bank.

Mandy pointed out where she'd walked and gave as many details as she could remember. From her past experience with a prior murder case, she knew he needed them. Quintana stayed silent and took notes during her narrative. She ended, red-faced, with, "Sorry about the puke."

Quintana pshawed. "Doesn't smell any worse than the body. We're used to it at violent death scenes. Usually from the first responder, who hasn't had a chance to prepare himself—or herself."

He pointed at the work gloves lying beside her. "You keep those on the whole time?"

"Yes," Mandy replied. "Until I got here."

"What about you?" he asked Steve.

"Same thing." Steve slapped the gloves stashed in one of his cargo shorts pockets.

"So neither one of you touched the body or anything near the campsite?"

"Right," they answered in unison.

"Good, don't need to worry about prints from you two, then. That your trash bag, Mandy?" Quintana pointed to the heavy-duty black trash bag next to where she'd thrown up.

"Yes, and that shovel next to it."

"What about that bag?" Quintana pointed to another trash bag, dark green and smaller, that sat farther away.

"No, that's not ours." Mandy stood and craned her neck to get a better look at it. It was open and some of the contents were spilled out. *So that's where the beer cans had ended up.* She sat back down. "Why would he pick up his beer cans and not the plastic rings?"

Quintana shrugged. "Could be he was only interested in recycling the cans. Could be he wasn't the one who collected the cans."

"You think the killer collected them?" Steve asked.

"Maybe. Maybe someone else." Quintana pointed his chin at a technician, who was carefully transferring a flowered garden glove from the ground next to the bag of cans into an evidence bag. "We'll see if any prints are on that glove or the cans and if they match the victim or not. We haven't found any direct evidence he had company at the campsite—yet."

He looked at Steve. "I'll need the reservation form, if there is one."

Steve raised a skeptical brow. "If there is one, I'll get it to you."

Mandy knew folks often used the AHRA campsites, especially Vallie Bridge, without making a reservation or paying. They played the odds, waiting to see if a ranger checked before coming up with a story about forgetting to pay and forking over the dough.

She had an idea. "I picked up some trash at a couple of the other campsites that may have been recent, especially those slimy bean cans. You should check if there are reservation forms for any of the other campsites. They may have seen something."

Quintana winked at her. "You beat me to it, Mandy. I was about to ask Steve for any other forms for reservations here this weekend. Now you're thinking like a cop."

Mandy felt her cheeks warming and glanced away. She noticed another technician collecting and cataloging a fly-fishing rod, waders, tackle box, a small cooler, and other gear. So the man had been a fly fisherman. The fly fishermen she knew were mostly gentle souls, the peaceful time on the river bleeding anger and angst out of their systems. Who would have wanted to kill him so violently, with so much rage?

She shuddered.

Quintana raised a questioning brow, but she feigned nonchalance, took a sip of water from her water bottle, and focused her attention back on the river. A ripple broke the surface, and a fin flashed. A splashy rise. The fish were feeding, probably on a late summer caddis fly hatch. The insects rose from the water in busy spirals.

Another man walked up, tall and rangy with a pock-marked face and a serious expression. Quintana made the introductions. "Mandy, this is Paul Unger, the county coroner. Paul, Mandy Tanner was first on the scene. You and Steve know each other already, right?"

"Right. Hi, Steve." Unger shifted his clipboard to his other hand so he could shake Mandy's. "Nice to meet you, Mandy. Sorry it couldn't have been under better circumstances."

He focused on Quintana. "You wanted an estimated time of death. Given the insect activity, I'd say sometime yesterday, probably afternoon. The pathologist might be able to narrow that down some after we get the body to the lab in Pueblo."

Quintana gazed at the river. "So the guy probably set up camp sometime Saturday, drank some beers, and ate some hot dogs."

"How do you know that?" Mandy asked.

"We found mustard and bags for buns and hot dogs in the cooler," Quintana replied.

Mandy remembered the plastic rings. "You think he drank two whole six-packs?"

"Over the space of two days, he could have, or maybe he had company." Quintana looked at Unger. "I'll need a stomach content analysis and blood alcohol level."

"Sure thing." The coroner made a note on his clipboard.

"Anyway," Quintana continued, "the guy slept here Saturday night, probably ate the Hostess cupcakes, whose wrappers are also in the cooler, for breakfast. Then he fished Sunday morning, releasing any he caught, because there's none in the cooler."

"Most fly fishers practice catch-and-release on the river," Steve said. "If they're fishing for food, they go to one of the lakes."

Paul cocked his head. "Why's that?"

"In the river, the fish tend to hang out in certain spots, and the anglers get to know those spots. If you take a fish from a spot, you can ruin someone else's fun."

"Back to our fisherman," Quintana interjected. "After lunch—probably the rest of the hot dogs—he lay down for a nap, which is when someone axed him. You agree with that scenario, Paul?"

Unger nodded.

Quintana smoothed his mustache again. "Any idea what the residue on his face is?"

Mandy gave them both a questioning look.

"You probably didn't notice," Paul said, "but something was sprayed on the man's face. Something slimy. It's obviously not bug repellant, because the flies aren't deterred."

"Sunscreen?" Steve offered.

Unger shrugged. "We'll do a chemical analysis on it."

"And we'll look for a spray can," Quintana said.

One of the techs at the crime scene, a woman, called for Unger, and he left. Mandy admired the woman's fortitude, which was obviously better than hers.

"Okay." Quintana clicked his pen. "Now I want to hear Steve's story. Then we'll go over both of them again."

Mandy sighed. At this rate, they'd be at this campground all day, being grilled by both the detective and the broiling hot sun.

———

Late that afternoon, after Quintana had released them, Mandy and Steve paddled their raft down to their take-out point on the Arkansas River and returned to the ranger district headquarters

11

in Salida. From there, Mandy drove her dusty, blue, nine-year-old Subaru wagon to the rafting outfitter business now jointly owned by her boyfriend, Rob Juarez, and herself. Her beloved Uncle Bill had died in June, leaving his near-failing rafting business to her. Given the sorry state of his operation, Rob and her accountant brother, David, had convinced Mandy to merge with Rob's rafting businesses.

All of her uncle's stock—rafts, paddles, wetsuits, lifejackets, vehicles, and more—had been moved to Rob's larger business location. He'd hired on Uncle Bill's rafting guides and transferred the trip reservations to his schedule, notifying customers of the change. David had combined the books of the two businesses, Rob continued as manager, and she kept her job as a seasonal river ranger and helped out when she could.

Mandy had been surprised at how easy the merger was—easy for everyone but her, that is. She still drove to her uncle's old house about once a week. She'd walk through the empty rooms and vacant equipment yard, yearning for a sense of his presence. She deeply missed being able to lay her troubles at his gouty feet, and gain comfort and unconditional love along with the down-to-earth advice only he could give her.

Mandy parked in the gravel lot and got out to look at the large, freshly painted sign across the top of the building that read "RM Outdoor Adventures." The initials stood for both of their names as well as for the Rocky Mountains. Rob had insisted on choosing a new name for the business, one that reflected their joint ownership. Mandy had balked at first at the cost of creating a new logo, revising Rob's website and letterhead, and mailing out notices to the customers and suppliers for the two businesses. But, looking up now at the sign and feeling pride well up in her chest, she was glad they had.

She walked up the steps to the wide wooden porch of the building Rob had repaired and painted himself when he bought it a few years back. She stepped aside to let a laughing, chattering group of tourists pass by on their way out. Obviously pleased with their rafting trip, they were passing photos around and commenting on them, barely aware they had almost mowed her down.

Smiling, Mandy pushed through the swinging saloon doors that gave the place a Western feel, along with the kitschy rusted ranch tools and horse tack Rob had hung on the walls. He kept a battered and stained ten-gallon hat in his office, too, to don when he greeted customers.

Standing behind the counter that ran along one side of the room, Gonzo Gordon pocketed his tip and waved at her. "Howdy, Mandy."

With his bushy blonde Rastafarian dreadlocks, sunburned face, baggy faded red shorts, and holey T-shirt, Gonzo epitomized the no-worries rafting guide. Though his voice was hearty, his eyes were still guarded. It had taken Mandy almost firing him to get him to finally start attending AA meetings for his drinking problem, and that still embarrassed him. But, he had stayed dry for the last couple of months, so Mandy had agreed with Rob to give Gonzo another chance.

She approached Gonzo and shook his hand. "Good run today?" She poked her thumb over her shoulder. "The customers looked happy."

He slapped his shorts pocket. "And they tipped well, too, so I'm happy."

"I'm sure you earned it. You're the best." Mandy knew Gonzo would need lots of assurances that she trusted him and valued his work before their friendship would be completely healed, but she was determined to do her part. "Where's Rob?"

"Out back, stowing some gear." Gonzo peered at her. "You don't look so good. Bad day?"

Before Mandy could reply, Rob walked in the back door, running a hand through his wavy black hair. When he spotted her, a grin split his face. "¡Mi querida!"

Though well-muscled, he could move fast. He caught Mandy in an embrace, lifted her off her feet, and whirled her in a circle, making her ponytail fly out behind her as she released a giggle. He set her down, leaned over, and planted a big smacker on her lips.

Mandy already felt a hundred percent better. She smiled up at him and ran her hands over the standing wave tattoos that danced when Rob flexed his biceps. "That's the first time you've lifted me since you were shot in the shoulder." Mandy still shuddered over the memory of how scared she'd been when Rob was shot in June, wondering if he would survive.

Rob rolled his shoulders. "Still twinges some. I don't have full mobility yet, but the physical therapist says I'm making good progress. She said today that I could start lifting heavier things than a bag of groceries, so I thought I'd begin with you." He gave her another sloppy kiss.

Even though they'd been dating almost five months, she still wasn't a hundred percent comfortable with his public displays of affection. "Good thing the customers have left."

"Aw, who cares?" He searched her face and the smile left his lips. He took a step back. "What's wrong?"

"Are my emotions written all over my face? Gonzo just finished asking if I had a bad day." Mandy released her hold on Rob and hugged herself. "Yes, I've had a very bad day. I discovered a dead fisherman at the Vallie Bridge campground this morning."

Gonzo let out a low, long whistle. "In the river?"

Mandy shook her head. "At a campsite. He'd been dead awhile and there were flies—" She stopped. "Let's just say it was gross. I lost my breakfast."

"Natural causes?" Rob asked.

"No, it was definitely murder. Quintana and his gang worked over the scene pretty thoroughly and kept Steve and me there the rest of the day, asking us questions over and over."

Gonzo came out from behind the counter. "They find any clues?"

"Maybe," Mandy replied. "Besides Steve's trash bag and mine, they found another one that had beer cans in it."

Gonzo sucked in a breath. "Anything else?"

"Yeah, a woman's gardening glove, which was odd. They're going to check the glove and cans for fingerprints."

"Bummer." Furrowing his brows, Gonzo pulled on one of his dreadlocks.

Mandy put a hand on his arm. "What? What is it?"

"I don't know if I should tell you." Gonzo gave her a worried glance then looked down, finding something very interesting all of a sudden on the bottom of one of his Teva sandals.

Mandy's grip tightened on Gonzo's arm. "If you know something, you should tell me—or the police. Otherwise you could be charged with aiding and abetting the killer."

Gonzo pulled his arm away from her. "No way would Newt kill someone."

One of Rob's eyebrows rose. "Newt?"

"Cripes, now I've done it." Gonzo shook his head.

Mandy planted her hands on her hips. "Spill it, Gonzo."

He sighed. "My good buddy Newt Nowak told me Saturday that he was going to do one of his recycling collection runs yesterday, from Rincon to Cotopaxi." His voice trailed off.

"And?"

Gonzo glanced up. "And he's got this pair of large old lady gardening gloves that he wears when he goes. I've teased him about them, but he says he found them in the rag bin at Goodwill and they work just fine."

"Flowered?" Mandy asked.

Gonzo frowned and nodded. "Flowered."

———

While Rob and Gonzo went out in the yard to finish hosing down and stowing the gear from the recent rafting trip, Mandy tried to call Quintana at his office. When he didn't answer, she left a message that she had something important to tell him. Then she helped the men finish up. After confirming their pool-playing get-together with the gang the next night at the Vic—the Victoria Tavern—a dour-faced Gonzo left.

Rob leaned back, resting his elbows on the counter, and cocked his head at Mandy. "You going to tell Quintana about Newt?"

"I have to. I'll stop by his office tomorrow morning." She noticed that on the counter next to Rob rested not only the trip schedule book, but also the ledger. "Let's change the subject." She pointed her chin at the ledger. "You've been going over the books?"

Rob tossed a glance over his shoulder at the books. "Yeah. I want to talk to you about that. You know, we've discussed expanding the business, adding adventure travel trips, so we could provide work for our best guides all year-round. I think we should start with climbing trips this fall and ice-climbing this winter. I've been pricing out the equipment and guide training, and we can almost swing it."

"Almost?"

Rob nodded and gave her a thoughtful look. "A few thousand more would do the trick."

"Where would we get the money?"

"There's a way we could get that and more." He pushed off the counter, came to her, and put his arms around her. "If you're ready."

Mandy had no idea where he was headed with this. "Ready to do what?"

"Ready to sell your uncle's place."

A hot rush of panic poured over Mandy, flushing her skin and turning her knees to rubber. She sagged against Rob, but he held her firm. "S-s-sell?" she stammered.

Rob led her to one of the waiting benches lining the wall, set her down, and clasped her hands. "I know you have a lot of attachment to Bill's place, but it's been sitting empty for a couple of months now. You're not going to live there; you've got your own place. And we don't need it for RM Outdoor Adventures."

He paused, as if evaluating her reaction. When she didn't respond, he said, "We could sure use the cash from the sale, though.

You know that making those unexpected repairs to your uncle's bus ate into our reserves quite a bit."

Mandy finally regained use of her tongue. "Yeah, sorry about that. All his equipment was on its last legs. You're probably sorry you ever suggested the merger by now." She gave him a rueful smile."

He squeezed her hands. "Never, *mi querida*. I like being your partner."

That was a loaded statement.

"Not all of the money from the sale needs to go into the business," Rob continued. "You could use some of it to fix up your place. You could invest some of it, start a retirement account or whatever. It would give you financial security." He paused, letting his words sink in.

Being a self-made man, financial security was very important to Rob. His advice was sound, but Mandy shook her head. "I'm not ready, Rob."

He cupped her chin in one hand, stroking her cheek with his thumb. "Bill's not there anymore, Mandy."

But I wish he was. Mandy leaned her face against Rob's roughened palm. She inhaled his familiar scent of soap, leather, and the grassy outdoors. "Still, I need more time."

His eyes were sad, understanding, but his teeth gnawed his lip in frustration. He stood up and shoved his hands in his jeans pockets. "Okay, take some time, but not too much. If RM Outdoor Adventures is going to survive long-term, it needs to expand—and soon. Your brother agrees."

"I'll think about it, Rob. Really, I will."

"Okay, that's all I'm asking." He checked his watch. "I'm due at Mama's house soon. Can you lock up?"

"Sure."

He gave her a quick kiss, then walked out the back door toward the equipment yard where his truck was parked.

Mandy knotted her fingers together in her lap. *What should I do, Uncle Bill?*

TWO

If fishing is like religion, then fly-fishing is high church.
—TOM BROKAW

A WET LICK ON Mandy's face awakened her the next morning. She rubbed her damp cheek against the shoulder of her lamb-print sleep shirt. "Cut it out, Lucky."

Her golden retriever was unrepentant. When Mandy peeked, the dog's tail was violently swishing back and forth, carrying his whole back end with it. He stared intently at her, mouth open in a wide grin and panting in anticipation of some morning play time. She gave up pretending to be mad at him and reached a hand out of the covers to scratch his ears.

The radio alarm clicked on.

"How do you do that, dog?" Lucky's timing was impeccable. He usually rose from his dog pillow at the foot of Mandy's bed just before the alarm went off.

She stretched and her hand hit the empty pillow next to her. Rob hadn't come to her place last night because he'd had his regular Monday dinner in Pueblo with his mama and whoever else showed up from his large, extended Hispanic family. He had taken Mandy with him a few times. She had enjoyed meeting some of the clan, though she still had trouble keeping all of their names straight. From the welcome she'd received, Mandy knew Rob's devoutly Catholic mama approved of her, though not of Rob sleeping with her before marriage.

Mandy got out of bed. Frowning, she wondered if Rob's mama had pressured him again last night about proposing. "I wouldn't be surprised, given the hints she kept dropping last time I was there," she said out loud.

Lucky tilted his head and lifted his ears as if trying to figure out what she was talking about.

Mandy laughed. "You know, the lady who gave me a large beef bone for you last time. She's already got you on her side, and you haven't even met her."

Lucky nosed her again with impatience. Morning sunlight was already streaming through the window, and he had business to conduct outside.

Mandy went through her morning routine—letting Lucky out in the fenced-in yard and feeding him, watering the marigolds she'd planted alongside her concrete patio—in between spoonfuls of raisin bran and milk. She tied her shoulder-length hair into a ponytail and donned her off-the-water ranger uniform consisting of black jeans and a black shirt with the AHRA logo. During it all, she mulled over Rob's suggestion to sell her uncle's place. It made a lot of sense, and her head agreed with him.

Her heart, however, was another matter.

On the drive to the Chaffee County Sheriff's Office, she popped in one of Pink's CDs. She turned the female pop rocker's music up loud so she wouldn't have to think anymore about selling Uncle Bill's home. She parked in front of the old blonde-brick Chaffee County Administration Building on Crestone Avenue that housed the whole county government. After entering the building, she climbed up the wide, worn stairs to the third floor where the detectives' offices were located. She tapped on the frosted glass door of Detective Quintana's office and entered after his "Come in" invitation.

He rose from his gray metal desk under the window to clear a stack of case files off the guest chair placed within easy reach next to his own chair. After pushing the guest chair back a few inches, he waved for her to sit down. "What's the 'something important' you need to tell me, Mandy?"

"I've got some information on the fisherman case." She told him about Gonzo's friend, Newt Nowak.

Being the first responder, Mandy was a member of the investigative team for this case, and she had a vested interest in getting it solved. She and Quintana would need to keep in touch until it was closed, so she could include whatever he found out in her incident report. Besides, the AHRA rangers and the Chaffee County Sheriff's deputies were good buddies. They trained together, invited each other to summer barbecues, and jointly investigated serious crimes that occurred within the park boundaries.

Quintana wrote down Newt's name. "I'll be sure to question him. Thanks for the lead."

"Did you find out who the fisherman was?" Mandy asked.

Quintana leaned back in his office chair, making it creak. "Howie Abbott. You know his niece, I think. Cynthia?"

"Yeah, yeah I do." Mandy nibbled on her lip. How was her best friend going to take the news about her murdered uncle? "Does she know?"

"I informed his closest relative, his sister Brenda Ellis, and her family yesterday. They may have called Cynthia after I left their house. It was not a good scene."

A memory of the grief that had totally incapacitated Mandy after her Uncle Bill's death washed over her, rendering her momentarily speechless. She blinked back threatening tears and clenched her hands.

As if sensing her need for a moment to compose herself, Quintana gazed at an email displayed on his computer monitor before giving her an appraising glance. "Do you know the Ellis family?"

Mandy shook her head. "Cynthia told me when her aunt's family moved back to Salida in the spring, but I only met Brenda's husband, Lee, briefly, at an Arkansas River Outfitter Association function in May. They've been living in New Mexico the past few years."

Quintana nodded. "They never got used to it, Brenda said, and they moved back to the Arkansas River Valley to be near family, her brother Howie and niece Cynthia. It was Cynthia's father who was related to Howie and Brenda, right?"

"Cynthia's dad was the oldest, Howie was in the middle, and Brenda was the youngest."

"And now she's the only one left. As I recall, Cynthia's dad passed away awhile ago."

"Yes, of lung cancer three years ago. Cynthia went back east for the funeral." Mandy remembered trying to cheer up her friend back then and wondered how badly this second loss would affect her. "Cynthia's parents were living in Connecticut. Her mom stayed there after the funeral, said she'd put down roots. Cynthia and her mom aren't close."

"Well, apparently Brenda and Howie were close. She seemed pretty broken up by the news. Plus, this bad news was a second blow to them. Brenda's fifteen-year-old daughter, Faith, ran away from home sometime Saturday night, and they haven't seen or heard from her since."

"Bummer. Was she unhappy about the move?"

"Seemed to be. Brenda said the girl became sullen and uncommunicative a few weeks after they moved here." Quintana extracted a thin case folder on his desk out from under the thick one with Howie Abbott's name on it. The thin folder was labeled with Faith Ellis's name. "Since Faith had been gone almost forty-eight hours by yesterday, I said I'd open a missing person's case file."

He pulled out a sheet of paper containing the photo of a teenage girl sitting on a large boulder with the sunlit choppy water of the Arkansas River behind it. "Maybe you can distribute this among the rangers and ask them to keep an eye out for her."

"Sure." Mandy took the photo. The girl was petite and thin but had a shapely figure. Her long, straight brown hair was swept back over one shoulder. A large mole under her left eye somehow added to her beauty instead of detracting from it. "Did Howie have a family of his own?"

Quintana folded his arms awkwardly over all the equipment on his uniform belt. "No, Brenda said he was somewhat of a loner, and had a temper on him. No woman seemed to tolerate him for long."

"Think one of them was mad enough to hatchet him?"

"I kind of doubt it. Brenda said he hadn't dated anyone steadily for a couple of years. But, I'll sniff around for old girlfriends, of course." Quintana leaned forward, resting his hands on his knees. "Here's something interesting. You remember Unger saying Howie had something slimy on his face?"

Mandy nodded. *Where is this going?*

"Well, once Paul gets a bee in his bonnet, he goes after it until he's satisfied with the answer. He had the lab test the substance right away. Guess what it was."

"Probably not something as mundane as sunscreen or bug repellant, but I don't know what else it could have been. Was it some kind of food he didn't wash off after eating?"

"Nope, it was all over his face." Quintana waited, stroking his mustache and obviously relishing his secret.

Mandy shrugged. "I give up."

"It was pepper spray." A wide grin split the detective's face.

"Pepper spray? Why pepper spray?"

"Curious, isn't it? And what's more, Paul says it was sprayed on after Howie was hatcheted. Droplets overlaid the wound's initial blood flow, and Paul found some inside Howie's mouth and on the handle of the hatchet."

"That's really odd. You think the killer did it?"

Quintana cocked his head. "Let's see if you reach the same conclusion I did. Why would the killer squirt Howie Abbott with pepper spray after swinging a hatchet into his neck?"

Mandy flinched at the violent scene Quintana's words invoked. "Because he was deranged or really, really mad at Howie?"

"Maybe. What other reason can you come up with?"

She closed her eyes and tried to envision the attack. She put herself in the role of the killer, wielding the hatchet, hearing Howie scream and stepping back to pull out the spray can....

Her eyes flew open. "You think the killer was afraid that if the hatchet didn't do the trick, Howie might come after him?"

Quintana slapped the arm of his chair. "Bingo. So what does that say about the killer?"

Mandy pondered this for a moment. "That he—or she—may be smaller, older, or weaker than Howie, not confident of defending himself or herself against the man, even though Howie's life was pouring out of his neck."

"And that not only did the killer bring a hatchet to the scene, he brought pepper spray, so this probably was a premeditated act."

"I'm not so sure," Mandy replied after a moment's thought. "Some women always carry pepper spray in their purses. And it can be used against bears, so both the spray and the hatchet might have already been at the campsite. The killer could have made a last-minute decision and discovered everything he or she needed right there. Did you find any evidence yet about who else was there?"

"No, but we do know someone else was at that campsite. We matched Howie Abbott's fingerprints to some of those on the beer cans that were in the trash bag, but we found other prints that don't match his. Neither Howie nor his friend reserved or paid for the campsite, though, so we don't know yet who was drinking with him."

"Could you match the prints to the CBI database?" Mandy knew the Automated Fingerprint Identification System maintained by the

Colorado Bureau of Investigation wasn't complete by any means, but sometimes they got lucky.

"Not yet," Quintana answered. "But we haven't finished pulling all of the prints off all the evidence. And, it takes time to do the comparison analysis."

"What about campers at other campsites?"

"Steve only found one reservation for last weekend at Vallie Bridge." Quintana peered at her. "You guys need to police your campgrounds better."

Mandy rolled her eyes. "Tell me about it. We know we're losing revenue like crazy, but it takes money to make money. Right now we can't afford to pay for extra ranger shifts to do campground checks. And the word is getting out that campers can get away with not paying."

"I sympathize. We've got the same problem with parking violations in Salida. Anyway, I assigned a patrol officer to interview the family who made that one reservation. Hopefully they saw something—or someone."

"So, nothing yet." Mandy sighed and stood. She tapped the photo of the missing girl that she held. "I'm going in to do the paperwork on the body discovery. I'll copy and post this photo while I'm at headquarters. We've also got some big meeting this afternoon about the fly-fishing tournament next week. You involved in any way?"

Quintana shook his head. "Too busy trying to catch a killer to catch flies—or fish, for that matter." He stood. "Thanks for the tip about Newt Nowak. We'll keep in touch. You going to see Cynthia soon?"

"Tonight."

"Please give her my condolences about her uncle."

While Mandy walked back to her car, she rehearsed what she could say to Cynthia about her uncle's death, but everything came out lame. Even though Mandy had been to hell and back after her own beloved uncle's death and could relate, Cynthia had never mentioned her uncle and how close she was to him. So, Mandy had no idea how upset her friend might be upon hearing about his death—by the hand of a hatchet and pepper-spray wielding assailant.

What a way to go! An involuntary shudder shook Mandy's spine.

———

Mandy slipped through the conference room doorway at the Arkansas Headwaters Recreation Area headquarters building a few minutes after two. Juggling a much-needed mug of coffee and a notepad and pen, she searched for an empty chair. All the chairs around the long oval table were taken, as were most along the two side walls and the back wall in the crowded room. Spotting an open seat along the far wall under the window, she shuffled sideways past knees and conference table chair backs, nodding to familiar faces, until she could plop her butt in the empty chair.

A fireman she'd gone through whitewater rescue training with that spring winked at her. "Welcome to the sardine can."

"Let's just hope it doesn't start to smell like one," Mandy replied.

She took a sip of her coffee and wished she'd thought to make it an iced coffee. With all these bodies, the room would heat up soon. The room was crammed with rangers, firemen, ambulance crew, sheriff's deputies, and anyone else involved with emergency rescue situations in the Arkansas River Valley who wasn't currently out on assignment.

Mandy spotted Steve Hadley standing at the front of the room. He was chatting with the Chaffee County Sheriff and the Fire Chief of the Chaffee County Fire Protection District, both of whom she knew by sight. Mandy didn't recognize the older woman with smartly coiffed gray hair, dressed in a stylish pant suit, who was standing with them.

The woman rapped her knuckles on the conference table to get people's attention. "Okay, let's get the meeting started so you can all go back to your important duties as quickly as possible. For those of you who don't know me, I'm Sandra Sechrest, Chair of the Chaffee County Visitor's Bureau. The purpose of this meeting is to brief all of you on the upcoming Rocky Mountain Cup fly-fishing tournament and make sure our emergency response plans are in place."

The woman went on to introduce her cohorts standing with her at the front of the room and to lay out the schedule. The tournament events would start the next Monday with judge and volunteer training, followed by two days of practice fishing by the competitors and two days of competition. The whole shebang would culminate in an award ceremony Friday night at the Salida SteamPlant, an electrical power plant that had been converted into a performing arts and events center. After Sechrest finished, each of the emergency response chiefs described their plans to support the event and what they expected from their troops.

When Steve's turn came, he started off with a question, "What's one of the most deadly sports in the world?"

Mandy knew the answer, but stayed quiet. Someone yelled out, "whitewater rafting," a good guess, but not good enough.

"It's fishing," Steve said, nodding while surprised murmurs filled the room, "usually from the fatal combination of boats, alcohol, and people who don't know how to swim. Now, given that we have serious competitors participating in this event, I expect that alcohol won't play a large part until after the award ceremony."

A few snorts and chuckles punctuated that remark.

"However," Steve continued, "we still have boats on the float-fishing practice and competition days giving us the same problems whitewater rafting boats do—hitting underwater obstacles and pitching their occupants into the water. And most of these teams are unfamiliar with the upper Arkansas, its rapids, and its hazards. So, I'm increasing river ranger patrols on the river during the competition.

"And then there are wading fishermen on the shore fishing days." Steve shook his head and tsked. "I hate waders. As the old-timers know, we usually have at least one fly-fisherman die each season, from either getting a foot trapped or tripping while standing in the river wearing waders. The fisherman falls in the river, the waders fill up with water, dragging the wearer underwater, and then he drowns."

A solemn silence descended on the group. Mandy, and no doubt many others, was remembering the most recent drowning of a local fly-fisherman that spring, leaving a widow and two teen-aged children.

"I want all of you river rangers to be on the alert," Steve said, "for boaters not wearing their personal flotation devices and for standing fishermen wading in too deep. If you see a boater without a PFD, you give them a warning. If you see someone wearing waders without a belt, suggest they put on a belt immediately. Tell them it will stop most of the water from flowing into the waders if they fall and may very well save their life. If they're standing in moving water past their knees, you give them a warning."

One of the river rangers raised a hand. "We're bound to get complaints."

"Don't worry about complaints," Steve replied. "I'll deal with them. We want folks going home from this competition with a memory of the big one that got away, not the big guy who passed away."

Ouch. Mandy cringed. *Had Steve rehearsed that line?*

He handed some sheets of paper to the first ranger sitting at the conference table. "River rangers, each of you take one of these. They're the shift schedules for next week. Some of you will be working extra shifts to make sure we have adequate coverage along all of the competition beats—that's river sections for those of you unfamiliar with the lingo of fly-fishing competitions. Given the economic times, I thought some of you might appreciate the overtime."

Mandy checked her schedule and saw she had an extra shift next week. She could always use the additional money, so she didn't mind. Poor Lucky would be left in the yard alone an extra day, but she would make it up to him. And Rob was so busy coordinating rafting trips for RM Outdoor Adventures, he probably wouldn't even notice she was working overtime.

After answering a few questions, Steve gave a nod to Sandra Sechrest, who stepped forward. She cleared her throat, looking nervous for the first time. "We've already had one death of a competitor. Howie Abbott was killed sometime Sunday. He was registered to compete in the tournament."

Mandy sat up straighter. This was news to her.

"Furthermore, Mr. Abbott was most likely cheating." Sandra frowned. "His body was found at the Vallie Bridge campground, with his fishing gear nearby, and that campground is within one of the beats. No one competing in the tournament is supposed to access the competition river sections for six weeks prior to the start of the tournament."

"Isn't that a float-fishing beat?" one of the firemen asked.

"Yes, but that doesn't matter," Ms. Sechrest answered. "Scouting out from the shore where the fish tend to gather is still against the rules. Now, I know our prizes can't compete with the large sums offered in European tournaments, but a ten-thousand-dollar first prize is nothing to sneeze at. The temptation to cheat is there, and the whole point of the rules is to squelch that temptation.

"My hope is that Mr. Abbott's death is unrelated to the tournament, but the suspicion that he was cheating has already cast a pall on the event. We don't want these competitors, who are flying in from all over the world, to leave Chaffee County with a bad taste in their mouths."

Well, well, well, Mandy thought. *Did someone catch Howie cheating? Was that motive enough for murder? And what about the other camper who was with him? Was that person a competitor, too, and also cheating?*

———

She made a mental note to get a copy of the list of the competitors to give to Detective Quintana.

THREE

The only time a fisherman tells the truth is when he calls another fisherman a liar.

—AUTHOR UNKNOWN

AFTER FEEDING AND PLAYING with Lucky and heating up a can of chili for herself, Mandy arrived at the Vic well after eight on Tuesday night. The historic tavern's heavy scroll-worked door was propped open to let in the fresh night air. A light breeze coming off the mountains to the west, a harbinger of an impending cool front, teased a few loose strands of Mandy's hair, tickling her cheeks.

The entertainment that night was warming up, and their reggae beat lifted her spirits when she stepped over the threshold. Once inside, the golden stamped-tin ceiling of the large barroom magnified the sound of both the music and chattering groups of people. Mandy worked her way to the long, polished wood bar.

She spotted Cynthia at the taps at the far end, pouring beer into pilsner glasses. Her bare arm flexed when she plugged the taps, twitching the green and red broad-tailed hummingbird tattooed on her bicep. With the back of her hand, Cynthia swiped at a lock of brunette hair that had come out of her French braid, then piled the glasses on a tray for a waitress standing at the ready.

Mandy shouted, "Cynthia!" and waved.

Cynthia flashed a thumbs-up and held up an empty beer glass.

Mandy returned the thumbs-up.

Cynthia retrieved a bottle of Mandy's favorite Fat Tire Ale from the cooler. After walking down the length of the bar with it, she plunked the glass in front of Mandy, and started pouring. "The usual for my best bud."

"Thanks." Mandy took a welcome sip, then feeling tongue-tied over what to say about Cynthia's uncle's death, she stalled with, "It's busy for a Tuesday."

"I think it's the band. Brought some groupies with them." Cynthia's trained eye scanned the bar. Seeing no one who required her immediate attention, she propped a foot up on a box behind the bar. "Ready?"

Mandy rolled her eyes, expecting another of the ritual blonde jokes Cynthia enjoyed teasing her with. Thankful for delay in talking about Howie Abbott and thinking Cynthia might need to work up to the topic, too, she smiled. "Fire away."

Cynthia pointed to the stained glass display behind the bar—multi-colored parrots and toucans hiding in lush green jungle foliage. "Here's why we don't have a mirror behind our bar. Once there was this bar that had a magic mirror. If you told a lie it would suck you in." She leaned on her elbows. "You with me so far?"

"I'm with you." Mandy took a sip of beer.

"Well, one day a brunette came into the bar." Cynthia patted her own hair for emphasis. "She walked up to the mirror and said 'I think I'm the most beautiful woman in the world' and it sucked her in." Cynthia slapped her hands together.

"The next day a redhead walked up to the mirror and said 'I think I'm the most beautiful woman in the world' and it sucked her in." Another clap.

"Then the next day a blonde came into the bar. She walked up to the mirror and said 'I think…' and it sucked her in." Cynthia slapped the bar, a grin splitting her face.

Mandy laughed. "Good one. Where do you dig these up?"

Cynthia waved her hand. "Oh, I've got a million of 'em. You blondes just keep giving the comics more material." Her smile slowly died while she polished away at an imaginary spot on the bar.

Mandy realized Cynthia was just going through the motions. "I guess your aunt told you about your Uncle Howie."

Avoiding her gaze, Cynthia scratched at a sticky spot on the bar. "Yeah, I heard."

"I'm so sorry for your loss and I feel terrible about it. I'm the one who found him."

Cynthia's head came up, concern in her eyes. "I didn't hear that. That must have been awful."

To get the sudden sour taste out of her mouth, Mandy took a drink of her beer. "It's part of my job. Eventually I'll have to get used to it. But that's nothing compared to what your family must be going through. Detective Quintana wanted me to pass on his condolences, too." She put a hand over Cynthia's, stilling her fingers. "And if there's anything I can do, just—"

Cynthia pulled her hand away and shoved the bar rag into her back jeans pocket. "There's nothing you need to do. Frankly, I won't be shedding any tears over good ole Uncle Howie." Her lips pursed as if she'd bitten into an unripe persimmon.

This wasn't the reaction Mandy had expected at all. "What's the story?"

"Nothing to tell. It's just … he and I weren't very close. I never saw much of him after I grew up, didn't have any need to, so I won't miss him that much." Cynthia shrugged, but it seemed forced. "I'm more worried about my cousin, Faith. She's been missing for almost three days now, and fifteen's awful young to be on your own."

"The cops are looking for her. Detective Quintana even gave me a flier to pass around at the ranger station. If she's anywhere in the county, I'm sure we'll find her."

"Thanks. I put some fliers up in the bar, too." She pointed to one near the front door. "I'm glad so many people are looking for her. I hope she's just playing hooky with a friend, and they're both having too much fun to realize how worried their families are." Cynthia chewed on her lower lip.

"About your uncle, though—"

"I don't want to talk about him anymore."

Before Mandy could reply, a waitress called Cynthia's name and waved an order slip in the air. Cynthia pushed off from the bar and stood. "Gotta go. Kendra and the rest of the gang are already back in the pool room."

Mandy stared at her friend's retreating back. What was the problem between Cynthia and her uncle?

———

Taking her beer with her, Mandy walked past the band on their tiny stage, covering the ear facing their loud instruments, and into the Vic's pool room. She spotted Gonzo in a Wave Sport kayaks T-shirt and baggy black jeans. Next to him sat Kendra in a shimmery jade green spaghetti-strap top that set off her black skin. On her left was Dougie with a faded Denver Broncos hat slung backward on his curly rag mop. All three rafting guides had worked for her uncle and now worked for the merged company run by Rob.

They were clustered around a table under the large wall-mounted shark, an incongruous item in a mountain valley bar. Still, it was somehow appropriate because the upper Arkansas River rapids could be man eaters. A couple of Mandy's fellow river rangers made up the rest of the gang. Since river rangers, like Mandy, were usually former rafting guides, the ties between the two groups ran deep.

Kendra saw Mandy and gave a whistle and come-hither wave. She and Dougie had a pitcher of beer and a couple of glasses in front of them. Gonzo was slurping a soda. When he finished, he glanced at the pitcher and licked his lips. He looked glum while Mandy settled into a chair that was vacated by a ranger who got up with his teammate to shoot pool.

After greeting the others, Mandy asked Gonzo, "What's up?"

"Newt told me Detective Quintana asked him to come into the station for an interview tomorrow. He's nervous about it."

Mandy took a sip of her beer, hoping she wasn't adding to the considerable temptation her alcoholic friend was being exposed to. "Does he have anything to be nervous about?"

"You mean, did he kill Howie Abbott? No way! He's just afraid the cops won't believe him because of his past history."

"What past history?" Dougie asked, rocking his chair back on its hind legs.

"Drugs." Gonzo took another drink of his soda. "That's how I met Newt, at an AA meeting. He's abused both dope and booze, so he can attend."

"Bummer," Mandy replied. "I'm sorry to hear that."

"Yeah, well, there're more of us than you might think," Gonzo said. "Newt's had a tough time holding down a job over the past couple of years. He's basically homeless—camps out in the summer, and when it gets cold, he goes couch surfing or sleeps at a homeless shelter."

"How's he get enough money to live on?" Kendra asked.

"He collects aluminum cans. Gets twenty cents a pound for them at Safeway." Gonzo glanced at Mandy. "That's what he was doing at Vallie Bridge. He's really an okay dude once you get to know him. Problem is, he has priors, mostly for possession."

Mandy leaned forward. "Detective Quintana doesn't strike me as the kind of man who will be influenced by someone's history. He pretty much sticks to the facts of the case."

"I hope so." Gonzo quickly downed the rest of his soda and stood. "I've gotta take a leak. I keep chain-drinking all these Dr. P's because I can't have what I really want."

At Mandy's stricken look, he added, "Don't look so worried. If the temptation gets to be too much, I'll just leave." He walked toward the restrooms.

Dougie caught Mandy's attention. "He's my designated driver, so I have a vested interest in making sure he keeps his vow. He's really doing pretty well for someone who's been dry just a couple of months."

Kendra nodded. "We're proud of him."

"Me, too" Mandy replied. "I know it's his journey to take. I just wish I could schlep his bags for him or something." Wanting to change the subject, she asked, "Either of you ever meet Newt?"

Dougie shook his head.

"I ran into him and Gonzo a couple of weeks ago in line at Mama D's counter," Kendra said, "and Gonzo introduced us. We shot the breeze for a bit, but I was getting take-out, so I booked."

"How'd he strike you?" Mandy asked.

"Seemed okay to me." Kendra shrugged. "Not as goofy as Gonzo. Grungy, probably from picking up cans that morning. Maybe a little jumpy. Kept telling Gonzo he had to get going."

One of the river rangers at the pool table shouted, "Hey, Kendra, Mandy, these guys are looking for a team to play eight-ball against. Want to take them on?" He pointed to the table next to him, where two sunburned, middle-aged men stood with cues at the ready.

The ranger winked at Mandy. He'd seen Kendra and her play many times, and play well, so she was sure some kind of side bet had been made. The strangers were probably thinking they could beat two women.

Kendra shouted, "Sure, why not? We'll whoop their sorry asses." She stood and signaled for Mandy to join her while she sashayed over to the table.

After they shook hands and introduced themselves, Mandy learned the two men were fly fishermen from Denver. They were visiting Chaffee County to practice for and participate in the tournament. While she chalked her cue, she decided to find out what they knew about Howie Abbott, if anything.

"Have you two ever competed in fly-fishing before?"

"Sure, lots of times," Fred, the tall one, replied.

"Do you know any of the other competitors in this tournament?"

"Most of the Colorado teams at least," Bob, the one with a bit of a paunch, said. "Some of the international teams are new to us." He removed the triangular rack from the balls and gestured for one of the women to shoot first.

Kendra took her place at the foot of the table and lined up behind the cue ball. Her break shot hit the balls with a loud crack, and the solid blue two ball dropped in a pocket. When the balls came to rest, though, the positions of the striped balls seemed better to Mandy's eye.

"Stripes?" Kendra asked Mandy.

Mandy nodded.

"You're giving us a head start?" Bob asked, surprise widening his eyes.

Mandy flashed a smile at him. "Not for long."

"And this isn't a call-shot game, is it?" Kendra asked the guys.

Fred laughed. "No way. You gals will need all the lucky shots you can get."

Kendra winked over her shoulder at Mandy.

While Kendra planned her next shot, Mandy asked the guys, "You two ever meet Howie Abbott?"

With a snort, Bob said, "That cheater? Sure. No wonder someone killed him."

Kendra easily sunk the red striped eleven ball in a corner pocket.

Mandy stepped back to let Kendra pass in front of her. "How did Howie cheat?"

"Well, you know he was scouting beats ahead of time if he was at Vallie Bridge. The section from Salida to Rincon was marked off limits."

"Also," Fred added, "Howie's been seen doing the 'San Juan Shuffle' in the past."

"What's that?"

"When you're standing in the stream and start kicking up the rocks to release the nymphs and excite the fish into a feeding frenzy."

Kendra's next shot pocketed the fourteen ball.

This 'San Juan Shuffle' was a new concept for Mandy. "That's against the rules?"

"Usually, and it's certainly frowned on when it isn't explicitly in the rules," Fred replied. "No fly-fisherman worth his weight in trout is going to admit he needs the help."

"So if Howie was seen doing it, what happened?"

The nine ball went whizzing by on its way into another corner pocket.

"When the judge called him on it," Fred said, with a worried glance at the corner pocket, "Howie came up with some lame story about getting his foot caught on a rock and losing his balance. So, the judge let him off with a warning to watch his footing in the future."

"Same way he came up with a story about having bait scent on him," Bob added.

Kendra put a hand on her hip. "You mean he stank? You're not allowed to stink?"

Bob laughed. "No, a judge found a tube of trout gel in Howie's tackle box. A little smear of that on your fly makes it smell better to the trout. Howie's story was that he took it away from a friend he was fishing with before the competition and forgot it was in his tackle box. Since the seal wasn't broken, the judge had to believe him, but he confiscated the gel. If he hadn't, I bet Howie would have used it."

With a clack, Kendra's cue ball hit the ten ball. It bounced off the rail and into the opposite side pocket.

"Good one." Fred scanned the table. "Hey, you gonna leave any shots for the rest of us?"

Grinning, Kendra moved around to the other side of the table. "Maybe."

Fred scowled at the two river rangers at the next pool table, who flashed wide, cocky grins back at him.

Mandy wondered how big the bet was and hoped the fishermen, who both seemed nice, wouldn't get fleeced too much. She turned to Bob. "Back to Howie. Has anyone seen him scouting beats before?"

"No," Bob said. "And doing it on a weekend, when more people are likely to be on the river, was a stupid move."

"Maybe Howie was getting overconfident," Fred said, while intently watching Kendra, "since he'd gotten away with so much cheating in the past."

Bob nodded. "That guy was a slippery eel, all right."

Kendra's next shot missed, and she gave a little bow to Fred. "Your turn."

Mandy politely waited for Fred to make his shot and sink a ball before she asked, "You know anyone who was particularly put out by Howie's cheating?"

Bent at the waist to line up his next shot, Fred looked over his shoulder at her. "Sure, he was a slime ball, but c'mon, who would take these competitions seriously enough to kill someone over one?"

———

Later when Mandy pulled her Subaru up the gravel driveway to her cottage, Rob's battered black Ford pickup truck was already there. He'd called her cell phone at the bar to ask if he could come to her house, and she'd left after finishing the pool game. She'd sunk two balls on her turn, and when Kendra's turn came up, she'd sunk the remaining striped ball and the eight-ball, even calling the pocket to show off.

Before Mandy left, she checked with the river rangers at the next table and found out the bet with the fishermen hadn't been too outrageous. She told them she didn't like being used to scam people and suggested firmly that the rangers buy the fishermen a round of drinks with their winnings. They sheepishly agreed.

After Mandy walked through the metal gate of her small fenced-in yard and swung it shut, she paused to look up at the star-studded sky. She stood hunched in her fleece jacket and picked out the Big Dipper, Cassiopeia, and a few more of the constellations her uncle had taught her to identify. The Milky Way was evident, even with the faint light pollution coming from the center of Salida.

Along the edge of its wide swath, thin ghostly fingers of cirrus clouds stretched from the Sawatch Range to the west, obscuring a few stars. The glow of the half moon tinged the edges of dark clouds piled up along the range. The wind had picked up, so Mandy surmised the cold front would pass over the Arkansas Valley during the night. Probably wouldn't dip below freezing yet, though, so her marigolds would last awhile longer. She took a deep breath of the pine-scented air, then walked in the front door.

Rob had let himself in with his key and was sitting on the sofa that Mandy had saved from her parents' house after they'd died in a car crash, leaving her at seventeen to be raised to adulthood by her Uncle Bill. While flipping through channels on the TV, Rob was vigorously scratching behind Lucky's ears. The dog's head lay on his lap with eyes closed and mouth open, obviously in nirvana.

When Rob saw her come in, he turned off the TV. "I'd get up and give you a hug, but I hate to disturb Lucky here."

Lucky opened an eye and panted a greeting at her, then returned to enjoying his head rub.

"Disloyal mutt," Mandy said to the dog then leaned over to give Rob a kiss. She smelled beer on his breath. After spotting the Pacifico can on the old scratched coffee table, next to Rob's stockinged feet, she picked it up and shook it. It was empty. "Need another?"

"Sure, thanks. It was a long day. Had to patch one of the rafts."

Mandy pulled out another of the Pacifico beers Rob kept stored in her fridge and saw the carton of eggs, jar of salsa, and package of flour tortillas he'd brought for breakfast tomorrow. His keys were on the card table in her kitchen that served as her dining table, his work boots lay on the mat by the front door, and his jacket was slung over one of the folding chairs.

A lot of his stuff had migrated over to her tiny house while they'd been dating, toothbrush and shaver in the bathroom, odd pieces of clothing, a battered guitar, some of his country rock CDs. Of course, she had a toothbrush, sleep shirt, and some other things at his place, too. If Mandy thought too hard about where this relationship was going, it got too scary, so she had resolved awhile ago to just take it one day at a time.

She knew Rob wanted more, a lot more. And with his mama pressuring him to make their relationship legal, Mandy wasn't sure how long he would be willing to wait for her to get comfortable with the idea of m, m, marriage. Imagining Rob's mama pleading with him to settle down and produce some grandkids for her to dote on, Mandy shuddered. She'd worked hard to become independent because she had to. And the thought of being responsible for raising kids scared the bejeebees out of her.

As if he could sense that she was thinking about him, Rob asked, "Did you get lost in la-la land out there?"

"I'm getting some water for myself, too." Mandy poured a glass and returned with the drinks. She sat next to Rob, on the other side of the sofa from where Lucky lolled.

Rob grinned at her over his beer. "I could get used to this kind of service."

Mandy blew a raspberry. "Was the raft you had to patch one of Uncle Bill's?"

He nodded while he drank his beer. "We'll probably have to replace a couple of his rafts once the season ends. You can only patch so many times."

"Damn, I hope you're not sorry about merging the two companies. Uncle Bill's tired old equipment wasn't worth much."

Rob stroked her thigh. "No, but his customer list was worth a lot, and the vehicles, and I sure value my silent partner." He pinched above her knee, making her jump, and his eyes twinkled.

Mandy laughed. "You mean your not-so-silent partner."

He leaned over and kissed her. "And she tastes good, too. Fat Tire?"

"Just a couple. Sorry you missed pool night." Mandy shifted to face him. "I found out some stuff about Howie Abbott, though." She filled him in on what the fly-fishermen had told her about the man's cheating.

Rob nodded. "I've heard rumors that Howie and his buddy Ira Porter were cheaters. Never really been caught. They were registered as a team in the tournament, and Ira's scrambling to find another partner. I hear tell no one's biting, though."

"Where'd you hear this?"

"A couple of the registered teams came in to rent rafts from us for the float-fishing practice and competition days. And I'll be guiding another team on the float practice day. This tournament is making some money for us."

Mandy shook her head. "I don't understand why someone would cheat in a fishing tournament, for Pete's sake."

"The purses can go pretty high," Rob said. "Not as high as those in bass fishing tournaments down south, but ten thousand dollars for the winning team isn't chump change. Even more important are the bragging rights."

When Mandy lifted an eyebrow, Rob smiled. "Being a woman, and a practical one at that, you wouldn't understand."

"Try me."

"The size of the fish implies the size of the catcher's willy, and the number caught is related to the fisherman's prowess at catching the lady folks."

Mandy laughed. "Oh, you've got to be kidding me!"

"I am a little bit, but these fishermen are deadly serious." Rob drank some beer. "You should've heard them talking at the counter today about past tournaments and who'd won what and who the tough competitors were."

"Don't women fly fish, too?" Mandy had tried it a couple of times with her Uncle Bill when she was a teenager, but she had neither the time nor patience to master the technique. After she'd hooked her thumb a couple of times, she gave up.

"Sure. There's a women's team in the tournament, too, but the sport's dominated by the *hombres*. But enough talk about fishing." Rob finished his beer, put it down, then gently pushed Lucky's head off his lap and stood. He held out a hand for Mandy.

As he lifted her to her feet, she could see from his languid gaze what he wanted, and she wanted it, too. But she was going to have a little fun first. "Be careful, or this fish might just wiggle off your hook."

When he drew her to him, she shimmied her hips in jest, but that only made Rob pull her in tighter against his chest, taking her breath away. "No catch-and-release tonight, my little trout. I'm going to heat you up and devour you."

Lucky gave a doggy snort of disgust and plopped down on the floor.

Giggling, Mandy let Rob draw her into the bedroom where they tumbled onto the bed.

FOUR

*There's a fine line between fishing
and just standing on the shore like an idiot.*
—STEVEN WRIGHT

REMEMBERING ROB'S LINGERING KISS before they had parted ways in her driveway, and remembering the evening before, Mandy drove to Detective Quintana's office the next morning with a satisfied smile.

You know, spending a lifetime with that sexy man might not be so bad. But that word "lifetime" was sobering. Would Rob still have the hots for her when she grew wrinkled and fat? A line from an old Beatles love song popped into her head, something about wondering if my lover would still need me when I'm sixty-four. What would Rob's answer to that question be? What would hers?

Mandy stuffed the questions in the back of her brain while she pulled into the lot in front of the county government building. She had more immediate concerns to think about, like the information she needed to relay to Quintana. She zipped up her black fleece ranger jacket before getting out of the car since the morning was cool and cloudy.

On her walk into the building, she noticed that the leaves of the oak trees planted on the parking lot medians were starting to turn yellow. Fall was on its way, as was the end of her seasonal employment as a river ranger. She was looking forward to working full time at RM Outdoor Adventures with Rob over the winter, but she'd also miss her river patrols and the camaraderie with her fellow rangers—and, surprisingly enough, with Quintana.

She found the detective filling his coffee mug in the break room and followed him back to his office. Once there, she handed him the list of competitors who had signed up for the fly-fishing tournament. "I didn't know if you had this or not."

He handed it back to her. "The tournament committee faxed one over yesterday afternoon, but thanks."

"I bet I've got some other information that you don't have, though. Howie Abbott and his partner Ira Porter are suspected of cheating in tournaments." Mandy gave Quintana a summary of what she'd heard from the pool-playing fishermen and Rob the previous evening.

By the time she'd finished, Quintana had emptied his mug and filled two pages of a lined notebook with writing. "Good stuff. I'd already planned on tracking down Ira Porter to see what he knew, since he was registered as Howie's teammate. But now I'll be directing my questioning a little differently."

"Do you think he could have been the other camper who shared some beers with Howie?"

Quintana nodded. "Likely, though Howie might have been drinking with someone who was angry about the cheating and who then ended up killing him."

Mandy was skeptical. "After drinking beer with him first?"

"Happens all the time." Quintana tapped the list of names. "I'll have to interview every one of these competitors."

"Including the women?"

"Especially the women. Howie's killer could have been a strong woman, either a fishing competitor or someone with a romantic interest. We found a few long brown hairs that weren't Howie's in his sleeping bag."

"Any way of telling whether the hairs got there this past weekend?"

"No, Howie could have shared his bag or loaned it to someone months ago."

"What about the autopsy? Did you get results from that yet?"

Quintana nodded. "Time of death is still late Sunday afternoon. Howie died from bleeding out of the neck wound. The hatchet opened up his jugular, so it only took a few minutes. Both blood and pepper spray were smeared on his hands, as if he tried to stem the bleeding."

Mandy grimaced, then had a more horrible thought. "Or maybe he held up his hands in front of his face to ward off the pepper spray, and they got splashed with the blood pumping out of his neck."

"That's certainly possible." Quintana smoothed his mustache. "What a way to go. Makes being shot sound downright pleasant."

Envisioning Howie's last moments was too bleak, so Mandy moved on. "What about the beer? Did Howie drink it all?"

Shaking his head, Quintana said, "There wasn't much alcohol in his blood, so the doc concluded Howie hadn't drunk any beer on Sunday and probably drank four at the most Saturday night. And the stomach contents pretty much matched the food wrappers we found. Another interesting thing in the autopsy report is that Howie had a tan line for a pinkie ring on his left hand, but we haven't found the ring. That's one of the questions I'm going to ask Newt Nowak."

He looked at his wall clock. "Speaking of which, he's coming in a few minutes. I'd like you to listen in on my interview with him, compare your recollection of the campsite layout with his and see if there are any differences."

"Differences? Why?"

"Could be an indication that Nowak's lying, or that someone was at the campsite in between your two visits, or something else." He shrugged. "Newt's words could stir something in your memory, too."

Mandy nodded. "Okay, I just need to clear it with Steve. He expected me to patrol the river today."

After okaying the plan with her boss, Mandy followed Quintana to the interview room and slipped into the observation room next door. Deputy Thompson, whom she had met during a previous investigation, was seated at the table behind the one-way glass that looked into the interview room. Mandy took the empty seat next to him. They shot the breeze until Quintana brought Newt into the interview room and seated him facing the glass. Thompson opened his notebook and clicked his pen while Mandy peered at Newt.

He was a thin, pale-skinned guy with stringy red-brown hair and dark shadows under his eyes, as if he'd been up all night. The shadows made him look like he was in his forties versus his late twenties. Newt was dressed in a holey T-shirt, stained camp shorts, and flip-flops. His fingertips started a nervous staccato beat on the tabletop, accompanied by a bony knee jiggling under the table. His tongue darted in and out of his lips while he glanced around the small room. Mandy could see where his nickname had come from.

When Newt's gaze rested on the glass in front of him, his eyes narrowed in suspicion. "Is someone behind that watching me?"

Quintana, who had seated himself at the end of the table so as not to block the view of Newt, answered with a placid face. "We always have another officer observe in case I miss something, but we figure most folks are more comfortable talking to one person. Just ignore the glass. Now, tell me about Howie Abbott. When did you see him?"

"Monday morning, about ten. I'd walked into the Vallie Bridge campground and was picking up cans." He grimaced. "Then I saw the body."

"You didn't go to the campground earlier, say on Sunday?"

Newt shook his head vigorously. "No way."

Quintana looked skeptical. "You sure?"

"Sure I'm sure!"

"Where were you from Saturday evening to Sunday evening?"

"Nowhere near Vallie Bridge." Newt half-rose out of his seat. "You're not trying to pin this on me, are you? I'm cooperating, for God's sake!"

"We're asking a lot of people where they were last weekend," Quintana answered smoothly, motioning with his hand for Newt to resume his seat. "It doesn't mean we suspect you in particular of anything. So, where were you?"

Newt sat but kept tapping the table. "I went to an AA meeting at six on Saturday, then hung out with my buddy, Gonzo Gordon, at his place. We grilled burgers, watched a movie, then he drove me back to my tent and I crashed for the night. All day Sunday, I was collecting cans at Hecla Junction. I took them to Safeway around seven and used the money to buy some bread and peanut butter and hiked back to my tent."

"Where is your tent, Newt?"

"Oh man, do I hafta tell you?"

"It'll go better for you if you do, and even better if someone else saw you there. I don't really care where you're camping out right now, though if it's illegal, I suggest you move."

Newt blew out a breath. "My tent's on National Forest land, and three other dudes have tents pitched there. Any of them could probably vouch for me, but I don't want to get them in trouble, too."

"I'm not going to haul them in, but I do need to question them," Quintana said. "Or would you prefer to have no alibi for the two nights you say you slept there?"

"Shit." Newt's gaze darted around the small room. "You've got me wedged between a rock and a hard place."

"We'll go to your campsite after we finish here, then. Will any of the others be there?" After Newt gave a reluctant nod, Quintana scanned his notes. "So, Gonzo Gordon can vouch for you Saturday evening, and hopefully one of your campsite buddies can vouch for you both nights. Anyone see you at Hecla Junction?"

Newt waved his hands wide. "Lots of folks, man, but I didn't know any of them."

"I'll ask around there today. Now, describe the scene at Vallie Bridge to me, everything you saw."

Newt went into a long description of the body, the campsite, and sleeping bag and fishing equipment scattered around, continually prompted for more details by Quintana. Mandy paid close attention, trying to match Newt's description with her memory to see if anything didn't jibe.

"Did you see anyone else at the campground?" Quintana asked.

"No, no one. Before I reached the dead guy's campsite, I saw some trash at another site, but no cans, so I just left the trash there."

Quintana finished making notes, then raised his head. "So where did you stash the ring that you took off Howie's hand?"

"What?" Newt's eyes widened. "I didn't take any ring. As soon as I saw the dead body, I dropped my bag of cans and ran."

"You didn't check to see if he was really dead, to see if you could help him?"

"Oh yeah, but when I went to take a pulse on his wrist, I could tell he was long gone. His skin was way too cool." Newt shuddered. "Then the flies grossed me out and I booked."

Mandy wrinkled her nose. The flies had grossed her out, too.

"What about the hatchet?" Quintana asked. "Did you touch that?"

Newt shook his head.

"I'd like to fingerprint you," Quintana said.

"Why? I had work gloves on the whole time, except when I checked for a pulse."

Quintana smiled. "Then you have nothing to worry about. We won't find any matches to your fingerprints on the murder weapon."

Newt looked skeptical, and his tongue flicked out to wet his lips.

"Describe your work gloves to me," Quintana continued.

"They're old lady gardening gloves that I scrounged up, yellow with pink flowers. Worked pretty well, though."

"You still have them?"

"One of them. I can't find the right one."

"That's because we found it at Vallie Bridge," Quintana said, and when Newt opened his mouth to speak, added, "And no, you can't have it back."

Newt sighed. "I suppose you're keeping the cans, too."

"Definitely." Quintana paused and scanned his notes. "Is there anything else you can tell me about what you saw or did while you were there? See any out-of-the-ordinary items, for instance, besides campground trash?"

Newt thought for a moment. "Well, when I first got there, I went through the day-use parking lot and picked up a few soda cans. You know where the stile through the fence is that leads to a shortcut path to the campsites?"

Quintana nodded.

"I found a few more cans on the ground under some brush next to the stile. A can of pepper spray was there, too, but since it wasn't aluminum, I left it. I remember that I thought it was odd for someone to leave it there."

"Good, that's helpful. Anything else?"

After Newt shook his head, Quintana said, "Okay, I want you to stick around town. I may have more questions for you later, especially if your alibis don't check out."

Newt's eyes widened. "I told you, man, all I did was spot the body and leave on Monday morning."

"But you didn't report it as you should have. That's suspicious in and of itself."

"With my priors, would you have reported it?"

Quintana just frowned, then thanked Newt for coming in, and escorted him out to be fingerprinted. He came in the observation room a few minutes later. "So, what do you think?"

"Doesn't sound like he's our killer," Thompson said.

"I agree," Mandy added. "He didn't seem to have any reason to kill Howie Abbott."

"Not that we know of yet." Quintana smoothed his mustache. "We've got some work to do before we rule him out, though."

He turned to Deputy Thompson. "Drive over to Vallie Bridge and see if you can retrieve that can of pepper spray. If so, bag it and bring it in. Then go to the Hecla Junction campground and see if you can find anyone who saw Newt picking up trash on Sunday. I'll take care of interviewing Newt's camping buddies and Gonzo Gordon."

The deputy nodded and left.

"Did Newt's description match your recollection of what you saw?" Quintana asked Mandy.

"Yes, and I really couldn't come up with anything more from listening to him. He actually saw more of Howie's fishing equipment than I did. Sorry."

"Something may still come to you later, and if it does, I want you to contact me." Quintana closed his notebook and slapped it against his thigh. "In the meantime, after I verify Newt's activities, I'm going to track down Ira Porter and have a nice long conversation with him. Fingerprint him, too."

———

Mandy treated herself to her favorite turkey avocado sandwich for lunch at the Salida Cafe. She ate it while sitting on the restaurant's deck overlooking the water park on the Arkansas River. Kayakers practiced their twirls and turns in their tiny play kayaks in the man-made rapids. She shucked her jacket to soak up some of the afternoon sunshine that had burned off the clouds and warmed up the air enough for folks to be in shirtsleeves again. This was the "Banana Belt" of Colorado, after all.

After lunch, she rendezvoused with Steve at the Stone Bridge campground to patrol the Arkansas River above Salida. Called the "Milk Run" by rafters, this slow section only contained one Class II-III rapid worth noting on the whitewater map. Thus, it provided some ideal fly-fishing spots. The upper half was designated as the wading section for the tournament, and teams would be dispersed along the bank at various beats marked with yellow-flagged stakes. Today, though, no competitors were supposed to be on the section, and Steve told Mandy that they had been asked to check for that.

When Mandy and Steve carried their raft to the put-in, they encountered Rob, Kendra, and Gonzo with two fly-fishing rods. All three wore waders that were belted at the waist. The neoprene booties of the waders were stuffed into waterproof boots. Rob wore a chest pack stuffed full of gear, and the handle of a cotton fish net was stuck through the waistband at his back.

Gonzo was trying to untangle a fly hooked on a bush. Kendra furrowed her brow while she concentrated on tying a fly on the end of her line, with Rob coaching her over her shoulder.

Mandy eased her end of the raft onto the river bank, in sync with Steve and his end. "Hi guys. What's up?"

Rob looked up and grinned. "I'm training these two how to fly fish. I'm hoping I can turn them into float-fishing guides, so they can work into the fall after the water levels drop and the summer rafters go back to school. I'll need to buy a couple of raft fishing frames, too."

Mandy met Rob's even gaze and nodded to show she'd received the implied message, though she didn't necessarily like it. Those aluminum frames provided raised, padded forward and aft swivel seats for fly fishermen, leaving a middle oaring seat free for a guide. They weren't cheap. Here was yet another need for the money that would come from selling Uncle Bill's place.

But how could she begrudge giving her friends some income during the lean shoulder season between summer rafting and winter skiing? Like many in the valley, Kendra and Gonzo had seasonal winter jobs at the Monarch ski area. Kendra had worked as a children's ski instructor last winter, and Gonzo, like Mandy, was a ski patroller. Though this year, with the need to help Rob manage RM Outdoor Adventures, Mandy wasn't sure she'd be able to do both. She'd barely been able to keep up her river rangering this summer.

Gonzo yanked on his line and ducked as the two hooked flies on the end sailed out of the bush and past his head. "Controlling this line is a lot harder than it looks. It's damned frustrating!"

"Hey, try tying on a fly with these triple-looped knots using skinny fishing line," Kendra retorted. Her tongue stuck out while she stared intently at the line in her fingers.

"You using dry-nymph combos?" Steve asked Rob.

"Yep. Got plain old San Juan worms hanging under green caddis flies." Rob pointed downstream a few yards. "As you can see, the caddis are hatching."

Mandy spotted the cloud of buzzing flies rising out of the water. Two black swifts circled overhead, a sure indicator of a hatch if you weren't close enough to see it yourself.

With an "Aaargh!" Kendra held out her line for Rob to inspect.

Rob rolled his eyes at Steve and bent over the tangle she'd managed to create. "We'll have to cut it off and start over."

"And this is supposed to be a relaxing sport?" Kendra replied.

Gonzo snorted in agreement.

Steve laughed. "It takes hours on the water to get the hang of fly-fishing. Don't beat yourself up about it. "

Rob turned to Steve and Mandy. "We spent the morning on the ballfield practicing casts, and I thought I'd give them some time by the river this afternoon. Being Wednesday, we only had one rafting trip scheduled to go out. Dougie and Ajax are handling it."

"I know you have a seasonal fishing license, Rob," Steve said. "What about these two?"

"I'm thinking positive and bought them both seasonal licenses, too," Rob replied. "Want to see them?"

"I trust you. Had to ask, though." Steve donned his PFD.

Mandy cinched her fanny pack with emergency medical supplies around her waist and picked up her PFD. "Well, I wish you all luck." She watched Gonzo fling a lopsided cast and grinned. "Looks like you'll need it."

"I'm not giving up on these two," Rob replied. "If we had some trained fishing guides other than myself, we could have gotten more guiding business from this tournament. A lot of the competitors came in a week early to fish the sections of the river that weren't blocked off for the competition."

With a wave and shouts of encouragement to Kendra and Gonzo, Mandy and Steve launched their raft and settled into a steady paddling rhythm. While they steered the raft in and out of the shade of cottonwood trees flanking the burbling river, Mandy's thoughts turned to her Uncle Bill. Whenever she was on this section of the Arkansas since he'd died in June, she was drawn to the memory of scattering her uncle's ashes at Big Bend just downriver. She felt his presence here almost more than when she visited his house, which had been her home for ten years.

As if reading her thoughts, Steve said, "Thinking of Bill?"

Manning the front of the raft, Mandy could feel that he had stopped paddling. She glanced back at him and nodded. "Yeah, I really miss him."

"We all do. He was an institution in the valley." Steve returned to his paddling, his silence respectful.

She and Steve continued this way through the long slow turn of Big Bend and past the County Road 166 bridge, which marked the end of the tournament competition section. The only sounds that broke the silence were the plunks of their paddles in the water and the nearby chittering of an irritated tassel-eared Abert squirrel. A cool, fresh breeze tickled the hairs on Mandy's forearms, but the warm sun kept her from getting chilled. They passed a section of river bank clogged with red-tipped willow and green alder bushes growing right into the water.

Up ahead, where the sandy bank was clear of bushes, two men in waders stood about thirty feet apart in knee-deep water over cobble bars of smooth, multi-colored river rocks. Their yellow fly lines sliced through the air in rhythmic arcs when they cast back and forth across the current. With a clear blue sky and sunlight strewing sparkling diamonds across the water, the scene would have made a perfect postcard advertising Colorado as an ideal fly-fishing destination.

Mandy noticed that one man's casts formed consistently perfect ovals in the air, letting the two flies tied to the end of the line drift to land with a light touch on the water's surface. The other man's casts, while still a good effort, were inconsistent, sometimes resulting in the flies plunking in.

"That one of the competition teams?" she asked Steve.

"The balding, middle-aged guy with the excellent form is Ira Porter," Steve answered. "I don't know the young guy, but I bet Ira recruited him to take Howie Abbott's place on his team."

While they drifted closer, Mandy wondered why, if Ira was so talented, he would resort to cheating with Howie Abbott, as the rumors said. She wasn't going to pass up this opportunity to talk to the man, though she knew better than to telegraph to him what Detective Quintana's questions would be.

"Could you introduce me to Ira?" she asked Steve.

Steve sat with the paddle across his lap, obviously admiring the beauty of Ira's casts. "Man, he's soft on the rod. I almost hate to disturb them."

Just then, Ira signaled to his partner to move downstream and pointed at a couple of small eddy pools there, likely spots to find lurking trout. The younger man pulled in his line, then took some tentative steps on the slippery rocks. He stepped in a depression, plunging into deeper water. He lost his balance, and with arms windmilling, fell to one knee. While he struggled to regain his footing, he held his chest high to keep water from pouring into his waders.

"There's a reason to disturb them now," Mandy said. "That guy could probably use a warning to stay in shallow water if he's so unsure on his feet."

"You do it," Steve answered. "I'd like to see how you handle the situation. And, if he has a problem with it and asks for your supervisor, I'll be right here to back you up. Paddle in real slow and easy."

By the time they had beached their raft on a high point on the cobble bar upstream of Ira Porter, the younger man had righted himself, and Ira had reeled in his line. The younger man's face was red. Ira was glowering, though Mandy wasn't sure if it was at his partner's slip-up or the intrusion of the rangers.

"Howdy, Ira," Steve said. "How's the fishing?"

"Not so good now," he said with a harrumph, "with your raft scaring them away."

"Sorry about that, but we've got to patrol the river. We tried to slip in quietly. The fish'll return after we leave." Steve pointed to

Mandy. "I don't believe you've met Mandy Tanner, one of our new river rangers this year."

Ira gave a curt nod to Mandy's hello.

"Who's your partner?" Steve asked.

Ira signaled to the younger man, who started slogging his way upstream toward them, "Wally Dixon, hails out of Silverthorne."

After Wally reached them and introductions were made all around, Mandy had a chance to study him. Red-haired and freckled, his looks were quite a contrast to Ira's darkly tanned middle-European features. Wally also had a pasty softness about him that made her think he wasn't a practiced outdoorsman.

"It's good to see you've found a new teammate for the tournament," Steve said to Ira, who frowned.

"Unfortunately," Wally replied. "I'm not as familiar with this river as the Blue. Ira's been giving me a crash course today."

Mandy heard an opening and took it. "Speaking of crashing, we couldn't help but see your fall. These cobble bars can be awfully slippery. Do you have a telescoping walking stick that you can use as a third support while you're moving around?"

"No."

"You might find one at one of the fishing supply stores in Salida," Mandy said, trying to keep her tone light. "In the meantime, I'd strongly suggest staying in water no deeper than your calves. Those waders can be awfully dangerous if they fill up with water."

Wally pursed his lips, obviously unhappy being given advice by a woman in front of the two other men.

Mandy turned her attention to Ira, the man she really wanted to talk to. "I'm always being asked by tourists where the good fishing spots are on the upper Arkansas. Got any suggestions?"

Ira pshawed. "You think I'm going to give away my secret spots to any yahoo from New York or Chicago?"

Mandy forced out a light laugh. "Of course not. I'm asking where you would tell them to go, where they might have a good chance of hooking a fish, but not disturb your secret spots."

"In that case, I'd say Stone Bridge, where you two probably put in, or Vallie Bridge downriver. Vallie also has the benefit of the campground if they want to stay overnight."

"You ever camp there?"

Ira gave her a sharp glance, but Mandy kept her face impassive. "Yeah, the campsites aren't bad. You get some shade from the willow trees. The section upstream from there that's in the competition has some good holes. But I usually fish well downstream of there, and I ain't telling you where."

Downstream of the campground was outside of the competition area, but who's to say he didn't venture upstream, too? "I found Howie Abbott in one of those campsites."

Ira's mouth opened in a little "o", then he clamped his lips shut and started fiddling with his reel. "Didn't know you were the one who found him." He shook his head. When he looked up, his eyes were red-rimmed. "I sure hope he didn't suffer much. He was a good fishing buddy."

An overall sense of awkwardness settled on the group, with none of the men looking at anyone else.

"I think his death was quick," Steve said, filling the silence. "Sorry for your loss."

"Did you know Howie well, Ira?" Mandy asked.

"Fished with him off and on for the past six years," Ira replied. "He's a hard man to get to know, very private, and kinda gruff most folks would say. He was sure fishy, though. May not have been able to read people real well, but he had a sixth sense about where fish were likely to be biting."

"I've heard he could rub people the wrong way. Did you ever have any problems with him?" When that question drew a suspicious glance from Ira, Mandy smiled. "I'm just trying to get a handle on his personality."

"Well, when we disagreed about something, like where to fish or when to move on to another spot, his temper could flare up, but I could hold my own. At the end of the day over a few beers, everything would be forgotten. I'll miss him." Ira shook his head and gazed off into the distance. "One thing's for sure, Howie could tie beautiful flies. I wonder who'll get his fly box. I hope that person will know the value of the contents."

After a respectful moment, Wally cleared his throat. "How about if you show me exactly where those eddies are that you were talking about, Ira?"

With admonitions to be careful, Steve and Mandy pushed their raft off the cobble bar. Giving the fishing duo a wide berth, they paddled quietly downstream. Mandy thought back on Ira's reaction. Was the man's grief genuine or was he faking it?

FIVE

Let your hook be always cast.
In the pool where you least expect it, will be fish.

—OVID

THURSDAY WAS MANDY'S DAY off, so she threw a load of laundry in the washing machine and took a nice long run with Lucky. After showering and breakfasting, she phoned Detective Quintana to tell him about her encounter with Ira Porter.

She ended with the question that had been niggling her all night. "Do you think Ira's really grieving over Howie's death, or do you think he might be the one who killed him?"

"Could be both," Quintana answered. "Ira's a much smaller man than Howie. If they got into an argument and it got out of hand, Ira could have resorted to the hatchet and then sprayed Howie with pepper spray if it looked like Howie would get up. And now he's regretting his rash actions and missing his fishing partner."

"But if they were arguing, why was Howie lying on top of his sleeping bag?"

"Maybe that's where he fell. Or maybe he was sitting there when Ira hatcheted him, or maybe Ira's temper simmered until Howie fell asleep and Ira got him then. Or maybe I'm just blowing smoke. Hopefully I'll find out something when I talk to him this afternoon. He's agreed to come in for questioning."

Mandy's dryer beeped, and she started unloading the clothes while cradling her phone against her shoulder. "Were you able to confirm Newt Nowak's alibi?"

"Gonzo confirmed that he spent Saturday evening with him," Quintana said, "but when I took Newt to his campsite, no one else was around. I almost wonder if they saw us coming and high-tailed it out of there."

"You going to go back there?"

"Yeah, sometime tonight. Though in the meantime, Newt could have concocted a story with his buddies. I would have preferred to talk to them last night."

Taking a break from folding her clothes, Mandy shifted the phone to her other ear. "Did Newt's fingerprints match any of those on the hatchet or beer cans?"

"No, but he could have worn his work gloves while doing the killing. Some of the prints on the hatchet were smeared. That could have happened when Howie tried to get it out of his neck with hands that were already slippery with blood. Or, a killer wearing gloves could have smeared the prior prints."

Mandy shuddered at the image of Howie clawing away at the hatchet. "Did you see any blood on Newt's glove?"

"Not from a visual inspection, but we sent the glove off to CBI. They'll see if it has any minute traces of Howie Abbott's blood or the pepper spray on it."

"And I suppose they'll try to confirm that it's Newt's glove by doing a DNA match on skin cells or hairs inside."

"Yep."

Mandy tugged on her ponytail while she mulled over the two suspects. "You know, I don't see how either one of these guys has a motive."

"Just because we haven't found one yet doesn't mean one doesn't exist." The sound of pages flipping came over the phone, as if Quintana was reviewing the case file. "From what I've been able to find out about Howie Abbott so far, he wasn't well liked. He tended to piss people off and didn't seem to care."

While stowing socks in her dresser drawer, Mandy said, "Yeah, he sure angered other fly fishermen with his cheating. But besides family and friends, did he piss off other people, too?"

"Some people he used to work for. He hasn't been getting as many calls for his carpentry skills in this economic downturn, so he owed money to a couple of folks. They aren't too happy he died before he paid off his debts. Something could have happened between him and Newt or Ira or one of his creditors that made one of them want to kill him."

"Or Howie pissed off someone else we don't know about yet."

"Agreed. I have a feeling there's a lot more to the Howie Abbott story than we know already."

At that point, Mandy heard the call-waiting beep signal on her phone. She figured she and Quintana were about done anyway. "Oops, I've got another call. I'll check in with you later."

"Thanks for the information about Ira. You've been real help-ful on this case, Mandy."

Feeling a glow of accomplishment, Mandy said goodbye and hung up on Quintana, then picked up the other call. It was the dispatcher from the ranger station.

"Sorry to call you in on your day off, Mandy, but we've got a body search situation where we need all hands."

Mandy stowed her laundry basket back in her closet and sat on the bed to scratch behind Lucky's ears. "What's going on?"

"A woman reported her husband missing last night. She said he told her he'd be camping and fishing at Ruby Mountain for a few days, but she noticed after he left that he'd forgotten his box of flies. When she drove to Ruby Mountain to deliver the box, his truck was parked there, but she saw no sign of him. He didn't re-spond to her shouts either. She searched for him along the banks for a couple of hours before it got pitch black, then she called in the report."

Damn, Mandy thought. Ruby Mountain was just upstream from Brown's Canyon, a rushing series of Class III and IV rapids that was the most popular whitewater rafting run on the upper Arkan-sas River. If the man's fishing waders filled up and he was washed into the canyon, his chances were slim to none. Worried it might be someone she knew, Mandy asked, "What's the man's name?"

"Arnold Crawford. You know him?"

"No. Did anyone try his cell phone?"

"His wife said he left it in his truck. He doesn't carry it when he's fishing."

"'Course if he had and it got wet, it wouldn't work anyway." Then Mandy realized that it was too early to start a search. "Why are we searching for him now? Don't we usually wait a couple of days on missing person reports?"

"A rafting guide picked up a Bronco's Super Bowl ball cap in lower Brown's Canyon this morning. It had Crawford's name written inside, so the guide brought it into the station. When it was shown to his wife, she burst into tears."

———

When Mandy drove into the parking lot at the AHRA headquarters, the two search and rescue trucks from the Salida and Buena Vista fire departments were parked there as well. Steve stood in the hot sun, consulting with the Salida fire chief and making notes on a clipboard. When he spied Mandy, he raised his hand in a wave to acknowledge her presence.

Mandy joined a group of her fellow river rangers who were milling about in the parking lot, readying gear and swapping stories. None of them seemed to know anything more about Crawford than what she'd already been told. The lot's black asphalt was already throwing off shimmers of heat waves under the blazing mid-morning sun. Only a few small cottonball clouds punctuated the clear blue sky. Beads of sweat had appeared on many foreheads, and some of the searchers crouched in the shade of the parked trucks.

After popping the cap on her sunscreen, Mandy started slathering it on the areas of her skin that weren't covered by her knee-length shortie wetsuit. She had figured there was a good chance she'd have to spend a long time in the river's cold water, so she'd worn that and wetsuit booties under her Teva river sandals. The rest of her gear was stashed at the ready in the trunk of her car.

Frank Canton, tall and thin with a shaved head, gave her a playful nudge with his elbow. "No hard feelings about Tuesday night, I hope?"

Mandy glanced at him, then at his companion in the pool game betting scheme, Lance Weston. Lance was a burly guy with a well-groomed mutton-chop mustache that had earned him the nickname Walrus. "As long as the fishermen were happy after the round of drinks you bought them, I guess there was no harm done."

Lance grinned. "By the end of the night, they were laughing about it, and we still went home with money in our pockets."

"Just don't do it again." Mandy poked Lance's beefy arm to emphasize her point. "Kendra and I don't take kindly to you two using us to scam tourists out of money."

"Aw c'mon, Mandy," Frank said with another elbow nudge. "It was all in good fun."

"You can still have your fun by suggesting that folks play us," Mandy said. "Kendra kind of liked showing off. Just leave the betting out of it."

Frank put a hand to his chest, while Lance mimed a swoon with the back of his hand to his forehead. "Cruel, cruel woman."

Before either one could say more, Steve hollered, "Listen up, folks."

The general chatter among the rescuers in the lot died down, and air thickened with tension. Everyone moved closer to the two men in charge. Steve and the fire chief divided their whitewater rescue-trained personnel into two search teams, each consisting of two AHRA rafts and six people. Mandy's team included Steve, Frank, Lance, two firefighters—one of whom was a familiar-looking female—and herself.

The two teams would leap-frog each other, searching for a live stranded or injured fisherman, or for a body trapped somewhere in one of the larger rapids. While that search proceeded, the Fire Chief would arrange for a rail car to be brought into Brown's Canyon, to be used to carry out an injured person on a backboard or a body in a body bag, since there were no roads running through the canyon.

After they all got their assignments, Steve sent a stack of fliers around. "Here's who we're looking for. This is a recent photo his wife gave us."

Mandy studied her copy. Arnold Crawford was forty-six years old, 5-foot-11, 220 pounds, white-skinned with glasses, a bit of a beer gut, and thinning black hair. She wondered how his wife was holding up and hoped the man was still alive. Somewhere.

Someone jostled her arm, and she looked up. Everyone was scrambling for their gear and climbing into the shuttle vehicles that would take the teams to the put-in at Fisherman's Bridge. The bridge was just upstream from the Ruby Mountain put-in, which was too small and hard to access with all their vehicles. Plus, putting in at Fisherman's Bridge would allow them to search the area upstream of Ruby Mountain, to see if Crawford had waded upstream and got into trouble there.

Mandy grabbed her gear and hopped into the back passenger seat of an AHRA van. She fastened her seat belt while Frank drove out of the parking lot, the raft trailer swinging behind them. Her stomach felt fluttery, a combination of nerves and excitement about being a part of a large search and rescue—hopefully a rescue—operation.

Steve talked on his cell phone in the front seat, relaying their plans to the county dispatcher. Then he said, "A couple of commercial trips have already started down the canyon. We told them to be on the lookout for the fisherman or any gear and to call you if they see anything."

When he started talking about communication protocols with the dispatcher, Mandy tuned him out and turned to her seat mates, the two firefighters named Janice and George. She introduced herself and asked about their training and experience. It was always a good idea to scope out who had what skills on a rescue team before an operation started. Therefore, Mandy had no qualms about answering their questions regarding her background, in turn.

As a result, she discovered why Janice looked familiar. They'd been in the same CPR recertification class two years ago. Knowing the rest of her team was well-trained alleviated some of Mandy's concern about how well they would work together. She just hoped she would measure up.

Before long, they arrived at the put-in. Mandy pitched in to carry rafts and paddles down to the water. The teams loaded the rafts with ropes, carabiners and pulleys, first-aid kits, provisions, and other equipment, all of which had to be tied down. There was an edge to their jokes and parried insults, as Mandy and the others tried to bleed off some of their nervous apprehension.

When they were ready, Steve directed the other two-raft team to paddle directly to the first major rapid in Brown's, the Canyon Doors. Once there, they were to set up a methodical body search operation among the huge sunken boulders. Mandy's team would follow more slowly, scanning the river and banks between Fisherman's

Bridge and the canyon entrance for any sign of the missing fisherman. Then they launched the rafts.

Later, while passing Ruby Mountain, a volcanic hill looming over the east side of the Arkansas River, Mandy remembered searching through the talus piles at its base with high school friends. They hunted not for the red garnets that gave the mountain its name, but for nodes of obsidian called Apache's tears that they'd take home and polish. Her Uncle Bill had explained where the name came from. In retaliation for raiding an Arizona settlement, the U.S. Army trailed a band of about seventy-five Apache warriors and launched a surprise attack against them. Nearly fifty died in the first volley of shots, and the rest leapt over a cliff rather than allow themselves to be killed.

Legend said the stones were the tears that wives and families shed for the dead warriors. Apache's tears were supposed to bring good luck. It was said that whoever owned one would never have to cry in grief again, for the Apache women had shed their tears in place of the owner's. Mandy hoped that the fisherman's wife owned some of the stones.

The normally boisterous Lance and Frank, who had teamed up with her in their raft, also seemed subdued by the seriousness of their task and content to focus on paddling and searching. Mandy was sure they were hoping, like her, that their search didn't yield a body in the river. She'd been trained in body retrieval in her river ranger class, but she hadn't had to put that training to the test yet.

They had chosen the left side of the river, while Steve and the two firefighters searched the right side in their raft. At every eddy or deep pool, Mandy slowed to peer into the water below. Sometimes she or Frank would probe the depths or beneath an undercut sunken boulder with a paddle if they couldn't see the bottom clearly. Lance, ruddering in the back, focused on searching the shoreline.

They passed riffles where Chalk Creek entered on the right and Seven Mile Rapid where Middle Cottonwood Creek entered on the left, but they found nothing. When they passed the railroad bridge that marked the beginning of Brown's Canyon, Steve had them eddy out above the Canyon Door entrance rapid while he radioed the team searching there.

"They're packing up their gear," he said to his team. "Didn't find anything. I told them to head down to Zoom Flume, searching along the way, and set up another body search there, while we take Pinball Rapid. Let's head out."

Pinball Rapid was a dicey technical boulder field with an S turn, a class III-IV killer. Mandy remembered the two most recent fatal incidents with some trepidation. A forty-seven-year-old man had died there in 2007 during a swimming exercise while training to be a rafting guide. And a forty-nine-year-old Texan was killed in July, 2009 after being thrown out of a commercial raft that hit one of the large boulders sticking out of the turbulent waters. This being late summer, the water level was lower than the busy early summer rafting season, but that only made Pinball trickier to maneuver through.

Mandy, Lance, and Frank and those in Steve's raft helloed the other team while they rocketed past their tied-up rafts below the Canyon Doors, riding the standing waves on river right. Soon after, they arrived at the entrance to Pinball, signaled by the profiles of large boulders hunkering in the water and the roar of water plunging over the drops.

"Beach the rafts by the railroad tracks," Steve hollered.

Once both rafts were pulled out of the water, they all walked downriver to scout the rapid. Numerous dark, shadowy holes and eddies could hide a body trapped in their depths.

"We'll set up a two-point system here, tying two lines to Frank and Mandy's raft." Steve turned to George, the large fireman. "You anchor the line on this side, with me as your helper. I'll try to stay high, so I can see the whole operation and supervise."

He put a hand on Janice's shoulder. "You and Lance ferry our raft over to the other side of the river and tie up there. Lance will anchor the line on that side, with you as his helper."

He turned to Frank and Mandy. "Frank, you steer the raft, and relay signals to us, and Mandy, you'll man the pole. Take your time probing all the eddies, holes, and backsides and undercuts of the rocks. We need this to be thorough."

Great, Mandy thought, *so if the guy's body is trapped under one of these rocks, I'm the one who retrieves it.* She envied Janice's role on the sidelines.

After they'd rigged two lines through D-rings on either side of Mandy and Frank's raft, Lance ferried his raft to the other side of the river, with Janice playing out the rope. They set up, with Janice holding onto the rope with work gloves, her feet firmly planted, followed by Lance acting as an anchor with the rope wrapped around his back. The remaining length lay coiled in an open bag at Lance's feet, so he could pick it up and carry it with them as they progressed downstream. Steve and George set up a similar configuration on their side of the river.

Mandy put on a pair of heavy latex gloves, hoping there wouldn't be a need for them, then a pair of work gloves to protect her hands from the fibers in the long fiberglass probe pole. She climbed into the tied raft with Frank and shouted, "Ready." She really wasn't. Her hands had started to perspire inside the gloves and her mouth had gone dry, but she wasn't going to admit that to the others.

With the raft pointed upstream and his back pointing downstream, Frank paddled out into the current. He let the raft slip over the tongue of water for the first part of the S, then blew once on his whistle and held his arm up, signaling a stop. Mandy held on while the two belayers on the shore leaned back on their ropes, halting the raft's progress. Then she leaned out over the front of the raft, resting her chest on the pontoon, and started probing the downriver side of the rapid with the end of her pole.

Using whistle blows and hand signals to the belayers, Frank signaled them to move the raft to the far right shore, then back across the current to the far river left until Mandy had probed under all the rocks and in all the deep eddies that might hold a body. "Nothing," she said to Frank, wiping sweat off her brow with her forearm. "Let's move on to the next drop."

"Good," he said, while he gripped his paddle. "I'm hoping this whole thing is a wild goose chase and the guy is holed up with a mistress somewhere."

Mandy cracked her first smile since getting on the river. "Wouldn't that be nice? Though, not so nice for the wife."

Frank snorted. "Yeah, then she might be wishing for him to be dead." With whistle and hand signals to the belayers, he ferried the raft over to the standing waves on the left side of the river, let it slip backward over the next drop, and signaled for another stop.

Mandy poked the pole in gravel and under the large boulders on either side of the river until her arms ached. She turned and sat back, shook out each arm, splashed some cool river water on her shoulders, and took a swig of her water bottle. "One more to go."

Frank nodded and ferried right. The last drop was the biggest, so Mandy hunkered down and held on tight while they bounced over the edge. Another whistle blast, and they shuddered to a stop. The current had carried them beyond the edge of the drop, so Frank blew two blasts, signaling the belayers to pull in rope, moving them upriver until Mandy could reach under the boulders with her pole.

She focused on a massive undercut boulder in the left center of the river. It had a deep pool behind it and was the most likely place in Pinball for something to be stuck. When she probed, she dislodged a couple of water-logged branches that popped to the surface. Her tense muscles jumped, too.

She soon settled down when she recognized what the branches were. While they floated downstream, she thought, *Phew, maybe that'll be all we find.*

Then a ghostly white shadow wavered on the bottom.

Her heart rate accelerating, Mandy bent over the side of the raft to get a better look. With the bright sunlight glinting off the ripples in the water, it was hard to get a fix on the underwater phantom. *Is it another branch, a fish, or something else?*

"What?" Frank asked, his voice rising. "What do you see?"

"Something whitish," she replied, then licked her dry lips and gave him a worried glance. "Might be an arm or a leg."

"Christ," he whispered. Then he blew three long blasts on his whistle, the emergency signal, to alert their teammates, who could neither see them behind the boulder nor hear their voices over the roar of the rapid, that they'd found something. Or someone.

Mandy regripped the fiberglass pole and ran it along the underside of the boulder, then back again deeper, until something softer than rock pushed back. The white shadow moved.

A shudder coursed through her.

She followed the contours of the soft mass under the boulder, trying to dislodge it with the tip of the pole, but with no luck. She pulled the pole out of the water and turned it around so the nasty-looking hook on the other end, the one she'd avoided looking at, faced the water.

"Get ready," she said to Frank, who was staring at the hook. "If I get this out, whatever it is—" She didn't want to admit yet to what her brain was telling her and swallowed back the bile that had risen in her throat. "—and it pops up, you need to help me hold it next to the raft so it doesn't float downstream."

He licked his lips and nodded, then pulled a pair of heavy latex gloves out of his fanny pack and slipped them on. He picked up his paddle and positioned it over the water.

She dipped the hook under the surface, aiming for the same spot. When it pushed against the trapped mass, she closed her eyes to focus on the feel of the pole in her hands. Running the curve of the hook along the form, she twisted the hook back and forth as she went, groping for a hold.

Suddenly, the end of the hook slid under something. She turned it and tugged gently. It wedged. "I've got it."

Steve appeared on the river bank nearest them, after scrambling down the shoreline. He had put on his latex gloves, too, and carried the other probe hook. "Take your time, Mandy," he yelled. "Make sure you've got a good grip on it."

"I do," Mandy yelled back, sounding more confident than she really felt. She took a deep breath and said to Frank, "Here goes."

She yanked hard, but her hands just slipped up the pole. She repositioned them, planted her feet against an inflated gunwale, and yanked again.

The mass moved. Another tree branch and some leaves and pine needles floated to the surface and bobbed downstream. And another white shadow, larger this time, emerged underwater.

Mandy was sure she saw a foot on the end. "Jesus!"

"What? What?" Frank yelped.

"Another limb, a leg." She glanced back at Frank, whose wide eyes probably mirrored her own. "We've definitely got a body."

Her heart hammering now, she pulled again, felt the hook slipping, stopped for a moment to reset it, then yanked hard.

With a sudden release that sent Mandy sprawling back, the body came free and floated to the surface. It was completely naked and face-down, the torso slightly bloated, with the hook wrapped around a thigh.

Before she could discern much else, Frank scooped his paddle against the body's shoulder and pulled it against the side of the raft. He reached out and grabbed the nearest arm.

Mandy quickly righted herself and pulled the legs in toward the side of the raft, too, with her hook. She held onto the hook with one hand and grabbed the nearest ankle with her other hand.

As soon as she made contact, even though her hand was gloved, a violent shudder ran through her. She gritted her teeth until it passed.

"You got it secured?" Steve hollered.

"Yes," Frank yelled back.

The two of them gaped silently at the body while Steve directed the belayers with whistle commands and arm signals to ferry the raft toward him.

Mandy gripped her pole and the ankle with clenched hands. Slowly, while she stared at the body, observations registered in her mind.

The person was too short and too thin to be Arnold Crawford.

Even from the back and with the torso bloating, the body appeared feminine.

Long brown hair, not short black hair, swirled around the head.

When their raft entered the eddy at the bank beside Steve, he splashed into the thigh-deep water and slid his hook gently around the body's waist. "Okay, we're going to turn it over."

With Mandy and Frank's help, he used a gloved hand and his hook to gently roll the body face up. Small breasts and a pubic mound appeared above the water surface. The body was that of a young woman.

Mandy's gaze traveled to the bruised face as Steve brushed the hair away. The young woman's expression was serene, the eyes closed as if she was peacefully sleeping. A large mole was visible under her left eye.

Slack-jawed, Mandy dropped her pole.

SIX

The fishing was good; it was the catching that was bad.

—A. K. BEST

FAITH ELLIS IS DEAD, Faith Ellis is dead.

The morbid mantra repeated itself over and over in Mandy's mind until she thought it would drive her mad. Her sweaty hands slipped on the steering wheel of her Subaru when she made a turn. Thursday was one of Cynthia's nights off at the bar, so Mandy was driving to Cynthia's apartment on the west side of Salida. As soon as she'd seen Faith's face, Mandy knew she would have to be the one to tell Cynthia.

Her stomach tightened while she mentally rehearsed and discarded what she might say to her friend about the death of her young cousin. The taste of cheddar cheese and tomato rose in her throat, from the sandwich hurriedly eaten at home while changing out of her wet river clothes and taking care of Lucky before getting in the car. To keep anything more from coming up, Mandy took a deep breath and blew it out slowly while she hit the brakes at a stop sign. She'd just have to trust that the right words would come at the right time.

While she accelerated, she flashed back to that afternoon. After they'd pulled Faith's body out of the Arkansas River and quietly zipped her up in the body bag that Steve had stowed aboard his raft, they radioed in the find. The other team continued down the river, searching for Arnold Crawford. Mandy later heard they had found nothing.

Lucky bastards.

She had already started thinking about Cynthia while they waited for a rail car to bring a fire department rescue crew to carry the body out. A sheriff's office detective also rode out on the rail car to see if he could retrieve anything else from the scene. Steve went back out in the raft with Frank to probe for clothing under the boulder, but only a few more branches, leaves, and other natural debris had surfaced.

The detective had brought a photo of Faith with him. It was clear to everyone that the body was hers. When he said he would notify the Ellis family, Mandy volunteered to tell Cynthia. It was the least she could do for her best friend—especially given what Cynthia had done for Mandy after her Uncle Bill died.

Mandy turned her Subaru onto the asphalt driveway that led to the detached two-car garage over which Cynthia's studio apartment sat. She parked on the left side, behind the bay allocated to Cynthia and not the homeowners, who were out in the yard, returning to their house with gardening tools and a half-full plastic bag.

The retired couple waved at Mandy when she got out of her car. "Dead heading," the husband said and held up the bag. They were meticulous gardeners.

Not wanting to get into a discussion with them, Mandy just nodded and gave them a return wave before they turned and went inside.

The last rays of the dying sunset picked out the pink and yellow zinnias blooming in front of delicate red penstemon spikes and blue caryopteris shrubs along the front of the main house. The beautiful combination was ideal for attracting butterflies and hummingbirds. As she walked to the garage, a hummingbird trilled past Mandy overhead on its way to the flower feast. In the deepening twilight, she couldn't tell if it was ruby-throated or rufous. She almost wished she could follow the tiny bird back to its nest and sink into a torpor with it, rather than face the heart-wrenching task ahead of her.

Mandy hadn't called in advance, but looking up, she saw that the lights were on in Cynthia's place. She took another couple of deep breaths while she climbed the wooden stairs leading up to the narrow deck running along one side of the garage. She stepped past Cynthia's small gas grill, a couple of plastic chairs, and pots of red geraniums. A tranquil scene, soon to be shattered.

Mandy knocked on the door.

Cynthia opened it, dressed in an extra large T-shirt and sweatpants. She held her calico cat, Mittens, draped over her arm. "Mandy! This is a surprise. Come in, come in." She stepped aside.

Mandy reluctantly entered the familiar cozy room with its brown plaid sofa and mismatched pink paisley side chair, both yard-sale finds. A small TV sat on a cinder block and pine board

84

bookcase, and a square wooden table and two matching chairs filled the other end of the room. On the table were the remains of Cynthia's dinner, an empty pot that had held some kind of soup, and half a package of Ritz crackers.

Cynthia closed the door and turned off the TV. She let Mittens leap out of her arms to rub against Mandy's ankles. "So, what brings you here tonight?"

Mandy sat on the sofa and clenched her hands in her lap. "I'm afraid I've got bad news. Maybe you should sit down."

Brow furrowed, Cynthia sat next to her and covered Mandy's hand with her own. "Mandy, your hands are like ice. What is it?"

Mandy licked her lips. "We were out on the river today, searching for a missing fisherman. We didn't find his body, but we found someone else's."

Eyes widening with sick, dawning realization, Cynthia said, "Oh, God. Who?"

"I wish I knew how to tell you this so it wouldn't hurt as much, but I don't, so I'm just going to say it." Mandy paused, her eyes already starting to burn with unshed tears. "It was Faith. We found Faith's body in the river."

Cynthia's hand dropped. Her body crumpled, and her face with it. "No. No. Not Faith."

Mandy put an arm around her friend's shoulders. "I saw her. I recognized her. It was Faith. I'm really, really sorry, Cynthia."

While she stared at Mandy in horror, tears welled up in Cynthia's eyes and overflowed down her cheeks. Her mouth dropped open, and out came a wail of pure misery. Starting softly, it rose in volume, growing into a howling scream that went on and on, raising the hairs on the back of Mandy's neck.

Cynthia gulped in a breath and screamed again. And again, her hands stiffened into claws raised to the heavens.

Shaken by the depth of Cynthia's reaction, Mandy grabbed her friend's shoulders and gave her a shake. "Cynthia?"

Staring at her without seeing, Cynthia went on screaming.

Mandy gave her another shake. "Cynthia."

Finally, Cynthia's gaze focused on Mandy, and she collapsed against Mandy's shoulders, deep sobs shaking her frame.

Mandy just held Cynthia and stroked her back and her hair, letting her tears soak into Mandy's long-sleeved T-shirt until it stuck to her chest. Mandy's own tears slid down her cheeks and dripped from her chin.

Mittens meowed plaintively and rubbed against her mistress's legs, but Cynthia paid her no attention.

Finally, as the sobs subsided, Mandy gently extracted herself from Cynthia's clutches. She stood up and grabbed the tissue box next to the TV, took a tissue for herself, and brought the box to the sofa.

After snatching a couple of tissues, Cynthia wiped her face, and blew her nose. She dropped them onto the floor and repeated the process. Her face was blotchy red and swollen and looked awful.

Cynthia pulled Mandy down next to her. "Tell me everything. Please."

"Are you sure you can handle it?"

Cynthia's grip tightened on Mandy's arm until it hurt. "Yes, tell me."

"I was the one who found her," Mandy said, while loosening Cynthia's grip. "Under the last huge boulder in Pinball Rapid."

"Do you know how she died? If she drowned or if someone killed her and threw her in?"

"No, we really don't know. Her body was bruised and scraped, but the river could have done that. I didn't see any large wounds, or a bullet hole or anything. Maybe the autopsy will tell us something."

Cynthia gasped. "They're going to carve her up?"

Mandy put her hands on her friend's arms and gently rubbed them. "It's not Faith anymore. She's gone." She sent up a silent prayer to her Uncle Bill, asking him to guide and comfort Faith's soul on her journey, if that was possible.

"What did she look like, besides the bruises and scrapes?"

"She looked peaceful, like she was sleeping. Her skin was so white and her hair was floating in the water, like a drowned princess or nymph or something. Beautiful, even though ..."

Cynthia dabbed at fresh tears. "Her skin? What was she wearing?"

"Um, nothing, actually." When Cynthia looked aghast, Mandy quickly added, "That's typical, though, for bodies found in the river. The rapids. They tumble the body. And ..." Unable to find a delicate way to word it, Mandy shrugged. "The clothes end up being torn off."

"Oh, God." Cynthia stuffed her knuckles in her mouth and took a moment to compose herself. Then she got up and started pacing the room. "I should have done something, something more. Warning her wasn't enough. Now she's dead."

"Warning her? What are you talking about?"

Cynthia stopped and stared at Mandy. Her mouth opened and closed, as if she were debating whether or not to say something.

Then Mittens meowed at her and batted her leg. Cynthia reached down, scooped up the cat, and started petting it, her lips pursed.

"Nothing," she said finally. "Faith was depressed. I tried to help her, but not enough. She wasn't safe yet, and now it's too late."

Before Mandy could ask more, a knock sounded on the door. The plaintive voice of Cynthia's landlady asked, "What's going on, Cynthia? Are you okay?"

When Cynthia rose, Mandy stood, too. "What do you mean Faith wasn't safe yet? Do you think she committed suicide? Was she depressed enough to throw herself in the river?"

"Maybe. Or she took a risk and someone killed her." Cynthia's grip on the cat had tightened, and it let out a yowl of pain.

"Sorry, Mittens." She loosened her hold and let the cat jump out of her arms, then opened the door.

The retired couple stood outside. Wringing her hands, the woman looked from Cynthia to Mandy. "We heard screaming."

"Mandy just told me that my cousin died," Cynthia said.

The woman gasped and put a hand to her face, while her husband gripped her shoulder. "We're so sorry," he said. "What can we do?"

"I don't know," Cynthia replied, rubbing her forehead. "I need some time to absorb the shock."

Mandy touched Cynthia's arm. "What kind of risk was Faith taking? What were you warning her about?"

Cynthia held herself, her fingers making white marks on her arms. "I can't talk about this. Not now."

"Can I make you some tea, dear?" the woman asked.

Cynthia's gaze flitted across the worried faces surrounding her. "I really need to be alone. Could you all just leave?"

"Sure, sure," the man said, and he turned to leave.

The woman made to leave with him, then turned back. "You call if you need anything. Anytime. And I'll check on you in the morning."

Cynthia nodded, then looked expectantly at Mandy, still clutching herself.

"Are you sure you want me to leave?" Mandy asked. "I'll stay the night. I'll do whatever you want or need me to, to help you through this."

"I know, and I appreciate it. Thank you for coming to tell me. I know it was hard. But right now, I just want to be alone."

———

The next morning, Friday, dawned bright and clear with a piercingly blue sky. Worried about Cynthia, Mandy called her and woke her up, but when she offered to bring breakfast by, Cynthia turned her down, saying she was going back to sleep. Mandy felt bad about waking her friend, but at least she knew Cynthia was alive and hadn't succumbed to her grief and done something drastic— like following her cousin into the river.

If that was how Faith died.

After driving to headquarters, Mandy rode with Lance in one of the ranger pickup trucks from Salida north to the Railroad Bridge put-in at the entrance to Wildhorse Canyon. Last Sunday, a commercial rafter had called in a strainer, a dangerous tangle of branches in the water, in the Frog Rock rapid. The river rangers cleared strainers as soon as possible because they could trap and hold a swimmer underwater. But since Wildhorse Canyon wasn't one of the popular runs on the Arkansas, the clearing of that particular strainer had been deferred. With the weekend coming up, though, it needed to be taken care of.

The tools and paddles rattling in the truck bed kept up a percussive beat to Lance's tone-deaf humming with the radio. Mandy tuned him out and watched the landscape of grassy ranchland stream past the window while she reflected on Cynthia's words about Faith the prior evening.

What did she mean when she said Faith wasn't safe yet? Safe from what? Was the teenager using drugs? Did she owe someone money for drugs? Someone who would get violent if they weren't paid? Or was she involved in a gang? Had she been sneaking out of the house to see some boy or to drink at one of the bars that wasn't careful about carding?

And what had Cynthia warned her young cousin about? The dangers of drugs and alcohol? Date rape or safe sex?

Or was Faith suffering from deep depression or some other psychological condition? Maybe it was the demons of her own mind that she wasn't safe from. Cynthia had said that "maybe" Faith committed suicide, as if she felt the girl was capable of it. But the alternative was even weirder. What "risk" would Faith have taken that would have gotten her killed? Mandy vowed to talk to Cynthia again, when she'd had a chance to process her cousin's death.

Lance gave her a poke in the arm when he turned off Highway 24. "We're almost there. What ya' been thinking about? That girl you pulled out of the river yesterday?"

"Yeah, sorta. Sorry I haven't been better company."

"Hey, I understand. It was a bad scene." He drove the pickup into the parking lot and maneuvered it so the small flatbed trailer behind them was near the ramp down to the river. He turned off the engine and rested a large hand on her shoulder. "Time on the river will help. It always does."

Mandy gave him a smile. "Yes, it does. Let's go."

She hopped out of the truck and started unlashing the catarafts from the trailer. Since it was likely they would need two boats to deal with the strainer, they'd taken two of the single-person craft that river rangers usually used for river patrols. Each one had an oaring seat clamped onto a metal frame suspended between two bright blue inflatable pontoons. Mandy and Lance stowed their lunches and the tools for cutting branches in dry bags in the equipment cages bolted behind the seats.

After they'd parked the truck away from the ramp and locked it and pushed their rafts into the river, Mandy took a deep breath and let the music of the gurgling water start working its magic. A large black rook let out a loud caw and flapped its wings overhead. A trout splashed near one of her oars, and a bright yellow butterfly fluttered among cattails along the bank sawing against each other in the slight breeze. When the sun warmed her back, she pushed up the sleeves of the splash jacket under her PFD and dipped her oars in the water again.

Yes, trouble had occurred in Mandy's human community of Salida, especially for Cynthia's extended family, with the death of two members—her uncle Howie Abbott and his niece Faith Ellis. Mandy knew firsthand how wrenching even one death in the family could be. But all was right with the world of nature, at least today here on the Arkansas River, and it made her feel glad to be outdoors and alive to enjoy it.

Lance whooped when they rode their two rafts over a class III riffle, and Mandy flashed him a smile.

"You know," he yelled over the rush of the water, "I've never understood why the commercial outfits don't run this section more often."

"It is beautiful," Mandy shouted back. "But let's keep the secret."

Soon, they reached Frog Rock Rapid and tied up upstream. They hiked down and studied the strainer. A couple of huge cottonwood limbs with lots of interlocking smaller branches were wedged between two large rocks. There was no way to get to the bundle from the shore, or to eddy out a raft near it. They decided to tie Lance's raft to a nearby cottonwood, let it drift down to the spot with Lance inside, then cinch up the line so the raft stayed there.

After that was accomplished, Lance leaned out of the raft and alternated using a hand saw and a pair of large clippers to cut the branches into sections. Mandy stayed on the shore and threw him ropes, when needed, to tie off and drag larger sections to shore. There she chopped or sawed the sections up into smaller pieces that would float down the river without getting tangled. All the while, she kept an eye on Lance and her throw bag within reach, because she was his downstream rescue backup if he ended up in the river.

They worked companionably, Lance being an easy-going and methodical guy, for a couple of hours until he shouted, "Done," and tossed the last section into the river. "Glad I didn't need the chain saw. I hate trying to control it in a bobbing raft."

Mandy made quick work of chopping that last section up, then stood and stretched her aching back. She shouted, "I'm done, too," and swiped sweat off her forehead.

"Meet you at the next eddy for lunch," Lance shouted back while he untied the line from his raft and oared his cataraft out into the current. He whooped while his raft bounced down the tongue of standing waves below Frog Rock.

Mandy hiked back upriver with her equipment and ropes. She retrieved the line that had been tied to Lance's raft, and stowed everything in dry bags in her equipment basket. After pushing her cataraft off from shore, she ran the now-cleared rapid with a "Whoop!" of her own.

She soon spied Lance waving to her from a quiet pool downriver and spun her cataraft into the eddy next to his. He had already tied off his raft to a tree on shore and secured hers to his.

He popped the cap on a bottle of Gatorade and held it up. "Here's to a job well done."

Mandy tapped her water bottle against his Gatorade and drank deep, then sank her teeth into her peanut butter and raspberry jelly sandwich. "You know," she said after swallowing, "nothing tastes as good as a smushed PBJ sandwich as long as it's eaten on the river when you're starving after a morning of hard work."

Lance laughed and held up his sandwich. "Except maybe a salami on rye in the same circumstances." He gave her a wink while he took a big bite and hummed while chewing.

While they were eating, a fly fisherman in waders came sloshing upstream alongside the opposite bank. He returned their wave, then went back to swishing his fly line overhead and casting it into eddy pools behind rocks lining the shore—favorite hang-out spots for river trout. He soon snagged a trout. He high-sticked his rod to hook the fish and bring it closer to him, then reeled in some line. As the trout flopped nearby, he reached behind him for the net stuck into his belt.

That's when something went wrong. He lost his footing, possibly because of a jerk from the good-sized trout, and fell forward with a splash into the main current. The current swept him downstream.

Yelling, "Don't stand up," Mandy untied her cataraft line from Lance's and shoved off with her oars. She pushed hard on her oars to catch up with the fisherman.

The man had flopped over on his back with his feet pointed downstream, the best position for self-rescue in whitewater. He paddled with one arm, trying to steer himself toward the river bank. Since he held on tightly to his expensive-looking fly rod with the other arm, though, he wasn't making much progress.

Mandy came up alongside him and shouted, "Grab hold!"

He rolled and threw his free arm over the nearest pontoon.

Mandy steered her now sluggish cataraft toward shore. She soon felt Lance's cataraft behind her, nudging against her raft to help propel the fisherman into the shallows.

When they reached a large shallow eddy next to shore, the man let go. He pushed himself off the bottom to stand on a calf-deep cobble bar. After grabbing hold of a bush overhanging the river bank, he took a few deep breaths.

Mandy oared into the bank and grabbed a bush to keep her cataraft in the eddy.

Lance pushed off and ferried across the river, where Mandy spied the man's net bobbing in a small whirlpool near the other bank.

Studying the fisherman, Mandy saw that he was middle-aged, but not overweight. Though he was breathing hard, his face was a healthy color, neither red nor ashen. But just to be sure, she asked, "You okay?"

"Yep," he answered. "Thanks, love. I thought I was a goner for sure."

The man's accent was foreign, maybe British, so Mandy asked, "You're not from around here, are you?"

He shook his head, scattering drops from his wet, sandy-colored hair. "Flew in with me mates from Sydney three days ago for the tournament. They're sleeping off too many pints last night, but I had to get out on the river." He held up the fly rod still gripped tightly in his hand, then did a double-take. "Blimey, the fish is still on the line!"

He efficiently reeled in some more line and grabbed the fish with his hand, since his net had floated away. He gently cradled the brown trout while sliding the hook out of its mouth. Then he eased it back into the water so it could swim away with an angry flick of its tail. "He was a beaut, wasn't he? Biggest brown I hooked today."

"That was a nice one," Mandy said, "and you look like you know what you're doing."

"Except for that dumb move back there," he replied, while he secured his line to his rod. "Should have planted my feet better. Sorry to trouble you. Name's Tim, by the way." He held out his hand.

Mandy reached over and shook it. "Mandy Tanner. I'm a river ranger, so plucking people out of the river is what I do for a living. You know, it's lucky we were here when you slipped." She saw Lance was ferrying his way back across the stream, then she turned back to Tim. "Can I make a suggestion? Go back to your motel and wake up one of your buddies to fish with you for the rest of the day. It's not a good idea to be on the river alone like this."

Lance drew his cataraft up next to hers and tossed Tim's net to him. "What Mandy says is damn straight. There's some wicked eddies downstream that can pull you right under. We can give you a ride on one of our rafts down to where you left your vehicle. You probably want to dry off anyway."

Tim looked down at his soaked shirt and gave a rueful smile. "I think the river gods are agreeing with you."

At Mandy's suggestion, he clambered onto the back of her raft and took an awkward seat on the equipment box. While she pushed off from the bank, Mandy asked him about his tournament experiences to get him talking. It was also a subtle way to check for shivering and hypothermia.

He rattled off a list of tournaments in his native Australia, Europe, and the U.S., then said, "Hey, I heard one of the locals who was going to compete got knocked off a few days ago. Someone axed him, supposedly."

"Yeah, I was the one who found his body," Mandy admitted.

Tim let out a long, low whistle. "I'm sure that was a pisser. From what the blokes were saying in the bar last night, though, the fellow won't be missed much."

"Oh? What were they saying?"

"There were some rumors he was a cheater, but no one seemed to have solid proof. Some of the Yank teams were saying 'good riddance.' And one bugger was even drinking to the man's death, saying now that his chief competition was gone, he had a good chance of winning. He doesn't know what he's up against, though." He thumped his chest. "We Aussies are gonna give that braggart a run for his money."

This was an interesting tidbit. Mandy glanced at Tim over her shoulder. "Did you get the name of the guy who was bragging?"

"Jesse Lopez, I think. Sort of a grizzled, squatty guy. Got the impression he was one of the old-timers hereabout."

Mandy had a vague impression that she'd heard the name before, but she couldn't conjure up a visual of Jesse Lopez. Maybe Rob or Detective Quintana knew the man. Regardless, she'd need to give Quintana this information. Before she could ask Tim anything else, he pointed to a small put-in off State Route 306 that she recognized.

"My rental car's over there."

While she ferried him over, she asked him where he was staying, so she could tell Quintana. "Maybe I'll see you at the tournament," she said when she dropped him off. "I'll be patrolling during it. Good luck."

He shook her hand. "Thanks, lovie, and thanks again for the rescue. I owe you a beer."

Mandy laughed. "It's all part of the job, but if I see you at Victoria's Tavern, I may take you up on that."

Tim gave her a thumb's up and sloshed his way out of the water up to the shore.

Lance brought his cataraft up next to hers. "We better get a move on if we're going to make it through Brown's Canyon and back to headquarters by the end of the day."

Mandy glanced at her waterproof watch. "If we have to do any more rescues, we may need to radio for someone to pick us up."

"Then let's hope we have a clean run down with no more rescues," Lance replied. "You've had more than your fair share of incidents lately."

"And more than my fair share of bodies, with no explanation for who killed them or in Faith Ellis's case, if she'd even been killed." Mandy shoved her oars through the water. *I've got to talk to Cynthia!*

SEVEN

Remember, a dead fish can float downstream,
but it takes a live one to swim upstream.

—W. C. FIELDS

MANDY AND LANCE ARRIVED at the boat ramp in Salida around five-thirty. By the time they stowed the catarafts and she drove him back to the put-in to fetch the truck, it was well past dinner time and her stomach was growling.

Lucky was miffed at her when she got home, barking at her through the fence. After she came through the gate, Lucky nosed his almost-empty water dish as if to say, "See how you abandoned me?" Feeling suitably guilty, Mandy gave him fresh water and fed him, tossing a biscuit on top to appease him.

She went inside and opened her fridge to see what her own dining options were. Half a jar of salsa sat on the top shelf, left over from the breakfast fixings Rob had brought by, and she remembered she had some frozen burritos. She took two out of the freezer and stuck them in the microwave to defrost. Then she went outside to toss a tennis ball to Lucky, taking her cell phone with her.

She tried Detective Quintana at his office first, hoping he might be working late on the case. He answered on the second ring. While Lucky dropped an increasingly slobbery ball in her hand to toss again and again, she told Quintana about her conversation with Cynthia. She felt uneasy about revealing Cynthia's statements that Faith was taking some sort of risk and wasn't safe, and that Cynthia felt some guilt about not helping enough. But she told him everything nonetheless, expressing her concern about Cynthia's fragility.

After Quintana promised that he would step lightly when re-questioning Cynthia, Mandy filled him in on Aussie Tim's revelation about Jesse Lopez drinking to Howie Abbott's death.

"Jesse Lopez," Quintana repeated. "Yeah, since he was on the list of Rocky Mountain Cup competitors, I've already gathered some information on him. He's a local and owns a gas station out on Highway 50, does some fly-fishing guiding on weekends. I already knew him somewhat. He wrestled in high school, as I did, graduated a year before me. He was real competitive back then, hated to lose, and had a temper on him. Would storm out of the gym if he was eliminated in a meet."

"Is he still that way?" Mandy asked. She thought Rob might know Jesse, too, since both were Hispanic business owners in town.

"I don't socialize with him, but I'm thinking probably yes. He's a fierce competitor in fly-fishing tournaments now. In fact, I remember now that he complained a few years back when Howie beat him out of a first-place purse. Even talked to the Sheriff's Office, but we had no reason to pursue it. He insinuated Howie hadn't earned the prize legitimately."

Mandy heard a scratching sound, as of a splintered pencil on paper.

"I'm making a note to bring Jesse in for an in-depth interview," Quintana said. "Did you find out where this Aussie was staying in case I want to follow-up?"

Mandy gave him the name of the motel.

"Thanks for the information. Also, I talked to Ira Porter. He says the last time he saw Howie was the Wednesday afternoon before he was killed, when they fished together. And supposedly he's got an alibi for Sunday afternoon. We're checking it out."

"What was his alibi?"

"That he was visiting his mother in an assisted-living facility in Colorado Springs that day. He said she's got dementia. So even if she vouches for him, she's not a reliable witness. I just got off the phone with the place. I asked for a copy of the visitor log for Sunday and also if I could interview their staff." Quintana cleared his throat. "Now, I've got some news that may help you with understanding Cynthia's reaction to her cousin's death."

"I'd appreciate anything you can tell me. Cynthia's comments were confusing and she's taking Faith's death really hard. I'd like to find some way to help her."

"This is confidential, so you've got to keep what I'm going to tell you to yourself."

Wondering and dreading what was coming, Mandy said, "Of course." She held onto the ball Lucky had just returned to her, waiting for the news.

"We sent Faith's body to the Pueblo County Coroner's Office. As a matter of procedure, their forensic lab took samples of skin and hair. The technician thought the hair looked familiar and compared it under the microscope to the ones we recovered from Howie Abbott's sleeping bag. They were an exact match."

Mandy dropped the tennis ball. "What? Had she borrowed her uncle's sleeping bag recently?"

"I talked to her family again today and asked them that question. They said no, that Faith had never used Howie's sleeping bag. She would have no reason to, having one of her own. So then I had to pursue another line of questioning, which didn't go over well. That maybe Faith had shared her uncle's sleeping bag Saturday night when she went missing."

A shudder coursed through Mandy. "Oh, ick. You think Faith's uncle was sleeping with her?"

Quintana sighed. "I've come across cases of incest before, unfortunately. If she was with her uncle when someone killed him, they may have killed her, too, and for some reason dumped her body in the river upstream."

Mandy ignored Lucky's nudges against her hand. "But why dump her body and not his?"

"She's lighter, a lot more portable," Quintana said. "And the killer may not have killed her right away. He may have assaulted her first. That's why I asked the coroner to use a rape kit when he did the autopsy this afternoon."

"Oh my God." Mandy plopped down on her butt in the middle of the yard. "And if he finds semen, it could be either her uncle's or the killer's or both."

"Correct."

"What did Faith's parents say to all this?"

"I didn't tell them my whole theory. No need to mention the possibility of assault by the killer if there wasn't one—or if she wasn't murdered. There's still the possibility her death was accidental or a suicide and totally unrelated to Howie's.

"However, I did ask them about the relationship between Faith and her uncle. Her parents and her brother all claimed not to know of anything odd or off-kilter between them, said it seemed to be a normal uncle-niece relationship. In fact, her father got pretty hot under the collar about the questions I was asking. I would expect denials, of course, even if they knew, but from their body language, they all seemed sincere."

When Lucky put his head in Mandy's lap, butting against her chest to get her to throw the ball, she covered the cell phone and whispered a fierce "No!" at the dog. Then she said to Quintana, "Could Faith have killed her uncle? Maybe if he was abusing her, she'd finally had enough and snapped."

"I considered that, but it would have taken someone fairly strong to wield that hatchet, a man or a large woman. Faith was a little thing. But we're looking into the possibility."

Lucky lay down with his head between his paws and whined at her. Mandy reached over and absently scratched behind his ears while she digested these revelations. Could the risky behavior that Cynthia mentioned last night have been an incestuous relationship between Faith and her uncle? Did Cynthia know about it?

"You're awfully quiet," Quintana said.

"Sorry, this is a lot to take in. You know, when Cynthia said Faith was taking a risk, one thing that came to mind was that Faith was using drugs. Did they find anything in her system?"

"No alcohol. The other toxicology tests will take awhile. Her body had been in the water quite awhile, but they should still be able to tell if she was abusing drugs." He paused. "Would you be willing to do something for me?"

"What do you need?"

"After you talk to Cynthia, let me know her reaction. You can tell her about the hairs matching. I want to find out if she knew anything about Faith and Howie. Maybe she had warned Faith to avoid her uncle. The risk she mentioned may have been that Faith was sleeping with her uncle and trying to keep it secret from her family. If Cynthia knows that we know about the hairs, she may open up some more to you. The chances of that are certainly higher than if I talked to her."

Mandy's hand stilled. "I'm not sure I'm comfortable snitching on my friend."

"The only people you'd be snitching on are both already dead."

———

When Mandy went back inside the kitchen with Lucky, she found lukewarm burritos waiting for her in the microwave. She zapped them for another minute, smothered them with salsa, and wolfed them down. Not a great tasting meal, but one that filled the gaping hole in her stomach. While she was washing her plate, her phone rang. It was Cynthia.

"Mandy, I hate to ask this of you, but my aunt and her family want to talk to you."

"Why me?"

"Well, um, because I told them you were the one who found both Uncle Howie and Faith."

"Damn it, Cynthia, I don't want to describe their bodies to grieving relatives. Not only would I feel really awkward about it, I don't think it would be helpful."

"Aunt Brenda wants this, and so do I, Mandy. You did say you'd do whatever I needed to help me through this."

Mandy sighed. "Yes, I said it and I meant it. Okay, I'll meet you at your place, and we can drive over together." Mandy hung up and looked down at Lucky. "Sorry, fella. I've got to leave you alone again."

Lucky snorted and padded off as if he understood her words.

Mandy called Quintana back to make sure it was okay for her to visit Faith's family. He told her that as long as she didn't divulge anything about the investigation and reported back to him with her impressions, it was fine. In fact, he encouraged it. Then she picked up Cynthia and followed her directions to the Ellis home on the outskirts of Salida. During the drive, Mandy tried to bring up her questions about Faith again, but Cynthia stone-walled her.

"Faith's troubles were private," Cynthia said.

"I hate to tell you this, Cynthia, but Faith's hair was found in Howie Abbott's sleeping bag."

Cynthia sucked in a breath, then she quickly recovered. "The whole family shares camping gear. That doesn't mean anything."

"Did you know about something going on between Faith and her uncle?"

Cynthia clamped her lips shut. "I told you. Faith was depressed and I was trying to help her."

"But you said Faith may have taken a risk. If whatever Faith was doing is related to her death, if it caused someone, like her uncle, to kill her, then the police need to know."

"But you don't. If the autopsy shows she was killed, I'll talk to the police." Cynthia turned her head to stare out the passenger window, signaling the conversation was over.

The Ellis home was situated on the lower flanks of Methodist Mountain south of Route 50, in an older neighborhood. The two-story half-brick, half-tan-siding home squatted among stands of gnarled pinion pine and juniper. It had no yard to speak of, except a small fenced-in flower garden in the front. The fence most likely was erected to protect the flowers from being eaten by mule deer. Late summer mums and impatiens bloomed among the fading petunias and dried stalks of iris.

A faded red extended-cab pickup truck with the logo of Lee Ellis's small rafting company on the door panel sat in the driveway. He'd bought the company from the struggling owner just prior to the family's move to Salida. Mandy vaguely remembered when her uncle introduced her to Lee at a gathering of the Arkansas River Outfitter Association members in May. Maybe Rob had had a chance to get to know the man better over the summer. While she crunched up the gravel path to the front door with Cynthia, Mandy made a mental note to ask Rob about Lee as well as Jesse.

Cynthia rang the bell. An older woman with light brown hair streaked with gray and wearing a checked flannel shirt over faded jeans opened the door and gave Cynthia a hug. While Cynthia made introductions, Mandy had a chance to study Brenda Ellis. The woman's features bore a slight family resemblance to Cynthia's and were an older, more flaccid version of her daughter's. Her eyes were reddened and her face puffy and strained as if she'd been crying recently. Rightfully so, Mandy thought, since Brenda had lost both her brother and her daughter in the past few days.

Brenda ushered them into the house and introduced Mandy to her husband. Lee was a tall, rangy John Wayne look-alike with a full head of gray hair and large hands that engulfed Mandy's when they shook.

"We've met," Lee said.

"Yes, last summer," Mandy replied. "When I came to an AROA meeting with Uncle Bill."

Lee nodded. "He impressed me when I met him. Folks around here really seemed to look up to him."

"Thanks." Mandy still missed her uncle every day, but it was good to hear how well he was respected in the commercial rafting community.

"And this is my son, Craig," Brenda said with a guiding hand on Mandy's arm.

Mandy shook hands with a younger version of Lee, who looked to be in his early twenties. "Nice to meet you," she said, then immediately regretted it, because the circumstances were anything but nice.

The Ellis family didn't seem to notice, though, as everyone settled into the overstuffed living room furniture. Lee and Brenda sat in matching La-Z-Boy chairs that were obviously their de facto reserved seats. On the end table next to Brenda's lay a stack of women's magazines and a box of tissues. A basket on the floor in front of the table was stuffed with a knitting project, something in blue and gray yarn. The end table next to Lee's chair held a fly-tying kit, a can of Bud, and the TV remote.

Mandy felt squashed between Craig and Cynthia, both stiff as boards, on the sofa. In the awkward silence that followed the greeting and seating ritual, she blurted out, "I'm so sorry for your loss."

Tears welled up in Brenda's eyes, and she reached for a tissue.

Lee covered her other hand with his. "This has been real hard on Brenda. To lose a brother and then a daughter so soon after is more than one woman should have to bear."

"No mother should outlive her child," Brenda said in a hoarsened voice. "It's heartbreaking. Absolutely heartbreaking."

Lee gave her hand a squeeze, swallowed hard, then looked at Mandy. "We understand you were the one who found her."

"Yes."

He shifted in his chair, as if it was suddenly too confining. "They called me in to identify her body."

"I'm sorry. That must have been awful. I didn't realize they'd ask you to do that since we all knew it was her, from her photo."

Another awkward silence. Next to Mandy, Cynthia dabbed at her eyes.

Brenda cleared her throat and glanced at Lee. "Lee said she looked peaceful. Is that how she looked to you when …when you pulled her out of the water?"

Mandy nodded, then took a deep breath, while the image of the girl's bruised but serene face appeared in her mind, her long brown hair swirling in the water. "Her eyes were closed as if she was sleeping."

The whole Ellis family leaned forward.

Mandy realized they needed to hear more. She didn't want to describe Faith's naked body, however, and the bloating that had begun to swell the torso. "Her face was beautiful, even with the bruises."

Brenda gasped and put a hand to her cheek. "Bruises?"

"From the river, most likely," Mandy hastened to add.

"What do you mean?" Brenda asked.

"The force of the whitewater. It bangs things, people, against the rocks. Even folks who fall out of rafts in the rapids wind up with bruises." Mandy winced. "Sorry, I'm not saying this very well."

"No, no, that's okay. I know this can't be easy for you." Brenda crumpled her tissue. "They told Lee that the river probably removed her clothes, too. What do you think? Can the rapids do that? I hate to think of her starting out that way."

Next to Mandy, Craig dropped his head and squinted his eyes shut, as if he didn't want to hear about his sister's naked body being churned by the river.

"I just started working as a river ranger this spring, so I don't have much experience with … situations like this." Mandy paused, tried not to squirm. "But my instructor said, in my training this spring, that it's very common for bodies, um people, to be found partially or totally unclothed. So, yes, that's probably what happened."

God, could I sound any more lame?

"And could you tell how she died?" Craig asked. "Did you see any, um, wounds, or anything?"

Mandy shook her head. She glanced at Lee, and he shook his head, too, so she added, "Hopefully, the coroner found something today during the autopsy."

"We want some answers, obviously," Lee said. "It's hard to believe little Faith isn't with us anymore. I keep expecting her to come flying in the back door, letting the screen bang, which she always did, no matter how many times I told her not to." A bittersweet smile rose to his lips then faded. "Kinda wish I hadn't harped on that so much now."

"I remember her practicing on that guitar," Cynthia said in a choked voice. She nodded at the acoustic guitar that leaned up against the brick fireplace. "She has—had—such a sweet voice."

A series of awkward reminiscences followed. Of Faith's first date in New Mexico and the tearful breakup that followed almost immediately after. Of her attempts at cooking under Brenda's guidance that included both a delicious chocolate cake and a burned pot of macaroni and cheese. Of her struggles with math, and Craig's attempts to help her when he was home on the weekends while earning his business degree at New Mexico State. And about how unhappy she'd been with the move that spring.

"I know Faith didn't want to move until the summer," Brenda said. "Didn't want to be drop-kicked into a new high school and class schedule with only a few weeks to go until the end of her sophomore year."

"Moving during the school year is supposed to be the best time for kids," Lee said automatically, as if they'd gone over this many times already, but he was repeating it for Mandy's benefit. "That's so they can make friends more easily. And if I was going to take over a rafting business, spring was the only sensible time to do it."

"I know all the good reasons for the timing," Brenda said, "and deep down, I think Faith did, too. But she was so unhappy. That's why I asked Howie to take her under his wing, show her the river, teach her fly fishing and such." Her hands tore apart the tissue. "I guess that was a mistake."

Lee scowled. "That detective had no proof of anything improper between Howie and Faith. And he won't find anything, because there's nothing to find."

"This isn't something we should discuss with Mandy here." Brenda whispered.

Cynthia squirmed next to Mandy, and Craig's hands gripped his knees so tightly his knuckles turned white.

Given the family's reactions, if Howie had been abusing Faith and one of them found out, Mandy could envision any of them reacting violently. She still felt she had to tread gently here, though. "Detective Quintana has to look into all possible leads," she said, "and since I'm a part of the investigative team, I know what he's doing. So if you want to talk—"

"He's barking up the wrong tree is what he's doing," Lee shouted, his face reddening and his hands clenching into fists.

Brenda put a hand on Lee's arm, shot him a look, then turned to Mandy. "As I said, we aren't going to discuss it."

A dead quiet descended on the room, until Mandy realized that if anything more was going to be said, she had to be the one to speak first. Even though she didn't want to, she felt she should offer information about Howie, since Cynthia had implied that they wanted to know. "Um, did you want to know anything about Howie's discovery?"

Brenda shook her head violently and looked away, her fist to her mouth.

This was the point where Mandy should have steered the conversation in another direction, but she couldn't think of anything besides the old standby, "How 'bout them Broncos?" and that was definitely inappropriate. She was saved by the cell phone ringing in her purse.

"Excuse me." She stood and walked into the hall while digging for her phone. "Hello?"

"Hey, Mandy," Rob answered. "You still up for listening to Ian's bluegrass band at the Vic tonight? Their first set starts in a half hour."

Mandy glanced at her watch. Almost eight-thirty. "Hold on a minute. I'm at the Ellis house with Cynthia. Let me ask her how much longer she wants to stay." She signaled for Cynthia to join her in the hall.

Mandy held her hand over the phone and whispered. "This is Rob. He wants me to listen to a friend's band play at the Vic with him. How long do you want to stay here and do you need me to stick around later? I'm happy to say no to him if you need me."

Cynthia shook her head and whispered back, "It's getting pretty awkward in there. I think they've asked all the questions they can handle right now. And it's about all I can handle, too. Let's use the call as an excuse and bolt." She put a hand on Mandy's arm. "And you don't need to stay with me, but thanks for the offer."

Cynthia went back to the Ellis family to say that they had to leave, while Mandy made plans to meet Rob at the bar. After a flurry of hugs and goodbyes, they left the house and got in Mandy's Subaru.

While Mandy put the car in reverse, Cynthia said, "Thanks. I know that was hard for you, but I think it helped. I know it helped me."

"If they want to talk about Howie later, I can come back," Mandy offered.

Cynthia stared out the passenger side window. "The less said about good old Uncle Howie, the better."

———

An hour and a half later, Mandy was whirling in Rob's arms in front of the small stage at the back of the Victoria Tavern, trying to keep up with his lively two-step. She gave a desperate wave to the acoustic guitar player, Rob's friend Ian, who laughed and kept on strumming. Just when she thought she'd have to beg Rob to rest for a minute, the song ended with a flourish from the banjo player. Rob and Mandy joined in giving a resounding hand to the band.

Ian announced the band would take a short break, so Mandy and Rob walked back to the table they were sharing with Kendra, Ajax, and Dougie. Kendra had a sheen of sweat on her brow, and Dougie's mop of hair was damp. The three of them had been dancing together on the other side of the dance floor.

Mandy took a long, cool sip of beer then sat back and smiled. "This is exactly what I needed after that scene at the Ellis home."

Kendra's brow furrowed. "How's Cynthia taking the death of her uncle and her cousin? I noticed she's not working tonight."

"She's a lot more broken up about Faith's death than her Uncle Howie's," Mandy said. "There seems to have been some bad blood between her and her uncle."

Ajax shook his head. "Damn shame that girl had to die so young. Any idea how her body ended up in the river?"

"Not yet." Mandy let her head loll back against Rob's large, strong hand while he rubbed the tension out of the back of her neck. "Man, you know just what I need, Rob. Don't stop."

He grinned. "Nothing like some down-home bluegrass dancing and a neck rub to bleed the stress out of a hard day." He leaned over to whisper in her ear. "And some down-home loving, too, *mi querida*." He nipped the tip of her ear.

Delicious tingles tickled Mandy's neck, but she managed to elbow him playfully in the ribs. "Down, boy. Save that for later."

Dougie rolled his eyes. "The lovebirds are at it. C'mon, Ajax, how 'bout a game of darts?"

The two of them wandered off, and a friend of Kendra's asked her to play pool, leaving Mandy and Rob alone at the table.

Rob draped his arm across Mandy's shoulders and searched her face. "Seriously, though, are you okay? That can't have been easy, talking about Faith with her parents."

"I'm okay," she replied. "It had to have been a lot harder for them. They're just starting the grieving process."

"And they aren't going to have much time to themselves in the next few days. Howie Abbott's funeral is Tuesday, then Lee and Craig are working the fishing tournament for the next four days before Faith's funeral on Sunday."

"They aren't taking time off between the funerals?"

Rob shook his head. "In this economy and at this time of year, an outfitter can't turn down any opportunity that comes his way to meet potential clients. That's why I volunteered, too. Lee especially needs to do it, since he just bought the business."

"How's his business doing?"

"I really don't know. I know he's running trips because I've seen his boats on the river and his vans and trailers on the highway. But I have no idea if he's making any profit."

"I had barely talked to him before tonight," Mandy said. "Have you?"

"We've both been too busy lately. Haven't had time to do much besides wave at each other."

Mandy drained her beer glass. "What about Jesse Lopez? Do you know him at all?"

Rob refilled her glass. "The Jesse who owns the gas station? Why're you asking about him?"

"Apparently he had a grudge against Howie Abbott."

"Jesse could hold a grudge all right," Rob said with a nod. "Especially when it was justified. I had to talk him out of filing charges against a couple of other gas station owners who always put up price changes on the same day. He groused about it for weeks afterward."

"Really? Why'd you talk him out of it?"

"The suit would have been thrown out. It wouldn't have gotten him anything other than a bad rep among other business owners in town. I told him that sometimes you've just got to let things slide, especially if you're a Hispanic business owner in this valley."

Mandy nodded. She had heard Rob say many times that he and other local Hispanic businessmen had to earn market share by being sharper than their rivals, reacting quicker to changing conditions. All reasons he wanted to expand RM Outdoor Adventures. "So you and Jesse know each other pretty well."

"I guess I'd say we're friends, though we're not that close. I've fished with him and his brother a few times. He's good." Rob finished off his beer. "Mostly, we just talk business, whether or not tourism's growing in the valley and by how much. When's a good time to expand. Things like that. Speaking of which ..."

Uh oh. Mandy stiffened.

Rob didn't seem to notice as he poured himself another beer from the pitcher. "Have you had a chance to think anymore about selling your uncle's place?"

"Barely." Mandy took a gulp of beer. "I've been a little busy."

"I know, and I know it's hard for you to give up a house that has so many memories for you. But if we're going to expand the business and offer year-round adventure trips, like we agreed, we've got to start. Before scheduling any climbing trips this fall, we have to enroll guides in training classes and order the equipment. Soon. And we don't have the money for that."

He studied her for a moment then reached into the pocket of his jean jacket that was draped on the back of his chair. He pulled out a business card. "The wife of one of the other outfitters is a real estate agent. I asked around, and people seem to think she's pretty good. Why don't you give her a call?"

Reluctantly, Mandy took the card. "I don't think Uncle Bill's place is ready to put on the market." *And I'm not ready to put it on the market.*

"That's something this agent can help you with. She'll do a walk-through of the property, tell you what needs to be done to make it show well. And she can give you an idea of what it'll sell for."

Mandy flipped the card over and over in her hand, as if it were a hot potato. She refused to read the name on it.

Rob put a hand over hers, stilling her fingers. "I know you're not used to the idea yet, but we can't afford to wait until you're a hundred percent comfortable with it to start the process. The agent will need some time to schedule the appraisal, draw up the papers, and arrange for whatever repairs are needed before you can put the house on the market. Let her start on that stuff, at least. Then when you're ready, the property will be ready."

Mandy stuffed the card into her jeans pocket. "Okay, I'll call her."

"She works on Saturdays."

Mandy blew out a breath. "Tomorrow, then."

"Excellent." Rob stood and held out a hand. "Now, let's go to my place. I have plans for you, *mi querida*."

EIGHT

Fishing is a delusion entirely surrounded by liars in old clothes.
—DON MARQUIS

MANDY WOKE IN ROB's arms Saturday, disoriented at first because she wasn't in her own bed. Sunlight streamed through the partially closed mini-blinds in Rob's bedroom window, striping the rumpled bedclothes. She smoothed her hand over the quilt that had been lovingly and painstakingly handmade by a generous aunt of his in Pueblo. Pieced in natural colors of orange, brown, and ivory, with accents of turquoise, the pattern was the Oso Grande or Big Bear. Rather than being scary, the large paw print design made her feel safe, comforted, and protected, much like being held by Rob made her feel.

She reveled a minute longer in his embrace, his soft exhales stroking her cheek, until she caught a glimpse of the alarm clock on his nightstand. Almost eight o'clock. Lucky would be pining for her, and if she wasn't mistaken, Rob had some mid-morning whitewater rafting trips to prepare for. She nudged him until he opened one sleepy eye.

"It's almost eight," Mandy said. "Don't you have a few trips going out this morning?"

He groaned and rolled onto his back, throwing an arm over his face. The movement exposed his bare, muscular chest and the dark hairs running down his abdomen.

Mandy stifled an urge to trace her fingers down the sensual path the hairs defined and instead swung her legs out of the covers. "And I've got to get home and take care of Lucky."

Before she could stand, he clasped her arm and gently drew her to him for a kiss. "Good morning."

She smiled. "Good morning to you, too." He released her and she got up and started picking up her clothes from the floor where Rob had flung them last night after removing them piece by piece—with his teeth.

The memory sent a delicious tingle down her legs and almost sent her back into the bed, but they both had places to go, things to do. With another glance at the handsome hunk in the bed, who lay there watching her, she scurried into the bathroom.

When she emerged fully dressed, Rob had thrown on some jeans and had the coffee pot perking. "Remember to call that real estate agent today."

"Sure, okay." She peeled a banana and refused to let the reminder annoy her. "I want to talk to Quintana, too. See what Faith's autopsy report has to say."

While Rob made toast, she pulled out the coffee pot to pour them both a cup then returned the pot to catch the rest of the coffee. He put out jam for himself and handed her the jar of peanut butter.

Mandy smiled at him while she slathered it on her toast. He knew one of her favorite breakfasts was sliced bananas and peanut butter on toast. Just as she knew he savored his mother's home-made jams. They were getting pretty comfortable with each other's likes and dislikes, she realized with a jolt. It was almost as if they could live together…

To get off that dangerous train of thought and to tease Rob, she stuck her finger in the peanut butter jar then put her finger in her mouth to slowly suck off the sweet treat.

He let out a low growl. "Woman, you are going to make me late to work."

Mandy removed her finger and sat up primly to take a bite of toast. "Whoops, got some crumbs on my chest." She swept her hand across the bare tops of her breasts rising above the low-cut slinky top she'd worn dancing the night before.

Rob's dark gaze followed her hand while Mandy trailed her fingers down her cleavage. When he glanced at her face, she gave him a sly smile.

He shifted in his chair and tugged at his jeans. "You are an evil temptress." He tore his gaze from her breasts and looked out the window while slurping his coffee then taking a deep breath.

"I'm just giving you something to think about while you're on the river." Mandy laughed lightly to change the mood and took another bite of her toast. "So what trips are going out this weekend?"

Showing his relief at being distracted, Rob quickly told her about the rafting trips scheduled for that day and Sunday while the two of them finished their breakfast. Sunday was nowhere near as busy as Saturday was going to be.

"How about if I fix you dinner tomorrow night?" Mandy asked, while she put her cup in the sink. "I haven't cooked for you in awhile."

Rob grinned as he stood to refill his coffee cup. "Is my little wildcat becoming domesticated?"

She gave him a kiss and slapped him on the butt before she walked out. "No way, José!"

———

After Mandy took Lucky for a long run and showered, she called Quintana to see if he was in his office and had the autopsy report. He said it was coming off the printer as they spoke, and if she came over they could read it together. Itching to know what the coroner had concluded, she hopped into her blue Subaru and zipped over to the sheriff's office. Soon, they were both pouring over the pages while sipping weak coffee from Styrofoam cups. Mandy knew the bitter brew was made from the cheapest tub of ground coffee the administrative assistant had been able to find.

"Estimated time of death is Saturday evening," Quintana said. "So Faith Ellis couldn't have killed her uncle, who was axed on Sunday afternoon."

Mandy set aside her coffee while making a face. She'd given it a chance, and it had failed miserably. "But could he have killed her?"

"Maybe."

The report was inconclusive on the manner of death. Faith had suffered a blow to the back of the head, enough to render her unconscious, but not enough to kill her. However, the forensic pathologist couldn't determine if the blow came after her body was in the river, from hitting something like a rock or a submerged tree branch, or if it came before. His official opinion of cause was drowning. She was alive and still breathing when she went into the water, because she had sucked water and river debris into her lungs. But he couldn't say whether the manner of death was accidental, suicide, or homicide.

Quintana leaned back in his chair and smoothed his mustache. "Faith could have fallen, or she could have jumped in the river herself. Her family told me she had been pretty despondent lately. And you said Cynthia told you Faith had been depressed."

"But how did she get into Brown's Canyon?"

"She could have caught a ride from almost anyone driving north out of Salida on 285. And whoever that was could have dropped her off at Ruby Mountain, Fisherman's Bridge, or Johnson Village. I've assigned a couple of patrol officers to ask around at those locations, to see if anyone saw her or gave her a ride. At least we know that she didn't ride her bike up there because it's still in the garage."

Quintana paused. "Did you read the rape kit results?" When Mandy shook her head, he found the page and handed it to her.

While she read the report, a wave of sorrow washed over Mandy. *That poor girl.* The physical evidence showed that she had been raped and lost her virginity no more than a few hours before she died. The forensic pathologist found semen inside her, too, protected from the river's waters by the tight seal of the vaginal sphincter. The swab had been sent to CBI for DNA analysis.

Mandy looked at Quintana. "So Faith wasn't having an ongoing relationship with her uncle or some young guy, because she had just lost her virginity."

"Not necessarily," Quintana said. "Sexual stimulation can take many forms. But the rape kit results also show she wasn't a willing participant in this encounter."

"Does this make you think someone raped her and knocked her unconscious, then threw her in the river?"

"Or an alternate scenario is that she threw herself in the river after she was violated, possibly by someone she trusted."

"Someone she trusted? You mean her uncle."

"That's precisely who I mean. I'm going to call CBI to suggest they compare Howie Abbott's DNA with that semen sample before they try matching it to anyone else in their databases."

While Quintana made the call, Mandy sat in stunned silence, her mind racing over the implications. When he hung up, she said, "So if Howie Abbott raped his niece and someone found out, someone who cared about Faith—"

"That someone could have been the one who killed Howie Abbott," he added. "But until I know there's a match, I can't make that conclusion and question Faith's family. Her rapist could have been someone else, maybe someone who gave her a ride out of Salida."

Mandy sat back, the damning report heavy in her hands. "This is awful. When do you think we'll know?"

"Not until Monday or Tuesday at the earliest. The lab techs don't work on weekends like we do." Quintana reached over and took the pages from Mandy, tapped them together with his pages and slid the whole report into his growing Faith Ellis file. "I did get some news, though."

"What's that?"

"Ira Porter's fingerprints matched some of those lifted off the beer cans at Howie Abbott's campsite."

"So his story that the last time he saw Howie was when they fished together last Wednesday afternoon is a lie."

"Maybe, maybe not. The beer could have been Ira's to begin with, and Howie ended up with it somehow. That's something to explore with Ira. I asked him to come in for questioning this afternoon, saying I wanted to follow-up on the last session. He agreed. I'd like you to observe, compare what he says today with what he told you on the river. Can you do it?"

The laundry she was going to do on her day off would have to wait, as would cleaning her bathroom. Oh well, if she closed her eyes while she showered, she wouldn't see the soap scum. "Sure."

Quintana checked his watch. "He'll be here at one. That should give you time to grab some lunch."

Instead, Mandy used the time to stock up on groceries, putting together a menu for the dinner she was going to fix for Rob from what she found on sale—ground bison for burgers, mushrooms and steak sauce, toasted onion buns, salad fixings, and brownie mix. She munched on an apple and a cheese stick while driving home and called that lunch.

After she put away the food, she spied the real estate agent's card in her purse, Ms. Bridget Murphy. She almost didn't call, but she knew Rob would ask if she had. She picked up the phone and dialed.

The agent listened while Mandy described the property then said, "I can take a look at it this afternoon, see what needs to be done."

"I've got business at the sheriff's office this afternoon. In fact, I've got to go there now. Maybe Tuesday? That's my next day off."

"I could get the key from you and look at the property by myself," Bridget replied. "Then we can talk later this evening. How about if I meet you in the parking lot of the county government building in ten minutes?"

"Uh, sure, I guess."

"Great. See you soon." She hung up.

Mandy stared at the handset. *Boy, the woman is in a hurry.* Come to think of it, if she wasn't out showing properties to clients on a Saturday afternoon or hosting an open house, she must really be desperate for listings.

When Mandy returned to the sheriff's office, a middle-aged brunette wearing a crisp white shirt and a gray pantsuit stepped out of a late-model tan sedan. "Mandy Tanner?"

"Yes," Mandy replied while walking toward her.

The woman shook Mandy's hand. "I'm Bridget Murphy. We just talked on the phone. Do you have the key to your uncle's property?"

Mandy fingered the key on her keyring. "I'd really rather go with you."

"Oh honey, you can trust me," Bridget said with a dismissive wave of her hand. "I wouldn't be a real estate agent for long in this town if I messed with people's stuff. I won't touch a thing, I'll lock the place up tight when I'm done, and I'll return the key to you tonight. Seven okay?"

"Um, I guess." Mandy gave Bridget the address, pulled the key off the ring, and placed it in the woman's outstretched hand.

"See you at seven." Bridget turned on her heel and strode to her car.

Mandy had the distinct impression that she was being railroaded.

———

By one o'clock, Mandy was ensconced behind the one-way mirror looking into the interview room in the sheriff's office. She had a pad of paper, a sharp pencil, and another cup of the raunchy coffee. She needed some caffeine to keep her alert after being up late the night before, and bad coffee was still better than tea.

The door opened to the interview room, and Quintana showed Ira Porter to the seat facing the mirror. Ira looked nervous, glancing around and wiping his hands on his pants before sitting down.

Detective Quintana sat and tapped his fingers on a thick case file, probably Howie Abbott's. While Ira squirmed in his chair, Quintana opened the folder, took out a paper with some typing on it, closed the folder again, and leaned back in his chair. He clicked his pen a few times and smoothed his mustache while studying the paper.

Ira squirmed again. "Well? Will you get on with it already?"

Quintana looked up, a placid expression on his face. "Oh. Sorry about that." He returned the paper to the file and leaned forward with his elbows on the table, crowding Ira's space.

"Can you tell me if Howie borrowed beer from you in the past few weeks or if you bought any together, divvied up a case, maybe?"

After a moment's thought, Ira shook his head. "Can't remember doing anything like that. We usually just take turns buying."

"So, tell me again about the last time you saw Howie Abbott."

Ira exhaled. "Why do we need to go over this again? It was the Wednesday afternoon before he was killed. We fished the upper Arkansas together, wading upstream from Granite."

"You sure you didn't see him after that? Maybe to share a few beers?"

"I'm sure."

"Here's the deal, Ira. The lab has matched your fingerprints with some that were found on the beer cans at his campsite at Vallie Bridge. Care to explain how that happened?"

Ira's eyes widened. After a long pause, words rushed out of his mouth, "Beer cans? Hell, I camp at Vallie Bridge all the time. There's good fishing there. Maybe I didn't pick up my trash carefully enough last time I was there."

"When were you there last, Ira?"

With a shrug, Ira said, "I don't remember."

Quintana stared at him, hard. "These beer cans also had Howie's fingerprints on them."

"Howie and I have camped there together lots of times." Ira crossed his arms.

"And, even more interesting is that not all of the beer in the cans had evaporated," Quintana added, cocking his head to one side. "The lab techs told me they had been recently opened, on the weekend Howie was killed."

Ira sputtered. "Well, they're damn wrong."

It was Quintana's turn to cross his arms. "You lied to me, Ira. You were with Howie Abbott last weekend. And lying about it sure seems suspicious."

"Howie Abbott and I were friends! Why would I kill my friend?"

"You've said the man can be kinda gruff at times." Quintana leaned forward again, getting into Ira's face. "While you two were sharing a few beers, maybe you got into an argument. Then that argument got physical. Alcohol can do that to people."

Ira sat back and waved his hands in front of him. "No, no, you're not pinning Howie's murder on me. I didn't do it."

"For me to believe that, Ira, you've got to come clean and tell me the truth about last weekend. The whole truth."

Lips pursed, Ira rubbed his forehead. "Dammit. I'll probably get thrown out of the tournament."

"Better that than getting thrown into jail."

"Shit. I've got no choice, do I?"

"Not if you don't want to be charged with murder."

"Okay, okay, here's the story. Howie and I camped at Vallie Bridge together Saturday night. We fished downstream during the afternoon, then had dinner and drank a few beers together that night."

Quintana lifted his pen from the paper where he'd been scrawling notes. "And?"

"Since only one family from out-of-town was camping there that night, Howie got the great idea to fish upstream, in the competition area, early the next morning."

"Which is cheating."

"Hell, yeah. I told him no way was I doing that, especially on a weekend, and we argued back and forth." Ira looked at Quintana and held up his hands, palms out. "But no, it didn't get physical. I said I wanted nothing to do with his scheme and moved my sleeping bag to the next campsite. I crawled in, turned my back to him, and refused to say anything else."

"Then what?"

"I heard him moving around a little, dousing the campfire. He kept mumbling things like, 'You'll change your mind tomorrow, Ira. I know you will. Hell, no one will see us.' I covered my ears. Finally, he got in his sleeping bag and I fell asleep. When I woke up Sunday morning, he was still sawing wood, so I packed up my stuff and left."

"You left? When?"

"It was around eight in the morning. I didn't want Howie to start up again and talk me into cheating with him. But, if word gets out that I was camping with him, no one will believe I wasn't cheating." His jowls drooping with dejection, Ira rested his chin on his hand.

"You see anyone at the campground Sunday?"

"Just that family, but they were all asleep when I left."

"How do you know they were from out-of-town? Did you talk to them?"

Ira shook his head. "Their van license plate was from Texas. We didn't really talk to them, just waved and said howdy."

"Did you find out how long they were planning to stay at the campground? Get their names?"

"They said they were pulling out Sunday morning. We didn't exchange names."

"Too bad," Quintana said. "They could have corroborated your story. What did you do after you left the campground?"

"I went to visit my mother in Colorado Springs, like I told you."

Quintana pulled a sheet out of his folder. "The visitor log shows you didn't sign in until almost three. What were you doing between eight in the morning and three in the afternoon?"

"I didn't get much sleep Saturday night. I was too steamed over the argument with Howie and worried that I'd have to find a new partner for the tournament. So when I got home Sunday morning, I collapsed into bed. Slept 'til noon, cleaned up, and headed out to Colorado Springs. I stopped at a Safeway there to buy a sandwich for myself and some flowers for Mother before I saw her."

"You use a credit card?"

"No, I paid cash." Ira paused and looked at Quintana's impassive face. "I swear that's the whole truth. There's no way I'd kill Howie. Even though the man could piss me off at times, we were friends, fishing buddies for life." His eyes filled and reddened. "His life was cut short, though."

"What about Howie's ring?"

"His ring? What about it?"

"Can you describe it to me?"

"You mean the one he wore on his little finger? It was his Salida High School ring, class of '79, but it didn't fit on his ring finger anymore. Gold with a brown stone."

"Was he still wearing it Sunday morning?"

Ira scratched his head. "I don't know. I didn't go near his sleeping bag, because I didn't want to wake him. He was wearing it Saturday night, though. He twirls it when he's agitated, and I remember him doing that. Why all these questions about his ring?"

Quintana ignored the question and tapped his pen a few times on the folder while reviewing his notes. "Okay, let's go over the story again. Construct a timeline."

Ira's eyebrows lifted. "You don't believe me?"

"Should I?"

"Fuck yeah!"

"I didn't say I didn't believe you. I just said I wanted to construct a timeline."

While the two of them rehashed Ira's story, Mandy looked over her own notes. She knew Quintana would make Ira repeat his tale at least twice to try to catch him in any slip-ups or inconsistencies. If the man had lied once, he could very well be lying again, changing his story to match the fingerprint evidence.

But he had teared up both during this interview and when she had talked to him on the river about Howie. Could he really manufacture grief so easily?

If Ira was telling the truth, that meant Howie Abbott was left alone from the time when the Texas family left the campground Sunday morning until he was killed that afternoon. Quintana probably would never find the family, and even if he did, they probably didn't see anything suspicious. If they had, wouldn't they have contacted someone?

Unless they killed Howie. A family with kids ax-murdering a stranger? Nah. Mandy would lay odds that whoever killed Howie Abbott knew him.

But who else besides Ira knew where Howie was on Sunday and wanted him dead?

NINE

Fly fishing is like sex, everyone thinks there is more than there is, and that everyone is getting more than their share.
—HENRY KANEMOTO

BY THE TIME MANDY got home after discussing Ira Porter's interview with Detective Quintana, the late afternoon sun's rays were slanting across her small yard and Lucky's outside water bowl was empty. Mandy refilled it and let the retriever inside to bounce around her, snuffling dog toys against her feet, while she sorted her laundry and threw a load in the washer. The two of them shared a hasty meal, kibbles for him and macaroni and cheese out of a box cooked with defrosted peas for her. She managed to clean up right before Bridget Murphy appeared on her front stoop and rang the doorbell.

The woman was kind enough—or astute enough—to put up with Lucky's obligatory crotch sniff, then reached down to scratch the dog's ears, sealing her friendship with Lucky for life. She stood and looked around. "Do you have a table where we can sit and spread out some papers?"

"In the kitchen." Mandy led the way. "Do you want something to drink?"

"Just a glass of water would be nice." Bridget dug a file out of her portfolio case and fanned out some pages on the table.

Once Mandy sat down with two glasses of water, Bridget started right in. "Your uncle's home is in pretty good shape. Needs a termite inspection and a thorough cleaning, but I can arrange both of those. If you want to sell it fast, I suggest we just list it as is. Were you planning to convey the furnishings that are left there?"

Convey? "I'm not sure what you mean."

"Oh, I mean that they'll be sold along with the house."

Mandy's brother had come up from Colorado Springs a few weeks after her uncle died, and they'd cleared out all of her uncle's personal items—clothing, toiletries, papers, foodstuffs, and so on. They each took home a few possessions to remember him by, and Mandy had sold some furniture really cheap to a few rafting guides fixing up a group rental home.

Before that, she and Rob had moved all of the rafts and outfitter equipment and supplies to Rob's place of business. But the two men had presumed she would want to finish the clearing out process, since she had the most sentimental attachment to the house. Without them pushing her on, she'd left the rest of the furniture alone, comforted by sitting in the same easy chairs she was used to whenever she visited the empty house.

"I don't know," Mandy said. "I don't have room for it all here."

Bridget looked around Mandy's small cottage. "I can see that. But maybe a few things? A couple of nice prints are hanging in the living room, for example."

"I really don't have time to go through everything and decide right now," Mandy said with dismay.

"I understand." Bridget patted her hand. "I tell you what. We can say that most of the furnishings will convey in the listing, minus a few items. I'll make up an inventory and bring you a copy, and you can put a checkmark by those things you want to keep. Easy peasy. I even have a guy who moves things for me, if you'd like me to arrange for him to bring the stuff you want to keep over here or to a storage unit."

This woman has all the answers. Mandy sighed. "I guess that'll work."

"Great!" Bridget pushed three property sale listings in front of Mandy. "I took the liberty of calling an appraiser. He'll do a quickie for us on Monday. In the meantime, I found these three comparables, given location and square footage. I suggest we list your uncle's property for the same price as the lowest one here. If the appraisal comes in significantly different from that, we can adjust accordingly."

Bridget sat back and took a discreet sip of water while Mandy looked over the listings.

The words blurred while Mandy tried to make sense of what she was reading, but all she could pay attention to was a tearful, childish voice in her head saying over and over again, "It's Uncle Bill's home. It's Uncle Bill's home." Then Rob's voice, full of reason and practicality, "It's just a building. Bill would want you to have the money, to build a successful business." She rubbed her aching head.

Bridget put a hand on her shoulder. "I know this is hard, honey. I've worked with a lot of clients who've had to sell the homes of their lost loved ones. I can tell you that putting off the decision just prolongs the agony. If you need to sell, you need to sell, and it's best to get it over with quickly."

With a last pat on Mandy's shoulder, Bridget removed her hand and slid a contract on top of the listings. "I'll do whatever I can to make this easy for you. Here's my listing contract."

Bridget's voice droned on while she explained each of the contract provisions until Mandy was ready to scream. When Lucky put his head in her lap, she saw a chance to escape. "Excuse me. I have to let Lucky outside. I'll just be a minute."

She almost ran for the back door and followed Lucky into the yard. The sun had dipped below the horizon and the first few stars were winking on as cobalt blue twilight gave way to inky darkness. She took a deep breath of the cool air, filling her lungs. Looking up at the North Star and the big dipper, she sent up a silent plea to Uncle Bill, asking for a sign.

What should I do?

No reply came, other than a neighbor clattering some trash cans to the curb, then moments later, the garage door closing. Lucky nudged her hand, and Mandy absently scratched his head. Then she had a thought. If she set the price of Uncle Bill's house to match the highest comparable instead of the lowest, maybe no one would make an offer for awhile, or if they did, it would be lower than the sale price, and they'd have to negotiate. Then she would be able to get used to the idea of selling it, and to visit the house a few more times.

Mandy gave a light slap to Lucky's rump. "C'mon, fella. Let's go inside."

She walked back into the kitchen and saw Bridget patiently waiting for her, hands in her lap.

"Okay," Mandy said, "Where do I sign?"

———

Mandy finally finished her laundry after midnight Saturday night, then crawled between the sheets while Lucky curled up on his pillow beside the bed. In what seemed like minutes, she was awakened by the doorbell, followed shortly by Lucky racing to the front door to bark at the visitor.

What the heck? She looked at the clock. After two a.m.

"Mandy, wake up!" Cynthia hollered through the front door. "And Lucky, shut up. It's me."

Groggy and rubbing the sleep out of her eyes, Mandy padded in her bare feet to the door and let Cynthia in. "What're you doing here so late?"

"I just got off work." Cynthia was wild-eyed, pacing and gesturing frantically. "I was thinking about Faith the whole time I was tending bar. I knew that if I didn't talk to you, I'd never get to sleep."

Mandy sat on the sofa and drew her chilly feet up under her. "So you woke me up instead."

Cynthia plopped down beside her. "I'm really, really sorry, but I know Faith's autopsy was done yesterday. I called Aunt Brenda from the bar, and she said Detective Quintana hasn't told them the result yet."

She clutched Mandy's arm. "I figured you and he were in cahoots, so he probably told you. I've got to know what they found out."

"I shouldn't say anything until Detective Quintana releases the report to the family."

"I won't tell a soul, I swear. Not even Aunt Brenda. But not knowing is tormenting me, Mandy. I can't wait any longer."

Mandy covered Cynthia's fingers and gently peeled them off her already bruised arm. She held Cynthia's trembling hand. "Why are you so anxious to know?"

"Remember when I told you I warned Faith about something, to be careful?" Cynthia bit her lip while Mandy nodded. "It wasn't something I warned her about. It was someone."

"What are you talking about?"

"Oh God, I don't want to tell you. I haven't told anyone why I warned Faith, not even her." Cynthia's eyes filled with tears. She hunched her shoulders, pulled her hand from Mandy's and tightly clutched her hands in her lap. "Maybe if I had, she'd be alive now."

A sick premonition crept into Mandy's gut. "I hope you aren't blaming yourself for Faith's death."

"That's exactly what I'm feeling!" A tear ran down Cynthia's cheek. "And that's why I need to know if that scum did to her what he did to me!"

"What scum? What did he do to you?"

"Uncle Howie. He raped me when I was fifteen, made me think it was all my fault, that I seduced him, that I was wicked and evil. He said if I told my parents, they'd send me away to juvenile

137

detention, where the guards and the other inmates would finish the job."

Horror-stricken, all Mandy could say was, "Oh, Cynthia, no." She tried to put a hand on Cynthia's shoulder, but her friend flinched.

Cynthia balled herself up tighter, drawing her knees up to her chest, as if trying to protect herself from attack. "He forced me to do all sorts of perverted things with him, in exchange for him keeping my secret. Finally I ran away from home when I was sixteen. I wound up in a youth shelter in Santa Fe. They let me stay and finish my GED even though I refused to tell them where I was from."

"But when I met you, you were here. How'd you make your way back?"

"My dad found me just before I turned eighteen, using a private investigator. He came down and brought me home. By then I'd toughened up, taken some self-defense classes, and got some counseling at the center. I called Uncle Howie after we got back and told him that if he ever touched me again, he'd be a dead man."

Mandy's eyes teared up, too, as she imagined the hardships a younger Cynthia had had to bear. "I don't know where you found the courage to do that. What did he say?"

Cynthia harrumphed. "He just laughed at me, said, 'Listen to the big girl now.' Then he lit into me, said he wasn't afraid of me, and threatened all kinds of grief if I ever told anyone what we'd been doing. He said he had no interest in me anymore anyway, that he'd already found someone else."

"Oh my God, not Faith!"

"No, she was just five years old then, hadn't matured yet to the age Uncle Howie liked his victims." Cynthia made a face. "Either he'd found some other teenage girl, or someone his own age, or he was lying to me."

"And you never told your folks or the police?"

Cynthia shook her head and dropped her feet to the floor. "I was too scared, embarrassed, even felt guilty. And I didn't want to think about what he did to me. I pushed it all way, way back in my psyche. I knew intellectually that none of it was my fault, that Uncle Howie was the predator. But emotionally, it was a lot harder to deal with."

As Mandy tried to imagine what she would have done if it had been her, a cold chill streaked down her spine. The ghastly memories. How would she deal with those? "You must have wanted to bury those memories."

"Yeah, I wanted to put it behind me, forget it all. I had started waiting tables, and after a few years, I decided I'd rather tend bar, that I'd earn more money that way. So, I went to bartending school in Denver, and came back here to work at the Vic, where I met all these great people. Salt of the earth, especially the river guides—and you. I'm so glad you're my friend."

Seeing Cynthia's body loosen up as good memories took the place of bad, Mandy hugged her. "And I'm glad, too. You're the best friend I could possibly have."

She pulled back a little to gaze at her friend's tear-streaked face. "But then you did dig up those memories. What made you decide to warn Faith? Because she turned fifteen?"

"No, it was more than that. Even though I tried to avoid Uncle Howie, we wound up attending some of the same family functions.

Once Faith grew up and filled out and her family moved back here, I caught him eyeing her."

"Oh, no."

Cynthia nodded. "Oh, no, is right. I would watch him from the other side of the room. Back in June, I pulled Faith aside, told her to watch out for Uncle Howie, that he was a pervert and she should never be alone with him."

"Did she listen to you?"

"I don't know. Problem was, I'm not sure she believed me, since I didn't, I couldn't, tell her how I knew he was a pervert." Cynthia looked at Mandy with tears shimmering in her eyes. "You see? If Howie got to her, if he raped her, maybe even killed her, then I failed. I failed Faith, and Aunt Brenda and Uncle Lee, and Craig and even myself. That's why I've got to know. I'm all knotted up inside."

Mandy couldn't prolong Cynthia's misery, but she wasn't sure she could alleviate it either. "All right, I'll tell you what I know. But you can't tell anyone that I told you anything about the autopsy."

"I swear I won't. Please, please…"

"You aren't going to like the result. The pathologist said Faith died Saturday evening, but he couldn't determine if her death was accidental, suicide, or murder. All he could say was that she drowned, that she was alive when she went in the river because she had water in her lungs. She had a blow to her head that might have knocked her unconscious, but he couldn't say whether that happened before or after she went in the river."

"So she died before Howie did."

"But we don't know if he killed her." Mandy paused.

Cynthia peered at her. "You know something else, something you're not telling me."

Mandy grimaced. "I can only tell you if you promise you won't have any contact with Faith's family until after Detective Quintana gives them the results."

"I promise." Cynthia had her arms wrapped around herself now, squeezing so tightly that Mandy imagined it must hurt.

Mandy took a deep breath and plunged in. "There was evidence of rape. We won't know until Monday or Tuesday whether the semen they found inside her matches Howie Abbott's DNA."

Cynthia pounded her fist into her thigh. "Damn him, damn that man! He deserved to die."

———

While Mandy ladled brownie batter into a pan Sunday evening for Rob's dinner, she felt deep sadness as the conversation with Cynthia ran over and over in her mind. She'd never seen her best friend so miserable and upset. Mandy had no idea how to help Cynthia recover from her present—and past—traumas and grief. She'd always thought of Cynthia as a happy-go-lucky gal, with her blonde jokes and willingness to listen to other people's problems at the bar. But now she couldn't help but think of her friend as a wounded victim. Maybe that's what made Cynthia so understanding of other people's woes.

Mandy pushed the pan into the oven and leaned back against the sink to lick the spoon while she pondered what to do. Lucky sat directly in front of her, his tail whapping against the floor, and stared at the spoon. Finally, Mandy scraped a bit of batter out of the bowl and held out the spoon to him. He started licking madly.

"It's easy to make you happy, isn't it Lucky?" She sighed. "If only people were so easy."

After knocking at the door, Rob opened it and stuck his head in. "How's my favorite river ranger?"

Lucky beat Mandy to the living room, but she got Rob's arms and mouth while the dog had to be content with rubbing against Rob's legs. After a thorough smooch, Mandy leaned against Rob's chest, reveling in the warmth and comfort of his strong arms around her.

Rob rested his head on top of hers. "Rough day? I didn't see you in Brown's Canyon this afternoon."

Mandy lifted her head to look into his worried eyes. "I patrolled Bighorn Sheep Canyon and Royal Gorge today. It was the usual stuff. Pulled some private rafters out of the water who were in over their head in more ways than one. Dealt with one mild hypothermia case. Even had the pleasure of unplugging a stopped-up toilet in the ladies' room at Parkdale."

She pulled back and took Rob's hand to lead him into the kitchen. "It wasn't my day that was rough. It was my night, early morning actually. I didn't get much sleep after Cynthia came by after the bar closed. I'll tell you all about it while I finish cooking. You can set the table."

While she fried the bison burgers, tossing in sliced mushrooms at the end to sauté them in the meat drippings, Rob set the table. He took the tossed salad and Italian dressing out of the refrigerator, along with bottles of beer for the two of them. And he listened quietly while Mandy first swore him to secrecy, then told him about her conversation with Cynthia.

He sat heavily while she carried the plates holding the burgers on toasted onion rolls to the table. "Damn. I never dreamed Cynthia was carrying around such a terrible secret."

"No one did."

"You'd think I would have picked up on it, though, given my sister's experience and what I went through with her."

Mandy stopped pouring steak sauce on her burger. "Your sister? Which one?"

"Nina, the youngest." Rob took a big bite of his burger. While he chewed, a smile spread across his face. "This is delicious."

"What happened with Nina?"

"You know she's divorced, right?" Rob gulped his beer.

"Yes. The marriage must not have lasted long, given that she's only twenty-three now. Your mother couldn't have been happy about it."

Rob frowned. "Mama doesn't approve of divorce, but this time she agreed that Nina should never have married that bum and she's much better off without him. He was abusing her."

"You're kidding."

"I should have seen the signs. They started coming less often to the Monday dinners at Mama's house. Nina kept thinking up one excuse after another. And when they did come, he spent most of his time drinking outside on the porch while she helped in the kitchen. She was quieter, too, didn't speak or laugh as much at the meals, and kept glancing at her husband when we sat down to eat. I thought it was because she was so in love with him. But she was trying to gauge his mood because she was so scared of his temper."

Mandy took a forkful of her salad. "How did you find out about the abuse?"

"Nina came to Mama one day, crying and hurting. He'd finally hit her where it showed, and she had a black eye and bruises on her arms. She told Mama that not only was he beating her, he was forcing himself on her. Mama called me, afraid that once Papa found out, he'd do something stupid and get himself hurt. I called Tomas and we confronted the bastard instead."

"Good for you guys! But Tomas. He's only twenty now. How old was he then?"

"Eighteen, and itching to avenge his sister." Rob stood to get another beer out of the refrigerator. "Frankly, so was I. We went over to their apartment, found the scumbag sitting on the sofa and watching TV like nothing had happened. We kicked him out. Literally. Threw in some good punches, too. We dumped his stuff on the sidewalk and told him that if he came anywhere Nina again, he was a dead man."

Looking at Rob's grim face, she was sure he meant to carry out the threat, if need be. "What happened next?"

"The coward slunk off with his tail between his legs. Nina moved back in with Mama and Papa and filed for divorce. Took her awhile to recover, but she's working now, has her own apartment that she shares with a girlfriend. She's even starting to date again."

Rob folded his arms and a pensive look overtook his face. "Looking back on it, I realized I should have known something was wrong when Nina stopped smiling. She has a beautiful smile, really lights up her face. But Cynthia still laughs, and cracks all those blonde jokes."

"Cynthia's abuse happened a long time ago. She's had more time to deal with it." A realization suddenly hit Mandy. "But she's not joking anymore. Not since she heard about Faith's death."

"You know, my sister's ex was scum, but Howie Abbott was worse, much worse. How could the family let him prey on his nieces like that?"

"I don't think they knew. There's no evidence that Faith told anyone, and Cynthia didn't either. That's what she's beating herself up about. She said that maybe if she'd told them, Howie wouldn't have gotten to Faith."

Rob finished his last bite of burger and picked up the salad bowl. While he scooped salad onto his plate, he said, "Someone got to Howie, though."

"Yeah." Mandy suddenly wasn't hungry anymore and pushed her plate away. "And I'm afraid someone in the family did it."

"If I was Lee or Craig and found out that Howie had raped my daughter or sister, I would have lit into him, just like I did with Nina's husband. A man takes care of his family."

Here was Rob's *machismo* speaking again, his belief that the man should be in charge that Mandy wasn't sure she agreed with. "But murder, Rob? With an ax? Could you really have done that?"

He silently drank his beer and lifted his hand, palm-up, as if considering wielding an ax with it. Then he sniffed the air. "When are those brownies going to be done? The smell is driving me nuts."

Mandy leapt up from the table. "Oh, damn. I never set the timer." She grabbed an oven mitt and pulled the pan out of the oven. The outside edges of the brownies had turned into a blackened crust. She tossed the pan on the stovetop. "They're ruined."

Rob stood and looked over her shoulder. "The middle still looks edible." He turned her in his arms and kissed her on the nose. "Thanks for making them for me. And for the delicious dinner, especially after staying up most of the night with Cynthia."

Exhaustion and worry finally caught up with Mandy, and she sagged against him. "I'm bushed."

"You go relax on the sofa. I'll clean up and bring in the brownies, the ones we can eat." Rob grinned. "They say chocolate is an aphrodisiac."

Mandy stumbled into the living room, with Lucky following behind. The idea of making love after their talk about abuse and rape felt weird, gave her the willies. She lay down and put her feet up. How was she going to break it to Rob that no matter how big a brownie he cut for her, she wasn't in the mood? Not in the least.

TEN

*I never drink water because of the disgusting
things that fish do in it.*

—W. C. FIELDS

TRAPPED IN HER CUBICLE doing paperwork in the AHRA Head-quarters building on Monday, Mandy kept getting up to refill her coffee cup. Then she'd go to the restroom and flush out the coffee. Each time, she would pass by the window so she could at least get a glimpse of the lovely late summer day outside. Maybe this was how zoo animals felt while pacing circles in their cages.

She envied the three river rangers who shared her office space and who weren't there. One had the day off, and the other two had gone out on patrol. It was a busy day on the upper Arkansas River for a Monday, because the fishing tournament controllers were out being trained and the organizing committee was staking river sections.

Thankfully Rob had understood how tired she was the night before, though he wasn't happy about it, and let her sleep long and deeply. She had made it up to him in the morning, so he left with a smile on his face. She smiled herself while she resumed work on an incident report. How would she describe the incident in her shower that morning? A swift water floundering, with two bodies rescued?

Oh, yeah.

Her pleasant reverie was interrupted by her phone ringing. It was Detective Quintana.

"I called for two reasons," he said. "First, I followed up on your Jesse Lopez lead. Questioned him yesterday. Yes, he was a long-term rival of Howie Abbott's, and yes, he was pretty upset about Howie cheating. But, he's got an alibi for Sunday a week ago. He was working at his gas station, same as he was yesterday. He manages the station on Sundays so most of his workers can have the day off; says he's not a church-goer himself."

"Can any witnesses back him up?"

"I've got a list of names from him, either folks who stopped by that he remembered or who paid with a credit card. We'll follow-up, but if any of them remember they were at the station when he says they were and remember seeing him there, his alibi is solid."

While Quintana was talking, Steve poked his head into Mandy's office, but she pointed at the phone, then mouthed to him, "Quintana." He nodded, pointed to his office, and left.

To Quintana, she said, "So Newt Nowak, Ira Porter, and Jesse Lopez have all come up with good stories for where they were on Sunday afternoon."

"Yep, anywhere but at Vallie Bridge. I'm hoping we find a hole in one of their stories."

"What about the family who had a reservation at another site?" Mandy asked. "Did your patrol officer get hold of them and did they have anything helpful to say?"

"They saw Howie and Ira on Saturday evening but just said hi in passing, like Ira said. They packed up and left Sunday morning about nine-thirty and said Howie was the only one they saw that morning."

"That backs up Ira's story that he left at eight."

"Or he could have just been somewhere else, fishing or taking a walk—or a piss."

True, Mandy thought. "What was Howie doing?"

"He had gotten up and was eating breakfast when they left, but they said he seemed to be in a foul mood, frowning and not saying much. They waved and said goodbye but he just gave a nod, and that was it."

"So they may very well have been the last ones to see him alive. Besides the killer."

"Unless Ira came back later. Or someone else." Quintana exhaled. "The pressure's on, with Faith Ellis's death hitting the news wires, too."

"Are the local press hounding you?"

"Them, the state press, and the Sheriff himself. I need a lead soon, on at least one of these two deaths. Though Faith's could very well have just been a sad case of accidental drowning or suicide. She certainly had good reason to be depressed."

Uh oh. That doesn't sound good. Mandy's stomach turned, and suddenly all of that coffee she drank during the day didn't seem like a good idea. "Does that reason have something to do with the second reason you called me?"

"Yep. I just got back from the Ellis home. We got the DNA results, and the semen in Faith Ellis's vagina came from Howie Abbott. I had to tell her family that her uncle had sex with her shortly before she died and we're pretty sure it was forced." He paused. "It was not a pleasant scene."

"I'm sure it wasn't." Mandy tried to imagine the horror and anger that Lee, Brenda, and Craig must have felt. To have confirmed the palpable fears she had felt when she visited them.

"The worst part was when I asked them all to come to the office to be fingerprinted."

Mandy remembered Rob's comment the night before about what he would have done if he had been in Lee's or Craig's shoes. "So you think one of them already knew about the rape and killed Howie on Sunday."

"That's why I watched their reactions carefully when I gave them Faith's autopsy and lab results. If any of them did know, they masked it well." He paused again, cleared his throat. "Speaking of family reactions, did you speak to Cynthia over the weekend?"

Mandy's stomach lurched again. "Yes."

"Well?"

"Remember I said I wasn't comfortable snitching on my friend?"

"And remember that I said the only people you'd be snitching on are both already dead."

"That's no longer true." Mandy shifted in her seat. "Cynthia told me something about Howie that I'm not sure I should share."

"Given what he did to Faith, I can already guess what she told you. I'm going to question her eventually, along with all of the members of the Ellis and Abbott families and their friends. I'll be fingerprinting her, too—already asked her to stop by the office. And," he added in a sterner voice, "if you know something relevant to these cases and you hold that information back, you could be obstructing justice."

"Shit." Mandy knew what that meant. She looked around. Her office mates were gone, but Steve or any of the other office staff could walk by or stop in at any moment. She got up and shut the door. "Okay, but if someone comes into my office, I'll have to finish later. I'm sure Cynthia doesn't want this news getting out."

"I'll keep what you have to say to myself," Quintana said solemnly.

Mandy took a deep breath then told him about Howie's sexual abuse of Cynthia and her fears that Faith had become his next victim.

After asking a few questions about the duration and frequency of Howie's abuse of Cynthia, which Mandy couldn't answer, Quintana asked, "How did Cynthia seem to you? Was she sad or angry about her uncle raping Faith?"

"Both. But probably more angry." Mandy hesitated, hating to incriminate her friend further, but Quintana had to know Cynthia's reaction. "Even though I told her we didn't know whose semen was inside Faith, Cynthia said, 'Damn him, damn that man! He deserved to die.'"

Mandy cringed as she had when she'd first heard the declaration. "But there's no way Cynthia would kill anyone. I know her. She'd never do that."

"Did you know she'd been abused by Howie before she told you Saturday night?"

"No."

"Then maybe you don't know Cynthia Abbott as well as you think you do."

———

Mandy was pacing the small river ranger cubicle space, debating whether or not to call Cynthia and what to say to her, when her phone rang again. She picked it up and said, "Hi again," thinking it was Detective Quintana calling back.

It wasn't. A woman's voice asked, "Is this Mandy Tanner?"

"Yes, it is."

"Hi, Mandy. This is Bridget Murphy calling."

The real estate agent was the last person Mandy wanted to talk to just then. "Oh hi, sorry, I thought you were someone else at first. What are you calling about?"

"Is this a bad time for you?" The woman sounded a little put off.

Mandy rubbed her forehead, where a doozy of a headache was building up. "I'm sorry. I'm not having a very good day."

"Well, then, I'll make it better for you! I have great news. We have an offer on your uncle's house."

Mandy sank into her chair. Her head began to throb. "Already? Didn't you just list it today?"

"Yes, and I invited a dozen real estate agents over for coffee and cookies and a tour this morning. One said she thought the house was a perfect fit for some clients of hers. They have a small gardening supply business and could use the equipment shed in the back for that. They're renting a storage space now. She showed her clients your uncle's home a couple of hours ago and they love it. Isn't that wonderful?"

"Sure, yeah." *Hell, no. How can I delay this?*

"There's only one minor issue to resolve. Because of the down economy, the couple is offering twenty-five thousand less than the asking price. Are you okay with that?"

Mandy sat up straighter. She had an idea. "Did the appraiser finish today, too?"

"Oh, yes, let me find the report." The sound of papers shuffling on a desk came over the phone. "Here it is. The appraisal came in at ten thousand less than your asking price, so this bid is only fifteen thousand less than that. You can feel real good accepting it, especially given this soft market."

This woman is just too eager. "Maybe. But I want to counter with the appraisal price. Let's see what the bidders do with that."

"Oh, well, if that's what you really want." Disappointment was evident in Bridget's diminished tone. "I'll contact the buyer agent and make the counter-offer. Are you sure you don't want to just accept, or maybe come down a bit on the counter, to halfway at least?"

"I'm sure." Then to appease Bridget, Mandy added, "Thanks for everything you've done. You've made this whole selling process very easy for me." *Too easy.* "Let me know what you hear from the buyers."

Mandy hung up the phone then sent a silent plea to the river gods that maybe the buyers would just walk away or find another property. She dug in her desk drawer for the aspirin bottle and swallowed two with the rest of her mug of coffee. She grimaced. The coffee had gone cold while she was on the phone.

After debating whether or not to refill her mug and deciding no way, that she was already stressed out enough, Mandy checked the clock and saw it was after five. She went to Steve's office, but he had already left for the day. Wondering what he had wanted, she spent a few minutes finishing her last incident report and tidying her desk. She decided to stop by Cynthia's place on her way home, see what her friend's reaction was to Detective Quintana's request to come in for fingerprinting.

———

When Mandy drove into Cynthia's driveway, she saw a man's mountain bike leaning against the wooden stairs leading up to the deck. A large riding helmet dangled from the handlebars, and the metal gleamed in the low rays of the sun dipping toward the horizon. *I should have called first.* Thinking Cynthia was entertaining a male visitor, Mandy considered turning around and going home.

But then Cynthia's door creaked open and her head poked out. "I heard your car drive up." She waved Mandy up the stairs. "C'mon up. Craig is here."

While Mandy ascended the stairs, she asked, "I'm not intruding?"

"'Course not!" When Mandy reached her, Cynthia whispered in her ear, "I'm glad you're here. He's in a foul mood. And he's drinking too much. Help me get him to stop."

Mandy walked into Cynthia's living room. Craig lay sprawled on her sofa, drinking from a can of beer. Three crumpled empties sat on the floor nearby.

Mandy raised an eyebrow at Cynthia then turned to Craig. "Hi, Craig, what's up?"

He sat up and rotated, taking his long legs off the sofa, and waved for Mandy to sit in the space he'd freed up. He tugged at his black stretch bike shorts, which didn't leave much to the imagination.

"I've just been fingerprinted is what's up. So were Mom and Dad." He showed her his fingers, which still had black ink around the nails. He rubbed the stains, as if trying to scrub them off. "After we got back from the county building, I had to get out of the house. Forgot my water bottle, so I stopped by here. Figured Cynthia would have some liquid refreshment." He gave her a wink and took another gulp of beer.

"Do you want something to drink, Mandy?" Cynthia turned to her kitchen.

"No thanks. Don't worry about me. Please sit." Mandy sure didn't want to encourage Craig to have any more beer by joining in with him. She waved Cynthia back toward her side chair, where Mittens waited expectantly for her mistress's lap.

When Mandy sank down on the sofa beside Craig, he added with a sneer, "So now the crack detectives at the Chaffee County Sheriff's Office think the whole Ellis clan are murderers, fingerprinting every God damn one of us. Hell, we're related to Uncle Howie, the sleazy rapist and committer of incest. We must have the stain of criminal behavior in our blood." He gulped the last of his beer and crumpled the can, letting it drop from his fingers onto the floor next to its brothers.

He turned to Cynthia. "Got another one?"

"How about a glass of water first, Craig?" Mandy said with a nod to Cynthia. "You probably need to be rehydrated before you drink another beer."

Cynthia dropped a miffed Mittens onto the floor and rushed into the kitchen to pour Craig a glass of water.

Craig didn't look too happy about the women's end run around his request.

"The sheriff's detectives are just doing their job, Craig," Mandy said. "I'm sure they don't think there's some family defect or anything. I mean, with this evidence that Howie … forced himself on Faith, you all could have had a motive for killing him."

Cynthia's hand shook as she put the glass of water on the end table next Craig.

"If any of us knew about it, you mean." Craig's lips twisted into a grimace of distaste. "He hid his perversion well. I never suspected a thing. I still can't believe he was so twisted and cruel. My own uncle. With my own sister, for Christ's sake!" He snatched up the glass and took a drink of water, spilling some down his T-shirt. He set the glass down hard on the table, sloshing out more, and swiped at his shirt.

Cynthia had settled back into her chair and sat twisting her fingers together. She glanced at Mandy, then nodded and took a deep breath. "Faith wasn't the only one, Craig."

Craig's eyes widened. "What do you mean?"

Oh, no, here it comes. Mandy clutched the arm of the sofa.

"He also raped me," Cynthia said softly.

As if he'd been physically shoved in the chest, Craig fell back against the sofa cushion. His mouth dropped open. "What?"

"It was a long time ago, when I was about Faith's age."

Cynthia choked out the whole sordid story, while Mittens meowed and rubbed against her ankles and Craig stared at her in stunned silence. His hands clutched his bony knees and his glass of water remained untouched.

"I warned Faith about him." She reached for a tissue to dab her eyes. "Told her to stay away from him, to never be alone with him. That Uncle Howie was a pervert."

"Did you tell Faith what he did to you?"

Cynthia shook her head. "I couldn't. Every time I tried to say something to her about it, I started to shake and sweat."

"Did she believe you when you told her Uncle Howie was a pervert?"

"I thought she did, but now I don't know. Maybe she didn't believe me. Maybe that's how he got to her. The memories are horrible, Craig. I didn't want to dredge them back up." She scrubbed her palms on her jeans as if trying to wipe away the past. "You're the first person in the family I've told."

Craig peered at Mandy. "What about you? Did she tell you?"

"Not until two days ago."

He dropped his head into his palms, and his fingers clutched his hair. After a moment of silence, he looked up at Cynthia, his eyes shimmering. "Do you realize that if you'd told Faith what he did to you, she might be alive now?"

A tear trickled down Cynthia's cheek, and she covered her mouth with her hand. Silently, she nodded.

Mandy's own throat was constricted so tight she couldn't speak either.

Craig sat up straighter and his voice rose, "Or if you told me, or Uncle Lee, or Aunt Brenda? Then one of us could have acted, protected her."

Cynthia's fingers pressed so hard on her lips that the tips went white. She nodded again.

Craig shot to his feet. "I hope you can live with that knowledge, Cynthia. I sure wouldn't be able to. I wouldn't be able to look at myself in the mirror." He was shouting now. "I'd hate the sight of my own lying face. In fact, right now I can't even look at you!"

He stormed out, the door slamming shut behind him. His heavy footsteps clattered down the stairs.

Mandy went to the window and watched him lurch onto his bike and pedal away, his legs pumping furiously. One foot slipped off a pedal and the bike wobbled, but Craig soon righted it and sped on.

She turned back to look at Cynthia who still sat in her chair, tears streaming silently down her cheeks.

"Do, do you think," Cynthia choked out, "he'll be okay on the bike?"

Mandy nodded. "He's controlling it all right. He should be able to get home. He only drank four beers, after all, and he's a big guy."

She approached Cynthia, kneeled next to her chair, and put an arm around her friend's shoulders. "I'm sorry you had to listen to him say such awful things. I'm sure he didn't really mean them, that it was his grief and anger talking."

Cynthia laid her head against Mandy's chest. "But everything he said was true. I killed her, Mandy. I killed Faith."

ELEVEN

The two best times to fish is when it's rainin' and when it ain't.
—PATRICK F. MCMANUS

THE NEXT DAY, TUESDAY, Mandy dressed somberly for Howie Abbott's funeral. When she donned the same mismatched black skirt and brown button-down shirt that she'd worn to another murder victim's funeral in June, her thoughts turned to the family of the man she'd pulled from the turbulent waters of the Numbers and who had died in her arms.

Like that family, the dark underbelly of the family of Howie Abbott and Faith Ellis was being exposed to the light. Unfortunately, this time her best friend was involved. If Cynthia's terrible secret was exposed to all, Mandy was sure her friend would be devastated. And the wounds would go much deeper than robbing Cynthia of her sense of humor—and the blonde jokes that Mandy had to admit she missed.

Mandy slipped on a pair of brown sandals—at least they weren't her river-running Tevas—and started searching for her umbrella. The day had dawned gloomy and gray, befitting a funeral, and by the time Mandy had gotten dressed, it had started drizzling. She knew she used to have an umbrella, but after ten minutes of fruitless digging she hadn't found it. And Lucky was no help, sticking his nose in the piles she was shoving around, pulling out random articles of clothing and shoes, and begging Mandy to play tug-of-war with them.

Finally she gave up the hunt, stood, shrugged on her AHRA splash jacket and pulled up the hood. At least she'd be dry from the waist up. She went in the living room to find her car keys, wishing she didn't have to attend Howie Abbott's funeral. But, she assumed Cynthia would attend, and she wanted to be there to support her friend. Also, Mandy was curious who else would show up. Howie's murderer was likely to be one of the attendees.

Lastly, she was the one who'd found Howie's body, so it seemed fitting to be present when he was laid to rest. Then maybe the nightmare images of the gash in his neck, the hatchet, the flies, and the congealed blood that had plagued Mandy's nights would also be laid to rest.

With an involuntary shudder, she thought, *I sure hope so.*

Lucky flopped down on the floor and watched her with sad eyes, his head between his paws, his mood echoing Mandy's gloomy one. Though Mandy had let him out to do his business in the yard earlier, he was unhappy because he was stuck inside now and his mistress didn't want to play.

At the front door, she turned back to give him a pat on the head and scratch his ears. "Sorry we can't go out and play, fella." But she couldn't bring herself to put on a happy face for the dog.

She drove her Subaru along wet streets to church central, the corner of 4th and D streets and the nucleus of Salida's church population. The Episcopal and Catholic churches were one block away. Clustered at this intersection stood the First Christian Church, the First United Methodist Church, and the First Baptist Church where Howie Abbott's funeral was scheduled to be held.

Mud-spattered cars and pickup trucks already filled the small parking lot of the church and lined the streets for a block in each direction. Mandy parked a block and a half up D Street. Before she got out of the car, her cell phone rang.

It was Steve. "I'm glad I caught you before you went into the service. I wanted to ask you yesterday to convey my sympathies and those of the whole ranger staff to the Ellis family."

"Sure," Mandy said, "and I'm sorry I didn't get back to you before you left."

"When I saw your closed door, I figured you were in a hot and heavy conversation with Quintana. Anything you can share with me?"

"Not now." *And maybe never.*

"I understand." Steve's tone, however, conveyed disappointment. "Let me know if you need anything, though, resources or my help, to close this case. I've been getting a lot of calls about it."

"I will. Thanks." While Mandy pocketed her cell phone, she thought, *so Quintana isn't the only one being pressured.*

She got out of her car and walked back to the church. The rain had washed its pearly white brick walls until they shone under the gray clouds, almost as if they were lit from within. The steep wood-shingled roof with its tall square steeple cleaved the sky.

A car drove by, splashing her legs with muddy water. *Great, just great.* If she hadn't already looked bedraggled, she sure did now. She tucked a damp tendril of hair back under her hood as she'd chosen to not tie up her hair in a ponytail as usual. With a sigh she hunched her shoulders against the rain.

Just outside the church, Mandy spied Detective Quintana in his knee-length official sheriff's office raincoat and plastic-covered hat. He was standing with Sandra Sechrest, the Chaffee County Visitor's Bureau Chair. The woman was perfectly attired in a black skirted suit and short pumps, with not a hair out of place. She stood under a large black golf umbrella, seemingly unperturbed by the wet drops splashing on the pavement around her. Quintana watched folks stream into the church while he gave a nod every now and then to Sandra's chatter.

After Mandy greeted the two, Sandra pulled Mandy under her umbrella. "Come share this with me, dear. You look like a drowned rat."

Mandy felt like one, too—a very unfashionable and gawky rat compared to the well-groomed sleek mouse next to her. "I'm a little surprised to see you here. I thought you might be out observing the first practice day of the tournament."

"Oh, I'll be at the check-in point this afternoon," Sandra replied. "I've lined up a reporter and photographer from the *Chaffee County Times* to interview some of the teams coming in off the river, especially the foreign teams. I think their reactions to our

162

lovely river and our beautiful town will make for good reading, don't you?"

"Sure, I guess so."

"I'm going to make sure the reporter sends the article and photos to the teams' hometown newspapers. It will be great publicity for the whole valley. And I'll make a statement about how we're a great tourism destination not only for rafting and fishing, but for all sorts of activities, from hot springs soaking to antiquing, bird watching to rock climbing, and more."

She smiled and patted Mandy's arm. "Sorry, I'm getting carried away with my little speech already. I just wish Howie Abbott's murder wasn't crowding the tournament news off the front page and casting a dark pall on our fair valley. Any progress, Detective? Making an arrest soon?" She looked hopefully at Quintana.

He shook his head. "It's still a very active investigation, but we haven't reached the point where we can arrest someone yet."

Sandra pursed her lips. "Too bad." She sighed. "Well, I suppose I should go in. Do you two want to join me?"

"I need to ask Detective Quintana something." Mandy stepped out from under the umbrella. "Thanks for sharing your umbrella with me, though."

"Oh, well…then I'll see you inside." Looking a little put out, Sandra turned and minced toward the steps leading up to the church's front door.

After Sandra left, Mandy turned to Quintana. "More pressure, huh?"

"Yep. She and many of our other civic-minded citizens would prefer that people's first impression of Chaffee County be for its superb fishing, instead of a macabre murder case."

"And I heard another complaint. I stopped by Cynthia's place last night and Craig Ellis was there, bitching about being finger-printed. Do you really think one of the Ellises killed Howie Abbott?"

Quintana pulled her onto the wet lawn of the church, out of earshot of those splashing by on the sidewalk and gingerly making their way up the slippery steps. "I questioned each of them individually about where they were and what they were doing the Sunday afternoon Howie was killed. Brenda said she was home alone doing chores and cooking dinner."

"So there's no one to vouch for her."

"Right, except when I questioned Lee and Craig, they said when they got home there were vacuum tracks on the rug, the bathroom towels had been laundered, and a roast chicken dinner with all the trimmings was in the oven. So, her story adds up."

"Where were Lee and Craig?"

Quintana smoothed his damp mustache. "Now there's the story that's a little fishy, in more ways than one. They said they were out on the Arkansas, fishing with a friend."

Mandy furrowed her brow. "So the friend can vouch for them. Why's that fishy?"

"Because the friend is the exact same fisherman who was reported missing by his wife—Arnold Crawford."

Mandy snapped her fingers. "Right, he disappeared Wednesday evening from Ruby Mountain. We were searching for his body when we found Faith's. What a coincidence."

"Yeah, his story is well-known because his wife is asking everyone and their cousin if they've seen him." Quintana shoved his hands in his pockets and rocked back on his heels. "It's a damned

164

convenient story that the two Ellis men were supposedly fishing with him when Howie Abbott was killed. Until or unless he shows up, their alibi is pretty weak. And it makes me wonder what happened to Arnold."

"Do you think he could be dead, too?" Mandy shivered. "God, I hope not. You know, we never did find any evidence of his body, clothing or otherwise, when we searched the river for him."

"And nobody else seems to have any idea where he is, or if he's even alive."

"Maybe Lee and Craig just chose him as an alibi precisely because he's missing. Because otherwise they had no alibi at all."

Quintana shrugged then nodded toward the church door. "It's almost time for the service to start. Shall we go in?"

While Mandy squished through the grass and preceded him up the steps, she wondered if Quintana thought Arnold Crawford was dead from accidental drowning, or if he thought the missing fisherman also had been murdered. *And by whom?*

After taking her seat, Mandy dug in her purse for a tissue and scrubbed at the muddy spots on her legs. While doing so, she looked around, noting the attendees in the pews. Beside her, Quintana was also surveying the crowd. Brenda sat stiff-backed up front, in a position of honor as the dead man's sister. Notably absent were her husband and son, and Cynthia. Mandy leaned over to ask Quintana if he'd seen them.

His reply was, "Nope. Interesting, huh?"

Mandy would have assumed that as Faith's mother, Brenda would be the most upset of the four at what Howie had done to her daughter. But maybe she felt that as his sister, she had to attend the funeral anyway. Then Mandy had an awful thought. Heaven forbid, what if the woman knew about her brother's sick proclivities, knew that he'd abused Cynthia, maybe even knew he was doing the same to her daughter? Maybe she tacitly accepted his actions or turned a blind eye precisely because they were related.

She whispered to Quintana again. "Do you think Brenda knew about her brother's—you know—behavior?"

"She said she didn't in our interview yesterday, very forcefully so, but—" Quintana gave another meaningful shrug. "Craig and Lee claimed to not know about it either."

"Well, Craig knows now, because Cynthia told him last night. He stormed out of her place, shouting that it was her fault Faith died, because she didn't tell the family about Howie's abuse before."

Quintana raised an eyebrow. "That family seems to be ripping apart at the seams."

Before Mandy could reply, the service started. She glanced at her program, curious whether Brenda would eulogize her brother, but only the minister was listed as a speaker. After an opening prayer and a haunting solo by a member of the church choir, the minister stood at the podium.

His speech was fairly generic. He droned on about how Howie Abbott would be missed by his friends and family, gave a list of the man's contributions to the local community, such as they were, and finished with benign platitudes. Howie was now enjoying the company of friends and family in heaven who had passed before him, since he had accepted Jesus as his savior as a member of the Baptist faith.

Mandy squelched a derisive snort. Surely the minister didn't even know Howie Abbott—and what he'd done. The man raped and abused his two nieces, and maybe others. How could he be welcomed into heaven, even with his faith, assuming he truly felt it? She hoped Howie Abbott was suffering in a special purgatory for sexual predators. She just couldn't maintain a spirit of Christian forgiveness when her best friend still suffered the effects of his monstrous behavior.

During the sermon, Mandy studied Brenda Ellis. How was she reacting to the minister's words? But the woman maintained her erect posture, never turning, so all Mandy could see was the back of her head. After the final hymn, the congregation remained seated while Brenda was escorted out by one of the ushers.

When the woman passed her row, Mandy could see that she was stone-faced and dry-eyed. Her gaze was focused straight ahead, as if she was avoiding having to look at any of the other mourners. Mandy likened the woman's stiff pose to a thin pane of delicate glass. One good poke, and she'd shatter into a million pieces. And if Mandy had to put a label on the emotion she saw on Brenda's face, she would have named it ice-cold anger, not grief.

When the mourners filed out of the sanctuary, they were directed by an usher downstairs to a meeting room, where the well-dressed, silver-haired ladies of the women's auxiliary were serving punch and cookies. While walking through the serving line, Quintana said to Mandy out of the corner of his mouth, "Keep your eyes and ears sharp. Let me know if you see or hear anything interesting."

Mandy nodded, then noted that he positioned himself close to where Brenda sat on a large easy chair, accepting murmured condolences from well-wishers who shuffled by. After collecting a glass of punch, Mandy circulated through the room. She didn't hear much of interest, however. The conversations were either awkward attempts to remember something nice about Howie Abbott or innocuous statements about the rain and its effect on the fly-fishing tournament practice sessions.

"It's not as pleasant for the fishermen," one woman with a weather-lined face said to an attentive acne-scarred young man across from her. "But rain doesn't bother the fish. It can even oxygenate the river by breaking the surface film, allowing the fly hatches to rise better."

"I never knew that," the young man answered.

A gray-haired man next to her nodded while he finished chewing a cookie. "And in wet weather, it gets harder for the flies to dry their wings so they can take off. They stay on the surface longer, so the trout have a better chance of feeding on them."

"But won't your dry flies sink?" the young man asked.

"Yes," the woman's voice rose excitedly, "and when your fly gets forced underwater, *keep it there*, because that's exactly what's happening to the naturals. Just wiggle your fly a little bit to imitate a struggling bug." She made small sharp movements with her hands, as if she was gently flicking a fly rod.

"I always reach for my terrestrials box when it rains," the older man added. "Grasshoppers, crickets, beetles, and ants can lose their footholds on leaves and grasses during a rainstorm, and get swept into the river. And here's one last tip." He tapped a finger on the young man's chest for emphasis. "The rain clouds up the water, distorting the fish's vision, so you can creep up a little closer to your prey. Yep, I almost prefer fishing in the rain."

Boy, these folks are really into the sport, Mandy thought. Of course, at a funeral for an avid fly fisherman, you were likely to run into more of the same. And fanatics were liable to talk about their obsessions anywhere, even at a funeral. None of this discussion was suspicious, though, so she moved to the other end of the room, toward the entrance.

Just then Craig Ellis came down the stairs, his gaze searching the crowd, probably looking for his mother. He was dressed in jeans and a polo shirt, obviously not funeral wear, and was nervously jiggling a set of car keys in his hand.

"Hi, Craig," Mandy said. "Looking for your mom?"

Craig looked uncomfortable, like he didn't want to meet her gaze after his outburst the night before. "Yeah. I'm here to pick her up and take her home."

"She's over there," Mandy pointed to the easy chair, where Brenda was accepting a plate of cookies that a woman had brought her. She was partially obscured by a line of people moving slowly by and bending over one-by-one to talk to her. "She hasn't finished talking to the mourners yet, so you may have to wait a bit."

"Mourners," Craig scoffed, his mouth turned down in a scowl.

A couple of people near them turned to stare at Craig.

Mandy took his elbow to steer him back into the kitchen. "Let me get you a glass of punch while you wait for your mom."

And keep you from upsetting people and making a fool of yourself.

The kitchen was fairly quiet, because all the cookies had been served and the church ladies were out mingling with the funeral attendees. Mandy steered Craig toward a folding chair and fetched him a glass of punch.

She plopped down next to him on another folding chair. "I haven't had a chance to speak to your mom, but Steve wanted me to relay the sympathies of the whole ranger staff to your family. Will you tell your folks for me?"

"Sure." Craig drank some punch, then held the glass awkwardly in his lap.

"So, I noticed that neither you nor your father attended the service."

Craig made a sour face. "If we had, it would have been the height of hypocrisy. I doubt I could have restrained myself from spitting on the man's coffin. Mom told me that if I couldn't behave respectfully, I shouldn't come." He put his glass of punch on the counter next to him and folded his arms. "So I didn't."

Mandy remembered that Howie's coffin, closed thank God, had been very plain—not quite a pine box but close, with a meager flower arrangement on top, comprised mostly of inexpensive carnations and greens. *Who had sprung for the flowers?* "It can't have been easy for your mother to come alone."

"Easier than staying at home, though."

"What do you mean by that?"

"Dad's been yelling at her, says he can't believe she knew nothing about Uncle Howie's abusive tendencies. He said that she must have been covering up for her brother and because of that, Faith's death is all her fault."

"Ouch. But then I remember you saying pretty much the same thing to Cynthia."

"Yeah," Craig said ruefully, banging his head back against the wall. "And hearing those same accusations coming out of my dad's mouth made me realize how hurtful they are. Even if Mom or Cynthia knew about Uncle Howie, his abuse of Faith isn't their fault. It's Howie's fault, and his alone."

Mandy nodded. "I've got to agree with you there. Are you going to apologize to Cynthia?" She put a hand on his arm. "Because I really think she needs to hear what you just said."

Craig blew out a breath. "You're right. I was pretty darn cruel, wasn't I? Think she'll forgive me?"

"You were hurting, still are, over Faith's death, so I'm sure she'll forgive you. I'm just not sure she'll ever forgive herself." Mandy lapsed into a moment of silence. "What about your dad? Do you think you can convince him to apologize to your mom? She doesn't look so good."

Craig rose to look out over the countertop. "No, she doesn't look good. And she hasn't been eating very much. I'll try to get Dad to see the light and stop yelling at her."

"Good." Mandy got up and stood next to Craig. Only two more people stood in line to speak to Brenda, and a glimpse of the woman's face showed that it was ashen and drawn. "In fact, I think you should take her home very soon."

"You know," Craig said thoughtfully while he stared at his mother. "If my uncle hadn't already been killed, I'd take great pleasure in doing it myself—as slowly and painfully as possible—for what he did to my sister." He started to walk out of the kitchen, then turned back to Mandy. "Too bad someone beat me to it."

TWELVE

*If you believe in your heart that you are right,
you must fight with all your might to do it your way.
Only dead fish swim with the stream all the time.*

—LINDA ELLERBEE

EARLY MORNING SUNLIGHT SLANTED through the window blinds in Detective Quintana's office and painted prison stripes across his face. The wind had pushed the rain clouds of the day before over Colorado's front range to pour what moisture they still held onto the cities of Denver, Colorado Springs, and Pueblo. Quintana smoothed his mustache and calmly gazed at Mandy. "I'm bringing her in for questioning."

Calm was totally out of Mandy's grasp, however. She gripped the arms of her chair. Her heartbeat scrambled along with her thoughts in all directions, like a panicked animal fleeing from a cloud of hornets buzzing out of a disturbed nest. "Why? Why would you bring Cynthia in?"

"We have a witness who overheard her saying to Howie that she would kill him if he touched her cousin. And then there are your reports about her abuse at his hands. She has motive out the wazoo." He spread his hands wide.

"But she's not a killer. No way! I already told you that. She just doesn't have it in her." Mandy leapt out of her chair, determined to convince Quintana he was wrong. Dead wrong.

"You know Cynthia's a really caring person, listening to people's problems at the bar. She rescued her cat from the street and nursed her back to health." Mandy stopped pacing and flung her arms in the air. "Heck, she even put up with Craig yelling at her in her own apartment, saying if she'd told Faith about Howie's abuse of her, then Faith might still be alive."

"I'm sure that upset her," Quintana said.

"Put her in tears! But when Craig stormed out, instead of being upset at him, Cynthia was worried whether he'd make it home okay on his bike after drinking. Does that sound like a killer to you?" By the time she finished her tirade, she was shouting.

Quintana just sat there with his arms folded across his chest, waiting for Mandy to splutter to a stop. "This is why I'm not inviting you to observe her questioning. You're too close to her. Too biased."

Mandy sank back into her chair. "God damn it! How can I convince you she's innocent?"

Inspiration struck. She sat up and slapped the corner of his desk "Wait. Didn't you say that Faith wasn't strong enough to swing the hatchet that killed Howie? How could Cynthia do it, then?"

"Cynthia's got a few inches and quite a few more pounds on her than Faith did. And she works out at Exer-Flex regularly. She could heft that hatchet."

Mandy's heart sank. "You've been checking up on her already?"

Quintana's face drooped with pity. "It's my job, Mandy."

"What about Faith's father and brother? Neither one of them attended Howie's funeral. And when Craig came to pick up his mom, he said to me that if his uncle wasn't already dead, he would take great pleasure in doing it himself—as slowly and painfully as possible. There's motive out the wazoo for you." Mandy stabbed a finger toward Quintana's maddeningly unperturbed face, punctuating her point. "What if they really found out about Howie's abuse of Faith before the weekend? And, didn't you think their alibi was flimsy for the Sunday when Howie was killed?"

Quintana nodded. "Yes, they're still possible suspects, and I questioned them, too. Now it's Cynthia's turn. She's agreed to come in and talk, so she has no problem answering my questions."

The implication was that only Mandy thought this was a problem. And she did. It was a big problem. Cynthia wasn't just being questioned as a witness. Quintana had made it clear she was a suspect. Mandy was deathly afraid that her best friend would wind up in jail. Was it because she was also deathly afraid that Cynthia had finally taken revenge on her uncle for abusing her? Did she secretly believe her best friend was capable of killing her uncle?

Mandy shook her head. *No, it wasn't possible.*

She slumped in her chair, deflating like a spent balloon. "When's Cynthia coming in?"

"In about an hour." Quintana squinted at her, as if assessing whether or not to tell her something else.

"What? What other bad news is there?"

He drummed his fingers on Howie Abbott's bulging case file on his desk, which lay atop Faith Ellis's thinner one. "Deputy Thompson found the can of pepper spray at the Vallie Bridge campground. We lifted a few prints off of it and the hatchet. Neither Newt Nowak nor Jesse Lopez's fingerprints matched any of those on either item."

"Have you matched the fingerprints to anyone else?"

"Some. Some on the hatchet were Howie's, smeared with blood and pepper spray. So, as we thought, he was trying to pull it out of his neck. A few on both the spray can and the hatchet we haven't IDed yet. They're small partials and hard to match. But we did find one almost-full thumbprint that was on the end of the hatchet handle, so it wasn't smeared by Howie's efforts."

"On the end?" Mandy asked. "You can't swing a hatchet with your thumb on the end."

"No, but it could get there any number of other ways, while picking it up, for instance. And since it was almost full, we were able to match it." Quintana paused, peering at Mandy.

She gripped the arms of her chair again. Something told her she wasn't going to like what he had to say. She licked her dry lips and gave a slight nod. *Go ahead.*

"The print matched Cynthia's right thumbprint."

———

Out on river patrol with Steve that afternoon, Mandy had a hard time focusing on work. Her mind kept drifting back to her conversation with Quintana, and she wondered how his interview with

Cynthia was going. Her cataraft drifted, too, and nudged against Steve's in the river current.

"Getting a little close there, Mandy," he said calmly.

"Sorry!" She swept one of her oars in the current to correct her heading and leave a few feet between the two rafts before lapsing back into silence. She'd already filled Steve in on the situation, as much as she felt she could share with him. He had expressed concern for Cynthia, but he couldn't offer anything else to Mandy but a sympathetic ear.

They were floating down the "Milk Run" section of the Arkansas River above Salida, so they could drift side-by-side and have no problem negotiating the few riffles they encountered. The section had been fairly quiet so far. Birds and squirrels were feeding in the trees, and fish were plunking after rising caddis fly hatches in the water, but there was little human activity. Since it was a weekday and this was a tame section, no rafting company trips were on the water.

They'd only passed one local woman lazing back in a small raft and reading while drifting with the current. When she spied them, she held up the book and said, "Thoreau's *Walden*. Perfect day for it," before returning to her reading.

Mandy envied her tranquility.

They'd seen one fisherman on the banks so far—a local, who Steve knew wasn't competing in the Rocky Mountain Cup. The competitors in the fly-fishing tournament were all supposed to be practicing on the float-fishing competition sections, or beats as they called them, from Salida downstream to Vallie Bridge. That was one reason Mandy and Steve were patrolling this part of the river, to be on the lookout for competitors breaking the rules and practicing on the wading beats. Though why they wouldn't want to take advantage of the float-fishing practice, Mandy had no idea.

They'd already passed the first set of yellow-flagged stakes that volunteers had put out on Monday to mark the first wading competition beat. But when they neared the second beat, Mandy saw that some stakes had been pulled out. One bobbed in an eddy between two rocks along the shore.

"Look at that," Mandy said to Steve, while she pulled on her oars to back-ferry across the river. She beached her cataraft near the eddy that had captured the uprooted wooden stake.

Steve beached his raft a short distance downstream, got out and tied it up. He walked back upstream and described the destruction to Mandy as he passed the evidence. Some stakes were missing, others were just uprooted and lying on the ground, and a couple of them were broken in two. He concluded with, "Looks like sabotage."

"Sabotage?" Mandy stood up after fishing the water-logged stake out of the eddy. "Why would someone want to sabotage a fly-fishing tournament?"

Steve shrugged. "Could be a grudge against the tournament by someone who was excluded or lost work or business because of it. Could be an animal rights activist, who thinks even catch-and-release is cruelty."

"But the competitors are required to use barbless hooks and cotton nets, and handle the fish gently." Mandy walked over to Steve to survey the damage herself.

"Some view any form of fishing as cruelty. It also could be an unrelated personal disagreement between someone and one of the tournament organizers or fishing teams." Steve reached for his radio and called in the damage.

"I'll patch in the tournament director," the ranger dispatcher replied.

After a delay, a man's voice came on. "This is John Squire. Can you tell me which beat you're on?"

"We're at the second one heading downstream," Steve said. "We'll check for damage to the other beats while we continue down the river."

"Okay, thanks. I'll send out volunteers to restake that beat. And here they thought their work was done for the day. Please radio in if you see any more stakes pulled up."

"We'll be sure to let you know."

"Damn! After the murder of that fisherman, this is all I need. Someone really wants this tournament to fail." He signed off.

"That's an angle I didn't think of," Mandy said while slapping the stake against her thigh. "That Howie's murder was part of an overall scheme to sabotage the tournament. Do you think that's likely?"

"I think it's a long shot. But someone could be both riled up about this tournament and have a hatred for Howie." Steve walked back to his raft and untied it. "We should be on the lookout not just for more damage but also for anyone behaving suspiciously."

Mandy laid the stake she'd retrieved next to another uprooted one and headed for her raft. "Better hustle, then. Maybe we can catch them in the act."

They got back in their catarafts and pushed off. After negotiating an easy class II riffle, Mandy spotted uprooted stakes in the next tournament beat section. She pointed them out to Steve, who radioed in the damage.

After rounding a bend, Mandy spied Kendra and Gonzo standing among knee-high grasses on the bank, both wearing waders and holding fly rods. One of the rafts from RM Outdoor Adventures was tethered to a cottonwood tree upstream from them. Gonzo was cursing a blue streak while he messed with the end of his rod, and Kendra was laughing. She managed to wave to Mandy before doubling over with guffaws.

Mandy beached her raft on a gravel bar midstream across from them, and Steve followed. "What's up?" she shouted to the two on the bank.

"Got a frigging wind knot in my fishing line," Gonzo shouted back.

"He refuses to cut his leader and restring it," Kendra added. "But he's got no hope of untying that knot."

Gonzo shot her an angry glare, but she just stuck her tongue out at him.

The wind had picked up while they'd been on the river. It was now tossing Mandy's ponytail and riffling the water. It would play havoc with the casts of these two beginners, blowing their tentative circles into strange shapes. "Maybe you two should pack it in and try again on a day that's not so windy!"

"Good idea," Kendra replied. "We haven't had a bite for over an hour. We just can't get the flies to land right."

"Has anyone floated down the river past here while you've been fishing?" Steve asked.

"Two guys in a private raft about fifteen minutes ago," Kendra said.

Mandy exchanged a look with Steve. "Notice anything suspicious about them?"

"Hard to say," Gonzo said. "They gave us a wide berth, avoiding our lines."

Kendra looked thoughtful. "Wider than they needed to, though, like they wanted nothing to do with us. And they didn't look like they were having a good time. Their expressions, and the way they paddled, were almost … grim."

"They didn't say hi or anything," Gonzo added. "Downright unfriendly, I'd say."

"What did they look like?" Steve asked.

"One was dark-haired and thin," Kendra said, "and the other was shorter and blonde. Both white, both wearing jeans and ball caps. No PFDs and their paddling technique sucked. Amateurs."

"Thanks." Mandy pushed off the gravel bar and into the main current. "Good luck with that knot, Gonzo!"

Gonzo threw his rod down on the ground, and mimicked shooting it with an imaginary pistol formed out of finger and fist. Kendra's peals of laughter floated after them as Mandy and Steve paddled around the next bend. At least Kendra was enjoying herself, but Mandy wasn't sure Gonzo had the patience needed to learn how to be a good fly fisherman.

By unspoken agreement, Mandy and Steve kept up a steady pace, using powerful oar strokes to push their catarafts downstream faster than the river current would carry them on its own. Mandy scanned the bank, looking for the stakes marking the next wading beat for the tournament.

Soon she spied a two-man green raft pulled up on the bank to her right, partially obscured by tall grasses and willow bushes. Two men wearing baseball caps were walking along the shore downstream of the raft, one tall and dark-haired and the other shorter and blonde. The shorter one carried a couple of yellow stakes under one arm. The tall one reached down to loosen another stake from the ground before the short one spotted Mandy and Steve's rafts and slapped his friend on the shoulder.

The tall one straightened, dropped his stake, and knocked the stakes out of the shorter one's arm. Then the two of them hightailed it for their raft, stumbling over rocks and clumps of high grass.

Mandy and Steve beat them to it. Mandy took their paddles and tossed them into her cataraft basket, so the men wouldn't be able to paddle away. Then she stood with crossed arms in front of their raft, trying to look as large and intimidating as she could.

Steve stepped out of his cataraft, a hand on his sidearm. Being a full-time ranger, he was one of the few on the AHRA staff who had been trained in firearms and was allowed to carry a weapon. As a seasonal river ranger, Mandy wasn't allowed to carry a gun. Steve positioned himself in between Mandy and the men.

"Hold it right there," he said to the two sprinting men. "Hands on your heads."

They stopped, panting, and eyed his handgun. They slowly raised their hands to their heads.

"We're rangers with the Arkansas Headwaters Recreation Area," Steve said. "And you're under arrest for vandalism." He tossed his radio back-handed to Mandy. "Call for backup."

She radioed headquarters and asked for two land rangers to come in one of their pickup trucks. Their current location was about half a mile from County Road 160, so the land rangers could transport the men out in their truck. The vandals probably hadn't realized how close they were to the road and that abandoning their raft and running for the road would have been a better choice.

In the meantime, the taller one was wheedling Steve. "C'mon, we were just out for a float down the river. Had to stop and take a piss, you know. We weren't doing anything wrong."

"And you need tournament stakes to take a piss?" Steve asked sarcastically. "Lie down on the ground."

The two exchanged nervous glances.

Steve tapped his handgun. "Am I going to have to draw this on you?"

"But our raft?" the short one said. "How're—?"

"Oh, shut up," the tall one said. "Don't say anything else. If we keep our traps shut, we can get out of this." He dropped to his knees then lay facedown in the grass.

Mandy put her hands on her hips, trying to look authoritative and hide her nervousness.

The short one looked at Steve, his gun, then back at his friend. Then he took off. He ran away from the river, high-stepping over the humpy ground.

Steve pulled out his gun. "Stop or I'll shoot!"

The short guy jerked and glanced back. That was his mistake. His foot caught and he plunged face forward onto the ground.

"Stay with the smart one," Steve said to Mandy, and he ran after the short guy.

Mandy looked down at the tall guy lying on the ground but stayed a defensible distance away in case he got any ideas of his own. He mumbled to himself, and she caught phrases such as, "God damn idiot," and "Fool will get us in jail."

Steve came marching back behind the short guy, who walked gingerly with his hands on his head and a frown on his face. Steve shoved him on the shoulder. "Sit down next to your friend."

The man gave a worried glance to his taller companion, who snarled at him, and sat at least five feet away from his buddy, well out of kicking range. He turned his head so he didn't have to look at his friend glaring at him.

"Okay, you can sit up," Steve said to the tall guy, whose T-shirt was already wet from the damp ground.

After he had rolled himself up to a sitting position, Steve said, "As I said, you're both under arrest for vandalism."

"They're just fuckin' plastic stakes," the short one muttered.

Steve ignored him and recited the Miranda rights to the two men. After getting their agreement that they understood, he said, "Two more rangers will walk you out to the County Road and take you to AHRA Headquarters in their truck. You'll be processed there. Mandy and I will tow your raft down to Headquarters with us, and you can pick it up after you're released. Any questions?"

They shook their heads glumly.

Steve and Mandy stood over them for the twenty minutes it took for the other rangers to arrive. Once, the short one opened his mouth to speak, but the tall one kicked his cohort's foot and shook his head. They didn't get another word out of the two of them.

When the two land rangers arrived, the full-timer handcuffed and searched the two men while Steve covered him. Then he drew his weapon and marched the saboteurs toward the road, following with his partner.

After they were out of hearing range, Mandy said to Steve. "Thank goodness they didn't put up much of a fight."

He led the way to the men's raft. "Yeah, I didn't want you handcuffing them, because you're not trained for that. The most dangerous moment during contact with a violator is when you're applying handcuffs. And I didn't want to give you the gun while I handcuffed them either."

"Whoo, now that would have been really dangerous!" Mandy envisioned shooting Steve by accident and shuddered.

Shaking his head, Steve said, "I hate having to draw my gun. At least I didn't have to fire it. Every bullet discharged has to be investigated." He pushed the men's raft to the edge of the water and started tying their bow line to one of his raft's stern D-rings. "They'll probably get off with just a fine and some community service hours."

"I wish they'd said what made them do it," Mandy said while she got into her raft. "I'm wondering if they had anything to do with Howie Abbott's death."

Steve stepped into his cataraft. "They didn't act like ax murderers."

Wondering, Mandy pushed off the bank into the rippling current. What does an ax murderer act like, anyway?

THIRTEEN

Men and fish are alike. They both get into trouble
when they open their mouths.

—JIMMY D. MOORE

WHEN MANDY WALKED INTO the Vic that evening for an impromptu Wednesday evening pool date with a gaggle of river guides and rangers, the place was hopping to the beat of a country rock band playing on the small stage in the back. Underneath the wails of the lead singer, Mandy picked out the twangs of a talented banjo player. Her pace fell in step with the drummer's rhythm and her hips began to sway. The music was going to be a great accompaniment to the stories her group always swapped in the back room about the outrageous antics of tourists.

But tonight, Mandy had another agenda—to ask Cynthia about her interview with Detective Quintana. Hoping Cynthia was in a talkative mood, Mandy approached the bar. Cynthia had three beer taps flowing into three mugs, with three more empties waiting. A waitress slapped a drink order on the counter in front of her, and Cynthia gave a quick nod. Mandy would have to wait for a lull in the action to talk to her.

She looked around for a place to park her butt. Conveniently, a couple left their barstools with drinks in hand to talk to friends across the room, so Mandy snagged one of their seats. She let the cacophony of bar sounds wash over her. Her muscles loosened as the tension drained out, and she started bobbing her head to the music.

Eyes half-closed, she was lost in the band's rendition of Jack Ingram's "Barefoot and Crazy" when Cynthia appeared in front of her, snapping her fingers. "Yoo hoo! Fat Tire?"

Mandy smiled. "Sure." She watched Cynthia pop the cap off a frosty bottle, pour half into a pilsner glass, and set both in front of her. The first swig went down real easy. "You got a minute to talk?"

Cynthia swiped a stray lock of damp hair off her glistening forehead and looked down the bar. All of the barstool drinkers' glasses were at least half full, and no waitresses were approaching with orders. She propped a foot up and leaned her elbows on the counter. She looked beat.

"I'm probably good until the band takes a break. Then everyone will want refills before they start up again. How was your day?"

"Interesting. Steve and I nabbed a couple of guys who were sabotaging the fly-fishing tournament, pulling up beat stakes. One of them took off, and Steve had to pull his gun to get his attention."

Cynthia raised an eyebrow. "Sounds like you're getting into this law enforcement stuff."

Mandy saw her opening and went for it. "Speaking of law enforcement, how did your interview with Detective Quintana go?"

"Okay, I guess." She looked down and started drawing circles on the bar with a finger.

Mandy laid a gentle hand over Cynthia's, stopping the circles. "I know it couldn't have gone okay. He suspects you of killing Howie Abbott! What really happened?"

Cynthia exhaled. "He said they found my thumbprint on the hatchet and asked me how it got there."

"And?"

She shrugged. "I have no idea. Maybe it was Uncle Lee's hatchet. We all share his camping gear. I borrowed his tent and some other stuff for that two-day trip to Ouray I took in July. I probably took the hatchet, too, since it's a good tool for pounding in stakes and cutting kindling. Maybe my thumbprint got on it then. I'm surprised Quintana didn't find prints on it from anyone else in the family, though."

"I thought that was odd, too." Mandy mulled it over while taking another sip of her beer. "But he did say there were partials on it that they hadn't matched yet."

Cynthia cocked her head and peered at Mandy. "You knew about the thumbprint?"

Mandy nodded. "That's why I was so worried, why I want to know what went down in the interview." She paused. "Quintana wouldn't let me observe since you're a friend."

"I wouldn't have wanted you there either."

"What's that mean? Why not?"

"It would have weirded me out. Who wants a friend listening in when they're being grilled by the police?"

"Did you say anything that you don't want me to know?"

"Maybe." Cynthia gave her a sideways glance, then stood up. "You want another beer?"

"Stop being evasive!" Mandy slapped the counter. "This is important. I'm trying to help. What did you say?"

"Look, Mandy, I don't want to give you all the details about what Uncle Howie did to me, and I'm sure you don't want to hear them."

"Okay, sorry—that I understand. But did Quintana believe your story about using the hatchet on your camping trip?"

"He said he'd confirm it with Uncle Lee." Cynthia looked around the bar. She seemed not just tired and busy, but haggard and distracted.

"It's pretty damning that only your print has been identified on the hatchet, Cynthia. If only someone else's was there, too, like one of the Ellis family. Or Newt, who we know was at Howie's campsite. Or Jesse Lopez."

"The killer could have worn gloves. Ever think of that?" Cynthia leaned in. "I overheard some fishermen talking in the bar last weekend about the rivalry between Jesse and Howie. It was pretty hot and heavy. Both had accused the other of cheating in one tournament or another, though Jesse was the most belligerent about it. Of course, Howie kept beating him, sometimes by just a few points, so Jesse had the most to prove."

"Unfortunately, Jesse probably has an alibi for the Sunday when Howie was killed, though Quintana's still checking it out. Did you tell Quintana about the conversation you overheard?"

"Didn't get a chance to. He was too focused on me."

Mandy nibbled at her lip. "That doesn't sound good, not good at all."

"Well, I'm still here." Cynthia spread her hands wide. "He hasn't locked me up yet."

"Don't say that. Jesus, don't jinx yourself. Do you think you gave him any more reasons to suspect you than he already has?"

"Like the fact that the bastard abused me?" Cynthia put a hand on her hip. "That's reason enough, isn't it?"

"Unfortunately, yes." Mandy didn't like the way this conversation was going at all. Cynthia wasn't swearing her innocence and didn't seem to have done any better with Quintana. *Does she know how big a hole she's digging for herself?* "I wish I could find someone else for Quintana to focus on."

With a flourish, the band ended their tune, and the crowd started clapping wildly. Once the applause died down, the band announced they were going to take a fifteen-minute break.

"That's my cue," Cynthia said. "I need to pour a couple pitchers of beer for the band, then be prepared to fill other orders. Kendra and Gonzo are in the back room, as is your honey bear." She gave Mandy a nudge with her elbow. "Go talk to them, instead. I'll see you later."

While Cynthia headed for the beer taps, Mandy watched her go. Her friend's shoulders were low, not high and jaunty as usual. And again, no blonde joke. There hadn't been one for days. Cynthia might be trying to hide it, but she was worried.

And so was Mandy.

———

Mandy walked past the band platform around to the back pool room, barely paying attention to the people she was passing as she kept replaying her conversation with Cynthia. Should she have asked her friend point blank if she killed Howie? Mandy thought it over and finally decided no.

She wanted to believe—needed to believe—that Cynthia wasn't a killer. And even if there was a niggling doubt, Mandy realized she was more concerned about keeping her best friend out of prison than punishing her. Cynthia should know that she had Mandy's support, one hundred percent of it.

And if she *had* asked that loaded question, in a crowded bar even, she would have created a legal mess, as a member of the investigative team. No, if it was going to be asked, Quintana had to be the one to do it.

As she entered the back room, she spotted Rob first, sitting at a table against the far wall of the room and talking to Ajax. Kendra and Gonzo were playing pool on opposite teams, so Mandy wished them both luck as she sidled by their pool table. She didn't want to play favorites.

When she approached Rob's table, he reached an arm around her hips and pulled her next to him. "I've been waiting for you, *mi querida.*"

He leaned his head against her, so she put an arm around his shoulders to keep her balance. He inhaled deeply of her scent, and she did the same—leather, musk, pine soap. Almost what you'd expect of a cowboy, but he was no cowboy. He was a river rat through and through, as was she. And he fit very comfortably against her like that.

Rob looked up at her and ran his hand up and down her hip. "What's troubling you?"

Mandy glanced at Ajax, who was diplomatically watching the pool game and chatting with a river guide at the table next to theirs. "I just had a talk with Cynthia that didn't go well, but I'll tell you about that later. But just wait until you hear about my day."

She disengaged herself and sat in one of the two chairs that Kendra and Gonzo must have vacated to play their game. One had half a glass of beer in front of it and the other had an almost empty soda glass. She told Rob and Ajax about collaring the tournament saboteurs, embellishing the story to make it colorful and take her mind off Cynthia's troubles.

"So what have you been up to today?" she asked Rob when she was through.

"Your story explains the call I got from John Squire today," he said. "John was rounding up extra volunteers to patrol the wading beats and make sure no one messed with the stakes—or the controllers or anything else. I told him I'd watch one of the beats tomorrow."

"Who's going to mind the shop while you're out?"

Rob pointed his chin at the pool table. "Gonzo."

Mandy lifted an eyebrow. "Gonzo? Really?"

"Really." Rob leaned forward and took her hand in his. He rubbed circles on her palm with his thumb, something that always made her heart beat faster. "Gonzo's been working hard to prove himself since he started AA. He's learned the cash register, been very polite and friendly to the clientele. I think it's time to show some more trust in him."

Rob sat back, released her hand, and took a swig of his beer. "Besides, it's a weekday and we only have one trip going out. An afternoon run down Big Horse Sheep Canyon with a contingent of Red Hat Society ladies."

"Aren't those a bunch of menopausal women who meet for lunches and teas wearing red hats and purple dresses? What are they doing taking a rafting trip?"

Rob laughed. "The whole point of the organization is to have fun and celebrate life. What better way is there to do that than take a roller coaster ride on the river? If this chapter enjoys themselves, I plan to ask the Queen how to get in touch with other chapters to offer them a special deal. It could be a whole new advertising campaign for us."

That was Rob, always thinking of new ways to expand and grow the business. But … "Did you say 'the Queen'?"

"Yep. She's like a chapter president. After they made the booking, I looked up the society on the web, so I could speak their lingo."

"But you won't be there. Gonzo will."

"Don't worry. I filled him in, and he's all prepared to butter up the ladies." Rob winked at her. "You know he's good at that. And I'll be there for the pickup shuttle, so I can chat up the Queen."

Mandy peered at Gonzo leaning over the pool table to line up a shot. He had managed to stay dry for well over two months, and he was drinking soda tonight. "I guess it is time to let Gonzo loose."

Rob leaned forward and gave her a peck on the lips. "Speaking of letting loose and queens, let's go make some honey, honey."

Mandy realized that after her rough day and the troubling conversation with Cynthia, she had no real interest in playing pool anymore. Rob's proposition sounded good, real good. She slipped her hand into his and stood, pulling him to his feet.

A slow, wide grin split his face. He tossed some money on the table. "That'll cover my share, Ajax."

Ajax turned from his conversation with a "Huh?" then took one look at the two of them grinning at each other and waved a dismissive hand at them. "Sure, whatever. See ya later."

Mandy and Rob walked out with arms around each other and gave a wave to Cynthia busy shaking a martini shaker at the bar. That reminded Mandy of Cynthia's mention of Lee Ellis and his camping equipment, particularly the hatchet. Rob said he hadn't talked to Lee lately when she asked him about Lee's business, but maybe he'd talked to Lee before, maybe even about camping. There was no better time than the present to find out.

When they stepped outside into the cool night air, she turned to him. "I have to ask you something. Before you and Lee Ellis got busy, what conversations did you have with him?"

"After we met him at the May meeting of the Arkansas River Outfitter Association, I talked to him at some other meetings, and he's asked me for advice on suppliers and such. We did the traditional beer for paddle trade a few weeks back when I picked up a couple of his paddles in Brown's Canyon. Chewed some fat at his business then. Sure hope he can make a go of it. It wasn't in very good shape when he bought it." Rob shook his head.

Just like Uncle Bill's business. "He ever talk about camping?"

"Yeah. He and Brenda and the kids used to camp a lot when Craig and Faith were little. He asked where some good campgrounds were up here."

A chill breeze blew off the river and Mandy shivered. "How are we doing this, anyway? And whose place are we going to?"

Rob chafed her arms to warm her up. "Ajax picked me up at my place, so you're driving. You need to take care of Lucky? Or do you want to go straight to my place? I stocked up on coffee ice cream and caramel syrup."

"Oh, yum." Mandy licked her lips. "We're going to your place for sure. Lucky will be okay until morning. He's been fed and run, and he's outside with a full water dish and a rawhide bone." She looked up at the star-studded sky. "It'll be a warm, dry night."

They jogged to her car and she started it up and pulled away from the curb. As they drove to Rob's house, she filled him in on her conversation with Cynthia. "So that's why I want to find out more about Lee Ellis and the rest of the family. I think they have just as much motive as Cynthia, and I want something to give Quintana so he'll turn his attention away from her."

Rob's brow furrowed. "I can't see any of them killing Howie. He was Brenda's brother, after all."

Mandy pulled into Rob's driveway and shut the engine off. "Can you see Cynthia killing him?"

"No, no I can't." He stared out the window. "Lee and Craig are working as controllers for the tournament tomorrow. Like me, they'll be carrying business cards, I'm sure, and chatting up the teams to try to get some future fish-guiding business. I'll talk to them in the morning when we all meet at the SteamPlant to get our instructions from John, see what I can find out."

"What time? Maybe I can be there, too, before I check in at AHRA."

"Early, six o'clock." He opened his car door. "We'd better hit the sack. Race ya!"

By the time Mandy had shouted, "You're on!" and leapt out of her car door, Rob was already at his front door. When she ran up giggling, he had unlocked it and pushed it open. He swept her up in his arms and carried her inside.

She reached out and pulled the door closed behind him. When he gently set her back down on her feet, she deliberately rubbed the full length of her body against his.

That got a rise out of him. His mouth was hot and hungry on hers in an instant. He kneaded her buttocks while their tongues fenced and he pulled her in even closer.

Mandy tugged his T-shirt out of his jeans and ran her hands up inside along the fine curls of chest hair until she found his nipples. She flicked her thumbs over them.

He groaned. "To bed, woman!"

They left a trail of clothing down the hallway as they raced to the soft, pillowy finish line.

———

Mandy sucked on her spoon, savoring the sweet caramel syrup as it melted on her tongue. She sat propped up in Rob's bed, the sheet pulled up under her armpits, luxuriating in the feel of the smooth, cool sheets against her bare skin. And she was feeling totally satisfied. Only one more luscious spoonful of coffee ice cream remained in the large bowl Rob had fixed her, and she was delaying the eating of it as long as she could.

He had long finished his bowl and lay propped on one elbow, watching her appreciatively.

The sheet puddled around his hips, exposing his muscled chest. Mandy decided she had the better view.

"You know," he said languidly, "having you over here full-time a few months ago was real nice. I could get used to that."

Mandy swallowed her last bite of ice cream and put her bowl on the nightstand. She pulled her knees up under her chin and put her arms around her legs. Yes, moving in to take care of Rob after he'd been shot in the shoulder had been nice, and having the fenced-in yard for Lucky was handy. But after two weeks of waiting on him hand and foot, she had jumped at the opportunity to move back to her own place when Rob regained enough movement in that arm to dress and feed himself.

She peered at him over her knees. "You know it wouldn't be the same. I wouldn't be at your beck and call, fixing all the meals and doing all the chores."

Rob grinned. "No? Darn! Seriously, though, we'd find a way to share the cooking and cleaning. I'd even volunteer to pick up Lucky's messes. What do you think?"

"More importantly, what would your mother think? She'd never approve."

That wiped the smile off his face, but after a moment, it slyly reappeared. "We both know what we could do to gain her approval."

"Yeah, I know, a huge church wedding, with a long white dress, eight attendants each, and flowers and incense and all that jazz." Mandy had tried to make a joke of it, but just in case, she added, "But it's waaay too early to think about that." *If ever.* "Merging two lives—and two households—is a big deal."

Rob's expression had grown more serious as she talked, until he was looking down at the mattress, scratching idly at the sheet. Mandy was just beginning to wonder if he was sad or disappointed in her, when he raised his head, his face wiped of emotion, and spoke.

"Not just two households. You still own both your house and Bill's. Any progress on selling your uncle's house?"

Mandy sighed. "Bridget Murphy called Monday and said a couple had made an offer."

Rob sat up. "That's good, isn't it?"

"Not so fast. The offer was twenty-five thousand less than the asking price."

"Maybe in this economy, that's as good as you'll get."

"Maybe, but it was still fifteen thousand less than the appraisal, so I asked her to counter with that price."

Rob frowned and rubbed the evening stubble on his chin. "I think that was a mistake. What if you scare them off? You may not get another offer."

"Well, if that's what happens, then that's what was meant to be. I'm still not really ready to give up the place. Having it on the market a few more weeks would give me time to get used to the idea."

"But then the money from the sale would come in too late to expand RM Outdoor Adventures into fall and winter adventure trips."

Mandy was getting irritated. "Is that all you care about, expanding the business?"

Rob looked at her, opened his mouth, then hesitated. "I also care about you, Mandy, your happiness, your financial security. That's why I suggested that you invest the rest of the money, set up a retirement account."

He was about to say something stronger. Mandy knew it. He was just smart enough to realize she was getting riled, even if he didn't fully understand why. "There's plenty of time for that. I'm only twenty-seven after all."

Rob blew out a breath. "But I thought you were interested in expanding the business, too. We made all these plans, then I selected equipment, found guide training classes. Have you changed your mind?"

"No, I understand why we need to expand. It's just, just..." She flopped her hands down on the bed as she struggled with the words. "The change is coming too fast."

"We talked about the timeline before—"

"I know that! But I didn't know how it would feel."

"But you contacted Bridget and started the process. So, I thought you were getting used to the idea. You seemed ready to sell." Rob peered at her. "Are you deliberately sabotaging the deal by countering too high?"

"Of course not!" *Or am I? No, no, I wouldn't do anything that underhanded.* And the implication that she would made her even madder, turning her voice steely cold. "Countering with the appraised price is a perfectly legitimate thing to do."

"Not if you really want to sell."

Mandy threw off the sheet and got out of bed. "It's not your house to sell, Rob. Stop questioning my decisions."

"I'm not!" Rob's brow furrowed in confusion. "I'm just trying to understand what you're thinking."

"That's the problem, Rob. By now, you should know not just what I'm thinking, but what I'm feeling."

Rob flung back the sheet and stood, facing her across the bed. "God damn it. I do know what you're feeling, and frankly, I don't like it one bit. You're using Howie's murder, your uncle's house, and whatever else you can come up with to avoid having to think about us!"

Mandy felt like she'd been slapped. "What?"

"That's right," Rob stabbed a finger at her. "You can't make a long-term commitment to our relationship, so you're throwing all this *stuff* in my face instead."

Quivering with anger, a hot flush reddening her naked body, Mandy stared at Rob, who was in the same state. "You are so wrong. That is *not* what I'm doing." She started picking up her clothes.

Rob watched her with dismay. "What are you doing?"

She walked into his bathroom with her clothes bundled in her arms. "I'm getting dressed and going back to *my* place." Then she slammed the door.

FOURTEEN

*. . . of all the liars among mankind, the fisherman
is the most trustworthy.*

—WILLIAM SHERWOOD FOX,
SILKEN LINES AND SILVER HOOKS, 1954

THE NEXT MORNING AT a quarter after six, Mandy hunched her shoulders against the early morning chill. She walked from her car to the Salida SteamPlant with her hands in the pockets of her black AHRA fleece jacket. She wasn't looking forward to seeing Rob after their argument last night, but she had to come. Talking to Lee and Craig Ellis was important.

Besides, she'd woken up with the infuriating realization that Rob was right, that she had been avoiding thinking about, and talking about, making a commitment to him. That's what had made her so angry last night. That he had pegged her feelings about their relationship better than she had herself. He had shoved them under her nose, where she couldn't avoid examining them any longer. It wasn't fair to Rob to string him along any longer if she wasn't willing to take the next step. But she didn't want to give him up. No way.

If only the next step wasn't so damned scary.

She took a deep breath, pushing her thoughts once again to the back of her mind, and entered the lobby. The SteamPlant's red brick walls were hung with watercolors by a local artist, but she was too intent on following the hand-lettered signs to the first meeting room in the Riverside Annex to enjoy the artwork. When she walked into the room, it was bustling with people all talking at once. As Mandy scanned the crowd, she could distinguish two types of people. Those wearing waders and bristling with gear were the competitors. Those wearing a hodge-podge of outdoor clothing and carrying clipboards and fish measuring tubes must be the volunteer controllers.

Behind a cafeteria table covered with paperwork and gear, a middle-aged man and woman stood talking to two controllers. As Mandy moved forward, she heard the fit and slightly sunburned man giving the wiry female controller across the table instructions on how to use the fish measuring tube. The tube was a lengthwise half of a large white PVC pipe, with one end closed off and hash marks at quarter-inch intervals along the middle of the inside.

"The angler will help you get the fish out of his or her net," he said to the nodding, white-haired woman. "But it's your responsibility to make sure the fish doesn't get away before you measure it. So, it's best to put the closed end of the tube into the net after the angler removes the hook from the fish's mouth."

He held the half-tube at an angle, defining the circle of an imaginary net with his other hand. "Gently roll the fish into the tube with its head down then lay your hand lightly on top of the fish until it stops flapping its tail. You can ask the angler to help you hold the fish still. Call out the measurement you see at the end of the tail and make sure the angler agrees before you release the fish."

"How do I do that?" the woman asked.

"Just lay the tube in the water and slide it forward and away from the fish. As soon as it realizes it's free, it should swim away. You know how to revive a fish if it's exhausted?"

She nodded. "Hold it upright in flowing water until its gills pump in some oxygen."

He handed the tube to the woman. "Think you've got it?"

"Yes."

The man glanced at Mandy and held up a finger, signaling he'd get to her soon, before returning his attention to the woman volunteer. By now, Mandy had pegged him as John Squire, the tournament director, and figured he would know if Lee and Craig had arrived yet. The brunette beside him must be his wife. Spouses and other relatives usually ended up getting roped into volunteering at their loved ones' activities, especially when budgets were tight. At least John's wife looked like she didn't mind it much.

"And you know the four species of trout that can be found in the Arkansas, right?" John asked the volunteer. "Brown, rainbow, brookie, and cutthroat?"

Cocking her head, the woman answered, "I'd better after being a recreational angler in these parts for over twenty years."

John put a hand to his chest, his expression pained. "Sorry about that. My wife recruited you from Colorado Women Flyfishers, didn't she? I should have known she'd only recruit the best."

His wife smiled and held a thumb up before resuming her conversation with the volunteer in front of her.

The woman volunteer pshawed and waved her hand. "No offense taken. I've never participated in a tournament, so this is all new to me."

"I'm sure you'll enjoy it. You may even want to compete next time." John winked at her. "Anyway, we're recording the species so we can recognize folks who catch all four for the Colorado Grand Slam later. But the species don't have any bearing on the final scores."

He handed her a clipboard. "The first few pages are for you to record catches. Write the two team member's catches on different sheets, because we're giving out individual medals, too. The last few sheets have the rules on them. Read them carefully, then come back to me if you have any questions."

"Okay," she said. "I'm really looking forward to this. Where's my team?"

John peered at a large chart on the table in front of his wife. "They haven't checked in yet. I've given you the Aussies. They're a lot of fun. I'll match you up with them once they arrive."

"Oh, goody." The woman flashed a smile at John and moved off to study her notes.

"Hello, ranger," John said to Mandy while holding out his hand for a shake. "Please tell me you're volunteering. Two volunteers have called in sick so far, and I've only got three standbys."

Mandy shook his hand and smiled. "Sorry, no. I'm working river patrol, so I might see you on the river later today. I'm Mandy Tanner. Nice to meet you."

John's face lit up. "Oh, you're the ranger who spotted those saboteurs. Thanks! I'm so grateful you caught them before they could do any more damage. Any word on why they were doing it?"

"I haven't heard anything yet."

"Please let me know when you do. In the meantime, let me introduce you to my wife, Carol." He interrupted his wife's spiel to introduce her to Mandy then asked, "So what can I do for you this morning?"

"I'd like to talk to Lee and Craig Ellis. I heard they're volunteering for you today. Have they checked in yet?"

John checked his chart. "Yes, about ten minutes ago." He scanned the room. "They wanted to work together, so I assigned them to the two North Carolina teams, who are going to fish together all day. The six of them headed off in the direction of the coffee pot to get acquainted, but I can't see where they are now."

John pointed to the far left corner of the room. "There're donuts over there, too. Feel free to help yourself." He glanced at his watch. "I'll be checking in folks for another twenty-five minutes or so, then I'll be addressing the troops, if you'd like to stay and hear what today's schedule is."

"Thanks," Mandy said. "I'm interested in learning how a fly-fishing tournament is run, so yes, I'll stay to listen to your talk. In the meantime, I'll let you get back to work."

She turned and threaded her way past a fishing team and two volunteer controllers who stood behind her, waiting to check in. When she passed them, she spotted Rob across the room, standing with a clipboard and tube tucked under his arm and talking to a couple of fishermen. Not feeling ready to talk to him yet, she turned in the direction of the coffee pot, hoping he hadn't seen her.

"Do you know Lee or Craig Ellis?" she asked a tall man next to her.

"Sure."

"Can you see where they are?"

Being taller, he could see over more heads than Mandy could. "They're over by the beat map." He pointed across the room, where a large USGS map of the AHRA hung on the wall, with bright red lines along the Arkansas River marking the tournament beats.

"Thanks." Mandy wended her way through knots of competitors and controllers until she reached the Ellis men, who were talking to four burly men with Southern drawls.

After a round of introductions, Mandy said to the North Carolinians, "Do you mind if I steal these guys for a few minutes? I need to ask them some questions."

"Not at all, darling," one of them answered, "as long as you return 'em before the starting bell rings."

Lee and Craig gave her some curious looks, but they readily followed her out to the mostly empty lobby.

Mandy led the way to a private corner away from the meeting room, below a large watercolor of cottonwoods leaning over the river, all glinting orange in a sunrise.

She took a deep breath and turned to Lee first. "I have to tell you that I'm really worried about Cynthia. Detective Quintana seems to be narrowing in on her as the most likely person to have killed Howie Abbott. I'm afraid he might arrest her soon."

Craig's jaw dropped and Lee's brow furrowed. "Anyone who knows Cynthia knows she's not capable of murder."

"Of course, but a lot of evidence is pointing at her." Mandy kept her growing doubts about her best friend to herself. "Did Quintana ask you about your hatchet last night, if Cynthia borrowed it for a camping trip?"

Lee nodded. "I can't find it, and the picture Quintana showed me of the one that was used on Howie matches mine. So, I assume Howie borrowed it when he went camping. Unlike Cynthia, he never asked when he wanted to borrow stuff. He just took it. I remember Cynthia asking to borrow some camping gear when she went to Ouray, but I couldn't specifically say that she took the hatchet then."

"What?" Mandy was aghast. "You couldn't back her up on that tiny point?"

Lee held up his hands. "That was in July. I just don't remember what all she took."

"Do you *want* Quintana to arrest Cynthia?"

"Hell, no," Lee said. "I wish he'd leave the whole family alone."

"You know," Mandy said, hands on her hips. She didn't like the answers she was getting, and decided to push the Ellis men—hard. "There are other fingerprints on that hatchet. They could match yours, or Craig's here, or even Brenda's."

"It was Dad's hatchet, after all. Why wouldn't our fingerprints be on it?" Frowning, Craig took a step forward. "What are you implying?"

"Maybe one of you wants Cynthia to take the fall for this, because one of you is the guilty party and doesn't want to admit it. Howie was abusing your daughter and sister, for Christ's sake!"

Lee's expression was pained. "But we didn't know about it."

Mandy glanced at Craig. "I almost could believe you didn't know, from the way you behaved Monday night. Either that or you're a darned good actor."

"Hey," Craig said, "That's a low—"

Mandy turned to Lee, fury pushing her past the brink of civility. "But it's just your word that you and Brenda didn't know. Maybe you found out right before Howie went camping and it ate you up inside, enough to take a hatchet to your brother-in-law."

"Mandy," Lee said, his hands making a calm-down motion. "I know why you're saying this. You're worried about Cynthia. But believe me, we had nothing to do with Howie's death. No matter how despicable the man was, I wouldn't kill him."

"Really? You wouldn't try to protect your daughter from a monster?"

Lee's face reddened. "Of course I'd try to protect her. But not by becoming a monster myself. I'd let the law put him away, in prison, where he belonged."

"What's going on here?" The voice was strident, shrill, and it was Brenda's.

She had come up behind Mandy, out of her field of vision. When Mandy turned toward her, Brenda was glowering, the lunch sacks she carried shaking in her hands.

Lee licked his lips. "Nothing to worry yourself about, dear. Mandy's just expressing her concern that the sheriff's office is targeting Cynthia for Howie's murder."

"That's not what it sounded like to me," Brenda said, her eyes wild-looking as if she was barely under control. "Sounds like Mandy's picking on a grieving parent, trying to get you to confess to something you didn't do." She poked a finger at Mandy. "Shame on you!"

Mandy's cheeks and neck flushed with heat. "No, no, I'm sorry if that's how it came across—"

"Don't try to excuse your behavior!"

"Mom." Craig took the lunch sacks. "Thanks for bringing our lunches. But you don't need to get involved here."

Lee walked over and put his arm around Brenda's shoulders, gingerly, as if he was afraid she would break.

The woman did look close to cracking as she shuddered and pointed a wavering finger at Mandy. "You're despicable. Leave my family alone."

"C'mon, honey." Lee turned Brenda toward the entrance. "I'll walk you back to the car. Craig, you go back in and listen to Mr. Squire's briefing. You can fill me in on what I missed after I get back."

"But, but, …" Mandy stuttered as the two of them walked away.

"I think we're done here." Craig glared at her, as he stood with a lunch sack in each hand. "I'm going back in the meeting room. John's probably about to start his talk."

While Craig walked away, Mandy took a deep breath to still her racing heart. She felt like sinking into a hole to hide her embarrassment over behaving like an ass. And she hadn't found out anything useful. Then she noticed that it had gotten quieter in the meeting room across the lobby. Deciding she might as well listen to the briefing, she rubbed her sweaty hands on her jeans and gathered her composure.

When she walked into the room, John Squire was standing on a folding chair. He held a hand out to help a woman climb onto a chair next to him. Another man held the woman's chair steady for her.

John held up a hand. "Folks, this is Emma Crawford, and she has something important to say to the group. Please give her your attention."

With a start, Mandy realized Emma must be Arnold Crawford's wife. She looked terrible, with deep dark circles under her eyes that hinted she hadn't slept much in the last week. Her limp, mousey brown hair looked like it hadn't been washed in days. Her lower lip trembled until she bit it and clenched her fists, obviously fighting for control. Finally she raised her chin and looked out over the respectfully silent group.

"Thank you, John, for allowing me to speak to everyone. As many of you locals know, my husband, Arnold, is an avid fisherman. He's been missing since last Wednesday, over a week now." She nodded at Carol Squire, who began handing out fliers around the room, the same flier containing a photo of Arnold Crawford that Mandy already had a copy of.

"Arnold went missing at the Ruby Mountain put-in," Emma continued. "If any of you see him, or see something suspicious in or near the river, such as an item of clothing or a shoe or …" She paused, her eyes glistening, and bit her lower lip again until she could continue. "Or, you know …"

At this point, Mandy finished the woman's sentence in her mind, as she was sure everyone else in the room was doing … *or his body*.

"Please call 911 to alert the Chaffee County Sheriff's Office. Thank you." Emma Crawford stepped off the chair then plopped down on the seat, collapsing like a rag doll.

Carol Squire returned to put an arm around Emma's shoulders while John added, "Or you can let me know. All of the controllers have my cell phone number on their sheets. I'm sure Mrs. Crawford would appreciate whatever assistance we can lend in finding her husband."

While John launched into a description of the day's schedule, Mandy watched Carol escort Emma out of the room and decided to follow. Lee and Craig had named Arnold Crawford as their alibi for when Howie Abbott was killed, after all.

Out in the lobby, Mandy spotted the two women sitting on a bench. She walked over, introduced herself to Emma and sat next to her. "I'm real sorry about your husband. I just wanted to let you know that I was part of the team that searched Brown's Canyon for him. We were very thorough. We're reasonably certain that he's not in the canyon."

"Thanks," Emma whispered, "that's one small comfort, at least." She heaved a great sigh and licked her lips.

"I'll get you some water," Carol said and walked away.

Here was Mandy's opening. "Your husband knew the Ellis men pretty well, I understand."

Emma nodded. "They fished together often. I feel real sorry for that family. Sure, my Arnold is missing, but they know their Faith is never coming back to them. And then there's Brenda's brother."

"Lee and Craig told the sheriff's office that they were fishing with your husband the Sunday afternoon that Howie was killed. Did you see them then?"

"No. Arnold just told me he was going fishing when he left the house that day. He didn't say who he was going with. He hardly ever does. Just like last Wednesday. I don't know if he was out there alone or if he was supposed to be meeting someone."

Carol returned with a water bottle, unscrewed the cap, and handed it to Emma. "Can I get you anything else?"

Emma took a drink. "No, I'll just head home. I spend a lot of time there these days, waiting for the phone to ring, hoping it's Arnold, or someone who's seen him."

While Mandy and Carol watched her leave, Carol shook her head. "That poor woman."

"Yeah," Mandy said, "but at least we didn't find her husband in Brown's Canyon. His body might be farther down the river, but there's also some hope that he's alive somewhere."

Carol nodded. "Guess we better get back inside and hear what else John has to say."

While Mandy followed Carol back into the meeting room, her mind raced. So Emma Crawford couldn't back up Lee and Craig's alibi story. And her husband, Arnold, had disappeared after Howie was killed. What if Lee or Craig picked him out as their alibi, then Arnold refused to lie for them. Would Lee or Craig have disposed of him, too? If one of them could kill a relative, why not an uncooperative friend?

———

Late that afternoon, Mandy was stowing her cataraft and equipment in the AHRA Headquarters garages after a hot but fairly uneventful patrol day on the river. She'd fished some garbage out of a few shallow eddies, so she was not only sticky with sweat, but grimy with dried river mud. She couldn't wait to clean herself up.

Steve came out of the back door of the building as she was throwing her dripping trash bags in the dumpster. "Have you heard how the tournament's going?"

After wiping her damp hands on her nylon river shorts, leaving more muddy fingerprints, Mandy checked her watch. "No, teams were supposed to check in at five, and it's a little after that now." She sighed inwardly but decided she'd better make a suggestion. "We could walk over to the SteamPlant and talk to folks ourselves."

"Good idea," Steve said. "And I bet we'll find quite a few of them at the Salida Cafe next door, having a beer."

Come to think of it, a cold beer sounded really good to Mandy, almost as good as a cold shower. And it's not like folks haven't seen someone with river grime on them in the Cafe. She fell into step beside Steve. The two of them walked to the end of G Street and turned left just before the boat ramp to approach the SteamPlant from the walkway along the river.

As they neared the event center, Mandy could see quite a crowd was gathered on the outdoor plaza. "John Squire must have moved his operation outside."

"I don't blame him." Steve raised his face to the warm rays of the sun that wouldn't set for a couple of hours yet. "It's a great afternoon to be outside."

Mandy shot him a look but clamped her lips shut so she didn't speak her thought, *not if you're fishing garbage from the river.*

Before she could think of a milder reply, she spotted Rob separating from the crowd, walking toward her. Stomach quivering with nervousness, she approached him. They both started talking at once.

"Sorry about last night."

212

"I'm sorry, *mi querida*. I said some things I shouldn't have."

"You were right, though, about a lot, but I was too angry to see that."

"I shouldn't be pushing you so hard."

"It was stupid of me to leave."

"Forgive me?"

"Forgive me?"

They both stopped. A slow grin worked its way onto Mandy's face, matching the one growing on Rob's. He held out his hands. "Come here."

"I'm all muddy."

"Like I care."

Gratefully, Mandy stepped into the warm circle of his arms and reveled in his hug. She lifted her face to his. "We're a couple of dumb bunnies, aren't we?"

He kissed her on the nose and stepped back, letting one hand slide down her arm to grasp her hand, which he squeezed gently. "Maybe not so dumb as bunnies. We can learn from our mistakes."

Mandy realized that the peck on her nose and his releasing her from the hug meant that Rob had remembered her aversion to PDA, especially in front of her boss. Steve, ever polite, had taken a few steps away and was staring at the crowd.

Yes, Rob was learning. Hopefully, she was, too. She gave his hand a squeeze back before letting go. "Want to try again tonight?" Then she looked down at her grimy self. "After I clean up, that is."

"Maybe I can help with that." He winked at her then leaned over to whisper in her ear. "There's nothing like make-up sex, they say."

A delicious shiver ran from Rob's breath on her ear down Mandy's neck. But this wasn't the right place or time. She forced herself to take a step back.

"Doesn't look like a happy gathering." Steve said with a frown and hands on his hips.

Men's voices shouting angry words at each other drew Mandy's gaze toward the crowd. Mandy couldn't tell who the men were, because a tense circle had formed around them. And their words were masked by a low buzz rising from the crowd, like the hum of hornets in a disturbed nest. Worried, she followed Steve and Rob as they pushed through the ring of people until they reached the inside of the circle.

Ira Porter and Jesse Lopez stood squared off against each other in front of John's check-in table. Ira's partner, Wally, had stepped away from his teammate and stood chewing on his lip. A slight, worried-looking Hispanic man, whom Mandy presumed was Jesse's partner, held his hand up as if to grab Jesse's arm, but it remained motionless, showing he was hesitant to touch his partner.

John stood behind his table, his hands making downward "calm down" motions. "Guys, guys, let's not get excited here. I'm sure we can work this out."

"But he's doing it again, John," Jesse said with a wavering finger pointed at Ira. "He's trying to get away with breaking the rules, just like he and Howie did when Howie was alive."

"But the rules don't say what to do when a partner dies," Ira said. "I'm in my rights to find a replace—"

"No, what you do is withdraw," Jesse spit out. "Clean and simple."

"Now, Jesse," John said, "Ira's right. The rules are unclear on this point. So we can be flexible."

Jesse stepped toward Ira, jaw jutting out. "Cheaters don't deserve flexibility."

Ira's fists clenched. "Who you calling a cheater?"

"This doesn't look good," Rob said to Mandy and Steve.

"Yep," Steve replied. "These two may get physical. Doesn't look like their partners are going to stop them, either."

"We all know Howie was a fucking cheater." Jesse made a wide sweep of his arm toward the crowd.

Mandy noticed some heads nodding in agreement while Ira shouted, "Not true, not true!"

Jesse glowered at Ira. "And anyone who partners with a cheater must be one himself."

"Fuck you, Jesse! You know you can't beat me. That's the only reason you want us out of the tournament. You're chicken." Ira tucked his hands under his armpits and pranced in a circle, making clucking sounds and flapping his imaginary wings.

That drew laughter from the onlookers.

"Big mistake," Rob muttered.

From her association with Rob, Mandy knew Hispanic men were a proud bunch, and from the purpling of Jesse's face, she knew Ira had gone too far.

While Ira's back was turned, Jesse rushed him, plowing into him. The two landed on their sides on the flagstones with a loud thump.

"Stop this! Right now!" Steve lunged toward the grappling fishermen.

Rob followed.

Ira and Jesse rolled and thrashed. Arms flew, trying to land punches. Voices from the crowd were yelling, "Fight, fight," and encouraging the two men.

John ran around the table toward them, yelling, "Break it up!"

Rob and Steve got there first. They each grabbed a combatant and pulled the men apart.

Ira and Jesse struggled against their captors while Steve shouted, "Help us out here!"

John grabbed Ira. Finally Wally and Jesse's partners acted, and both ran toward their teammates.

In Jesse's case, it was too late. He squirmed out of Rob's grasp and threw a wild roundhouse punch, connecting with Rob's face.

Rob staggered back, blood gushing out of his nose.

Hollering, "ow, ow, ow," Jesse jumped up and down, holding the knuckles of his punching hand. He looked at Rob. "Oh, crap, Rob, I didn't know it was you."

"Rob!" Mandy rushed to his side and helped him ease down onto the ground.

"Shit, I think he broke my nose." Rob put a hand up to his face. Blood flowed out between his fingers.

Mandy scrabbled in her first-aid fanny pack and pulled out a packet of gauze. While she ripped it open, she glanced around. Both Ira and Jesse were being firmly held a good distance apart by two men each. John was telling the crowd to back off and go home, while Steve was berating the fighters. Ira's and Jesse's shoulders were slumped, the fight drained out of them.

Mandy refocused on Rob. "Breathe out of your mouth. Now, this is going to hurt."

"It already hurts like hell."

She stuffed the gauze under his nose, pushing some into his nostrils as gently as she could.

Rob reared back and hollered.

It was hard for Mandy to tell, but Rob's nose looked crooked to her. "We need to go to the emergency room. I think your nose needs to be set."

He glowered at her. "No, just take me home."

"Like hell I am!"

Bob and Fred, the pool-playing fishermen from the Vic, approached, and Bob said, "Anything we can do to help?"

"Yeah," Mandy answered. "Help me get him to my car so I can drive him to the hospital."

"I told you—"

"I heard you," Mandy said, "and I'm not listening." She signaled Bob and Fred.

The two men pulled Rob to his feet while Rob held the gauze in place. Mandy directed them to G Street then shouted to Steve, "I'm taking Rob to the ER."

Steve nodded. "I'll handle these two. They're both going to be charged with assault, especially Jesse."

"He didn't mean to hit me," Rob said.

"Doesn't matter. He was aiming for someone."

After Bob and Fred helped ease Rob into the passenger seat of Mandy's Subaru, she thanked them and drove as fast as she could to the Heart of the Rockies Regional Medical Center. She hurried with her arm around Rob to the emergency walk-in entrance, while he held onto the gauze with his head tilted forward. A sense of déjà vu ran through her, but thankfully Rob wasn't seriously hurt this time.

There weren't many patients in the emergency room, so he was soon led back to an examining room. Some time later, he let out a loud howl that Mandy could hear in the reception area. She winced. That probably came from the doctor resetting his nose. After another wait, the doctor led Rob out. He was holding an ice pack to his nose and looking decidedly pissed.

"How are you?" Mandy asked.

"Sore and mad as hell," Rob said, his voice sounding stuffy since his nose was packed with gauze. "Mad at that idiot Jesse for punching me, mad at myself for not ducking, mad at you for bringing me here, and mad at the doc here for not warning me before he wrenched my nose back in shape." He breathed heavily through his mouth between each phrase.

The doctor grinned. "Believe it or not, it's less painful that way, because you're not tensed up. You got acetaminophen or ibuprofen at home?"

"Both," Mandy said.

"Good." The doctor handed a prescription for antibiotics to her and an information sheet labeled "Treatment for Broken Nose" at the top. "Get this filled for him and follow the directions on this sheet."

He turned to Rob. "You can come back here or get your regular doctor to remove the gauze in two days. In the meantime, I suggest lots of sleep."

"Great," Rob said, "and I've got a business to run."

"We'll manage," Mandy said. "I'll call in Gonzo to run the office again tomorrow. Good thing he's done it before. And it's my day off, so I can come in, too."

She steered Rob back to her car, stopped off at the pharmacy to fill the prescription, then took Rob to his house. She fixed him a can of chicken noodle soup to have with his painkillers and antibiotic while her own stomach growled in protest. As she watched him eat, misery in each slurp, she said, "I've got to go home to clean up and take care of Lucky. I'll come right back after that."

"Don't bother," Rob said. "I'm just going to hit the sack."

So much for make-up sex. But it wasn't Rob's fault. She'd feel lousy with a broken nose, too. She stood and tousled his hair and kissed him on his forehead, the only place on his face that didn't look bruised. "I'll miss you."

"Me, too, *mi querida.*"

While she drove home, Mandy replayed the fight in her mind. Jesse Lopez got mad enough to punch Rob, one of his friends, hard enough to break his nose. Could his temper lead him to kill his arch rival? A man he called a cheater, whom he obviously hated?

FIFTEEN

The gambler is like the fisherman, both have beginner's luck.
—CHINESE FORTUNE COOKIE

WHEN MANDY WALKED INTO Detective Quintana's office Friday morning, he put down his coffee cup. "I heard about the fight outside the SteamPlant yesterday. How's Rob?"

Mandy slid into his visitor's chair with a sigh. "He was not a happy camper last night. I thought I'd let him sleep in this morning, so I haven't checked on him yet."

"I'm sure it hurts like hell," Quintana said. "I remember when mine was broken in a wrestling match in high school. The worst part is not being able to breathe except out of your mouth until the swelling goes down."

"Hopefully he'll sleep a lot today," Mandy answered. "Gonzo's working the front desk for us. What concerns me, though, is how mad Jesse Lopez got. He was so blind with anger that he didn't realize he was punching one of his friends. Made me wonder if he could have axed Howie in a rage, too."

Quintana nodded. "Maybe, but we've contacted quite a few of his gas station customers from the Sunday when Howie was killed. Most of them remember Jesse being there."

"But not all of them, huh. Is there a time window when he could have gotten to the campground and back?"

"It takes about twenty-five minutes to get there from his station, so I figure he would have needed over an hour to make the round trip and kill Howie in between. Some of the customers' memories were hazy as to when they went to the station, but I haven't found a gap that long in their sightings. Jesse's alibi seems pretty solid."

Damn, Mandy thought. *With the other suspects falling by the wayside, the noose around Cynthia's neck is getting tighter.* "What about those saboteurs? Did you guys find out why they were pulling up beat stakes? Could they have killed Howie as part of their plan to derail the tournament?"

Quintana leaned back in his chair, making it squeak. "Funny how a murder accusation will loosen tongues. As soon as we asked Mutt and Jeff what they were doing the day Howie was killed, and they realized they were suspects in his murder, too, the sorry asses fell all over one another to explain themselves. Turns out one of the North Carolina teams had gotten into a shouting match with them at a convenience store last week over which state, Colorado or North Carolina, produced the best fly fishermen."

"But why would they take out their anger on the tournament instead of directly on the team?"

"Because their brains are the size of these nuts." Quintana pulled a jar of dry-roasted peanuts out of a desk drawer, poured some in his hand, and offered the jar to Mandy.

When she shook her head, he continued. "The North Carolina guys outnumbered and outweighed them, so Mutt and Jeff didn't take them on that night. That was one thing they were smart about. But they weren't competitive fishermen themselves, so they knew they wouldn't be able to beat the other guys in the Rocky Mountain Cup. They wanted to defend the glory of our fair state, though, so they kept scheming—over lots of beers—about how they were going to ruin the Southerners' trip to Colorado. Finally they hit on the idea of sabotaging the tournament so the North Carolina guys wouldn't have a chance to take home a prize."

"Which shows their lack of faith in the Colorado teams! Do you believe their story? Did they have an alibi for the Sunday Howie was killed?"

Quintana finished munching on his handful of peanuts. "We're checking their alibis, but I expect they'll hold water. These two were ready to piss in their pants when they thought they were going to be booked for murder instead of just vandalism."

Mandy exhaled. "Darn. Any other news on the case?"

"CBI confirmed the gardening glove was Newt's, found some of his hair and skin cells inside. But they didn't find anything of Howie's on the outside. And after three visits to his campsite, I finally caught one of his buddies, who confirmed Newt was there both Saturday and Sunday evenings."

"Could the buddy have been lying for him?"

"Possibly, but remember, Howie's time of death is Sunday afternoon. A tourist staying at Hecla Junction recognized Newt's photo, too, and said that he was there Sunday afternoon. She remembers seeing him still sorting through trash when they sat down to supper, because it disgusted her."

"So he's no longer a suspect either." Mandy sank lower in her chair. This was not going well. Then she remembered her conversation the day before with Emma Crawford. She straightened. "You know, I talked to Arnold Crawford's wife yesterday morning, and she has no memory of him going fishing with Lee and Craig Ellis on the Sunday Howie was killed. And with Arnold still not turning up, I'm wondering if he might be a victim, too."

Quintana smoothed his mustache. "How do you mean?"

"Well, what if Lee or Craig killed Howie then picked out Arnold to be their alibi? Suppose Arnold refused to lie for them and maybe even threatened to go to the police. Could one of the Ellis men have killed him, too? If Lee or Craig could kill a brother-in-law or uncle, why not a friend who was going to snitch?"

"Interesting theory," Quintana said, but before he could continue, someone knocked on his office door frame and walked in. When he saw who it was, Quintana's eyes widened.

Mandy turned, and her jaw dropped.

The man held out a hand to Quintana. "Heard you were looking for me. I'm Arnold Crawford."

When Quintana didn't respond immediately, Arnold looked from him to Mandy. "What's up with you two? You look like you've seen a ghost."

Quintana recovered first and shook Arnold's hand. "In a way, we have. We were just discussing whether or not you were dead. Where the hell have you been, man?"

Mandy blinked. Yep, Arnold Crawford was still there. Same glasses, bit of a beer gut, and thinning black hair as in his photo on the Missing Person fliers. She realized he was staring at her. She clamped her jaw shut and licked her lips. "Sorry, I'm Mandy Tanner, river ranger. I was one of those who searched the river for your body."

They shook hands while a flush crept up Arnold's face. "I owe you all a huge apology. I was gambling in Cripple Creek." He rubbed the back of his neck and gave a sheepish grin. "With my girlfriend."

"Your girlfriend?" Quintana repeated, then raised a brow at Mandy.

Mandy found it hard to believe that Arnold could attract a mistress, but she hadn't seen the woman yet either.

"Could we talk in private?" Arnold asked Quintana, with a nervous, sidelong glance at Mandy. "Man-to-man?"

"Mandy's a member of our investigative team, so she needs to hear this, too," Quintana replied. "But you can close the door before you tell us about your trip."

Looking even unhappier, Arnold shut the door and eased his back against it. After hemming and hawing some, he said, "My girlfriend picked me up at Ruby Mountain and drove us to Cripple Creek. The plan was to spend a few days there, with Emma thinking I was camping and fishing. Then I'd go home with no one the wiser." He looked down and dragged a shoe across the floor. "Didn't quite work out that way, though. And now I don't have a home to go to. Emma kicked me out."

Good for her, Mandy thought. "But it's been more than a few days. What happened?"

"During what was supposed to be our last night there, I hit a winning streak, and it went to my head. The casino comp'ed us a room, and we were living high, drinking a lot, too. I forgot about everything except chasing the next big win. Over the next few days I lost all the money, and more. I woke up this morning hung over and broke and realized I was supposed to be home ages ago."

He scratched a hand across the stubble on his unshaven cheeks. "Boy, the shit hit the fan once Emma got over her surprise at seeing me. In between her crying and shouting and cussing, she told me how you river rangers and the fire department had searched the river for me."

He nodded at Mandy. "I was trying to avoid the doghouse at home, and I didn't realize all the other trouble I was causing until I got back. I'm sorry about that."

Mandy was so aghast at Arnold's tale that she had no answer for him.

"Anyway," he continued after an awkward pause, "when she said the sheriff's office was looking for me, too, I figured I should get over here and straighten things out. Why were you looking for me?"

Quintana stood and folded his arms across his chest. "For one thing, we thought you had died in Brown's Canyon. A very expensive search was conducted for your body."

Arnold raised his hands out then let them fall to his sides. "As I said, I'm real, real sorry about that. But I heard that during the search you found a young woman's body."

"Yeah, but that doesn't let you off the hook. I hope you're also planning to go by the fire station and ranger's offices and apologize."

225

"Sure. You think bringing some donuts would help?"

Mandy snorted. "Maybe if you brought them every day for two weeks!"

"Another reason we were looking for you," Quintana said, "is that we need to know what you were doing Sunday before last."

Arnold frowned. "The day Howie Abbott was killed? Why?"

"So you heard about that." Quintana put his hands on his hips. "Just tell me what you were doing."

"I went fishing with Lee and Craig Ellis."

"Where and for how long?"

"All day. In the Department of Wildlife day-use area north of Granite. We were wading up the river all day, except when we stopped for lunch."

"Catch much?" Mandy asked

"Quite a few brookies," Arnold replied, "a rainbow, and Lee caught a good-sized brownie. Didn't keep any of them, though. It was all catch-and-release."

To Mandy's eye, the man didn't seem to have anything to hide. "How come your wife didn't know who you were with?"

"You know, that's all part of our problem. She has no interest in fishing or my fishing friends, so I gave up long ago telling her anything about my trips. I just tried to tell her when I'd be home."

"I suppose your girlfriend fishes," Quintana said.

Arnold sighed. "No, she doesn't. Gambling's her thing, and I'm beginning to think that woman's passion is too expensive for me, in more ways than one. I've made quite a mess of things."

"Can't disagree with you there," Mandy said.

"Yeah, well, is that all you need me for?" Arnold asked.

Quintana gave a curt nod. "Let me know if and when you plan to leave town next, though, in case I need to follow-up."

Arnold gave a sad smile. "Don't think I'll be going anywhere for awhile. I'm broke, and behind on my plumbing jobs, so I'll be working every day for a long time."

"Maybe you should look into some counseling, too," Quintana said. "About the gambling. Before it becomes an addiction."

"I hear ya." Arnold turned and walked out.

"Well, how about that?" Quintana said to Mandy while he re-settled back into his chair.

"Quite a surprise," Mandy answered, worried about the way Quintana was studying her.

"And now the only one in the Ellis family without any sort of alibi is Cynthia," Quintana said. "And no one outside the family is a valid suspect anymore either."

Mandy's stomach dropped into her shoes. "You can't think Cynthia actually killed her uncle."

Quintana held up three fingers. "She had means, with access to the murder weapon and the strength to use it." He pushed down one finger.

"She had motive, with Howie's abuse of her and the probable discovery that he was abusing Faith." He pushed down the second finger.

"And she had opportunity, with owning a car and having access to Vallie Bridge. With no alibi for the Sunday Howie was killed, she could have been there." He pushed down the last finger and leaned forward.

"Her thumbprint on the hatchet is the clincher, Mandy. I can't build a case for any other suspect, and I've got physical evidence

227

pointing to her. I've got no choice but to bring Cynthia in and arrest her for the murder of Howie Abbott."

———

Like a caged tiger, Mandy paced a circular path in her backyard later that afternoon, waiting for Cynthia to be processed into the Chaffee County Detention Facility. Lucky had long ago given up on begging Mandy to play with him. He lay in the shade with his head on his paws and watched his mistress go round and round.

Mandy clenched her cell phone in her hand, anxious for Quintana to call. He had told her that he'd put her on the list of Cynthia's official visitors. That way, she wouldn't have to wait to see her until Saturday afternoon, when friends and relatives could visit. And he promised to call once she could get in to talk to Cynthia.

Thank God for small favors. Mandy kicked a stick out of her way and circled again while thoughts flitted in and out of her brain. How had it gotten this far? How soon could she get Cynthia out of jail? Would the bail be something she could afford? Would Cynthia's mom or the Ellis family help pay it? And how could she prove Cynthia's innocence?

There was one question Mandy refused to ask herself. *Did Cynthia do it?*

The phone in her hand rang, causing her to stumble over a stick as she halted her pacing. She flipped it open. "Hello?"

"Hello Mandy, this is Bridget Murphy."

Shit, not now. But Bridget didn't give Mandy a chance to speak.

"I've got some wonderful news," Bridget said, her voice high with excitement. "The couple who are interested in buying your uncle's place have countered with a bid that's ten thousand more than their first offer. That's only five thousand less than your counter and the appraisal."

"I need some time to think it over," Mandy began. "I've got a lot going on, and—"

"This couple is looking at other properties, Mandy. I don't think we have the luxury of waiting. This is a good offer, and I urge you to accept it."

"Look." Mandy tried to keep testiness from creeping into her voice. "A friend of mine was just arrested—for murder. That's all I can think about right now. Send a copy of the offer letter to my email, and I'll get back to you Monday with an answer."

"Oh my, yes, I guess you do have a lot going on. I'll try to stall the other agent. Can I say what the reason is, or should I just say you need the weekend to think it over?"

Mandy rolled her eyes. "I really don't care what you say."

"No, I don't think I'll give the reason," Bridget said almost to herself. "Shouldn't mention the word 'murder' to potential buyers. That wouldn't be seemly. I'll just say you're really busy. You're involved in that fishing tournament, right? Yes, that'll be a good excuse."

"Fine. I've gotta go now."

"Wait, wait," Bridget said quickly. "Please look the offer over carefully sometime this weekend. I'll call you first thing Monday morning. And I'm keeping my fingers crossed that your answer will be yes! Good luck with your friend."

"Thanks. And goodbye." Mandy swooped down, picked up the stick that she had reached again in her circuit, and hurled it over the fence. "God damn it!" she shouted.

Dealing with a counteroffer on her uncle's place was the last thing she wanted to do at the moment. But before she could vent anymore, her phone rang again. This time it was Quintana.

"Cynthia's been processed in," he said. "You can visit her now."

"How did she seem?"

"Subdued, almost as if she expected it," he replied.

What Quintana didn't say, but that Mandy heard in his voice, was that Cynthia's reaction only made him more certain he had the right person pegged as Howie Abbott's killer. Cynthia was just digging a bigger hole for herself.

"Okay. I'll be right there."

———

An hour later, Mandy sat on one side of a gray metal table in a small private visitor's room at the jail, used primarily by inmates to talk to their lawyers. She drummed her fingers on the table while waiting for a guard to bring Cynthia in. A noise at the door made her stop.

A female guard swung the door wide, and Cynthia walked in, clothed in a bright orange jumpsuit. "Sit there," the guard said, while pointing to the chair on the other side of the table.

Cynthia sat.

"Don't move from that chair." The guard turned to Mandy. "I'll be watching right outside this door. Just shout if you need anything." She closed the door, and her face appeared in the small glass window embedded in the door.

"So much for privacy," Mandy said, in an attempt to cut the thick tension in the air.

Cynthia huffed. "You should see the open toilets in the cells. And some guard got the privilege of watching me get undressed and poking her gloved fingers where they didn't belong. Privacy doesn't exist inside these walls."

Mandy peered at Cynthia, who refused to meet her gaze directly. "You okay? Really?" Visions of jail assault made Mandy shudder. She leaned forward. "Any signs that anyone's going to, you know, come after you?"

"It's not like I haven't been raped before."

"Cynthia! C'mon, if anyone's harassing you, guard or prisoner, I can tell Quintana. Get him to protect you."

"Don't bust a gut. I'm okay. For now." Cynthia rested her chin on one hand and drew circles on the table with the other. "They put me in a cell by myself, since I've been arrested for murder. That's the one saving grace from the charge."

"Okay, that's a small relief. When's your arraignment? I want to find out how much bail the judge sets and get you bailed out of here."

Cynthia sighed. "By the time they finished processing me, the judge had taken off for the weekend. Gone fishing, they said. He won't be back until Monday, so my arraignment's scheduled for Monday morning."

"Damn! You have to spend the weekend here? I'll contact Quintana, see if anyone knows how to contact the judge." Mandy pushed off from the table and rose.

"Don't bother," Cynthia covered Mandy's hand on the table with one of her own. "Sit, as the guard out there so eloquently put it. Spending the weekend here won't be so bad, and I don't want you making waves because of me."

Mandy lowered herself back to her seat. "But you'll miss work, and—"

"I called my boss already. He's cool. Even offered to help with bail."

"That's another thing I want to talk about. Who can help pay. I'll organize a group to chip in the money. So there's your boss, and me, and I'll call the Ellis family and your mom."

Cynthia's eyes went wide and she sat up straight. "No, don't call my mom."

"Why not?"

"I don't want to be beholden to her. And I need to explain this mess to her. If she hears it from someone else, she'll go ballistic. I'll call her after I get out, though I'm sure not looking forward to it."

"Okay," Mandy said warily, "if that's what you want."

"Yes, that's what I want." She paused. "Thanks. For understanding about my mom. For being willing to chip in for bail and organize the others. For everything." Cynthia's eyes reddened. She turned her gaze toward the ceiling and swallowed a few times.

It was Mandy's turn to cover Cynthia's hand on the table. "That's what friends are for, Cynthia. I just wish I'd been able to convince Detective Quintana he was arresting the wrong person."

"Who's the right person?"

"That's the problem. I don't know. I just know it can't be you."

"But it could have been me." Cynthia withdrew her hand from under Mandy's and dropped both of her hands into her lap.

Aghast, Mandy asked, "What do you mean?"

Cynthia leveled a steady gaze at her. "If I'd known that good ole Uncle Howie had already raped Faith, I would have killed him, no question. I couldn't kill him to save myself, but I know I would have done it to save her. The man was a predator, evil incarnate. He deserved to die for what he did to her." She looked down. "For what he did to me."

"But you didn't, did you?"

Cynthia searched Mandy's face. "You aren't sure, are you?"

"Of course I'm sure. You're my friend. I know you. There's no way you'd kill someone." Despite her words, Mandy could feel the heat creeping into her cheeks.

"But I just told you I could. In fact, I should have killed Uncle Howie before he got to Faith." Cynthia raised her balled-up fists from her lap to pound them on the table. "I knew he was sniffing around her like a hound dog after a bitch in heat. Do you know how many times I've regretted NOT killing him?"

Mandy's mouth hung open as she watched rage consume Cynthia's face, hardening her features, blackening her eyes. Then she had a horrible thought. "Oh God, you shouldn't be saying things like this to me. What if I'm subpoenaed to testify at your trial?"

"Don't worry about it. I probably do deserve to be in here," Cynthia continued. "You know, it's a pretty sobering thing to find out about yourself—that you're capable of murder, murder of a relative, even."

"Maybe, under the right circumstances, anyone is capable of murder," Mandy said, though she wasn't sure she believed it. She just hated to see Cynthia beating herself up. "But with a hatchet, with all that blood? Could you have done that?"

Cynthia's gaze focused on the wall behind Mandy, as if she was visualizing the scene. "I can imagine getting a lot of satisfaction out of watching the bastard bleed to death. I hope it hurt. A lot.

Someone else did it for me, but not soon enough. Not before Faith was scarred, before she threw herself in the river."

"You really think she committed suicide?"

Cynthia nodded. "Remember, he abused me, too, when I was about Faith's age. I know what she was feeling. He was a master at making it seem like it was all my fault, making me think I was evil, that I was the one who seduced him."

She held up a thumb and forefinger an inch apart. "I came that close to throwing myself into the Arkansas. That's why I eventually ran away. To put some distance between me and the river and that man before I did do it."

Cynthia flattened her palms on the table. "I was too afraid to kill him back then, just as Faith was too afraid, I'm sure. If only I was strong enough, then, or fast enough, now, Faith might still be alive."

A pregnant silence grew and filled the room as Mandy tried to process the venom that Cynthia had just poured out against her uncle. An uncle who seemed to be the evil opposite of Mandy's own caring Uncle Bill. "God, Cynthia, what you've been through. I wish, I wish—"

"What?" Cynthia cocked her head to one side.

"That I'd been able to help you somehow back then, but I didn't even know you."

"Well, you can help now, by getting bail together, once we find out how much it is."

"And I won't stop looking for the real killer," Mandy added. Though she had severe, gut-wrenching doubts that she would be able to find anything that Quintana had overlooked.

Cynthia pushed off from the table and stood, prompting the guard to open the door. "You'd have to find someone who wanted Uncle Howie dead as much as me, Mandy."

As the guard came in and put a hand around her arm, Cynthia said, "You know, I can't blame Detective Quintana for fingering me, not at all. The man's a good cop." With that, she turned and walked out with the guard, leaving Mandy shaken to her core.

Was what she had just heard the convoluted confession of a killer? Was Cynthia telling her that no one wanted Howie Abbott dead as much as she did? But she kept saying she "should have" and "could have" killed her uncle, not "did." Did only innocent people talk like that, or did killers do it, too, trying to distance themselves from their crime?

What if Detective Quintana was indeed a good cop and had found his murderer after all?

SIXTEEN

It has always been my private conviction that any man who pits
his intelligence against a fish and loses has it coming.

—JOHN STEINBECK

MANDY WALKED INTO THE ballroom of the Salida SteamPlant
Friday evening for the festivities closing the Rocky Mountain Cup
fly-fishing tournament, but she sure wasn't in a festive mood. She
was emotionally wrung out after her session with Cynthia. The
roar of many conversations going on at once assaulted her ears
and threatened to overwhelm her.

She moved woodenly into the chow line and let servers pile
barbecued beef strips, coleslaw, and a sandwich bun on her plate.
After collecting a glass of lemonade, and an oatmeal-raisin cookie,
she looked around for a place to sit. She spotted Rob and Gonzo
at a table talking to Tim, the Aussie fisherman she'd rescued a
week ago. Another large, ruddy-skinned man, presumably one of
Tim's fishing buddies, sat next to him, shoveling coleslaw into his

mouth. Mandy wended her way through the buzzing crowd to the table and sat in an empty seat next to Rob.

Before she could say hello, Tim whacked his friend on the arm with the back of his hand, sending a forkful of coleslaw sliding onto the floor. "Speak of the devil, here she is, the lovely lady I was telling you about who fished me out of the river." He introduced his companion as Vince.

Mandy shook Vince's hand. "Were you Tim's partner in the competition?"

"Yes, and a finer fisherman can't be found in all of Down Under. You should have seen the huge rainbow he pulled out of the river this morning."

Tim nodded. "Lurking in a hole, he was, but he was more than happy to take a snap at my San Juan worm. Who would've thought that a cheap bit of plastic like that would look so tasty to a big, old trout? Got Rob here to thank for that. He told me a few days ago how partial your local trout are to dry-nymph combos. You two know each other?"

Gonzo, who was drinking a soda, gave a snort then grabbed a napkin to wipe his face.

Rob smiled and showed his palm to Mandy, indicating the floor was hers.

"You could say that," Mandy said to Tim with a wry smile. "We know each other *very* well. We've been dating for a few months."

"Exactly five months tomorrow," Rob added.

Mandy raised a brow at Rob. "I didn't know you were keeping track of the days so closely."

"Hey, I would, too," Tim said, "if I was dating a looker like you." He held up his left hand to display his wedding ring. "But don't get me wrong. I've got a good woman at home myself who knows how to keep her bloke happy."

Vince gave him an elbow nudge. "Like giving you a kitchen pass to fly halfway around the world for a fishing tournament."

Tim just grinned while Rob gave Mandy's thigh a gentle squeeze under the table.

Mandy used the break in the conversation to study Rob's face. Every color of the rainbow, it seemed, appeared in the bruises under his eyes and in his puffy cheeks. Under the bandage, his broken nose still looked swollen, though less than it had the night before. "How's your nose?"

Rob shrugged. "Still hurts like hell, but at least I can breathe some now. I took the stuffing out right before I came over here."

"We saw the fight yesterday," Vince said. "You really copped it fair in the face. Glad to hear you're on the mend. I bet you're still pissed at the bloke who whacked you, though."

Rob shook his head. "As soon as he saw me walk in here tonight, Jesse came over to apologize. He said he was so mad at Ira that he didn't know who he was swinging at. He even offered to bring over a six-pack of Pacifico, which I didn't turn down."

Mandy bristled. "A six-pack is hardly apology enough. How about paying your hospital bill?"

"We'll talk about that over the beer," Rob said quietly.

Mandy knew from his tone that the subject was closed, and the two men would resolve the issue between them, so she turned to Gonzo. "How'd it go in the office today? I meant to come in and help, but I ended up visiting Cynthia in jail instead."

"It went fine," Gonzo said. "We only had one trip, and Kendra stayed to help clean up."

"I'm sure you handled everything well." Rob gave Mandy's thigh another squeeze.

Realizing this was her cue to add her compliment, too, Mandy said, "Yes, it's great that we can count on you when we can't come in. Thanks so much, Gonzo."

Gonzo sat up a little straighter. "How's Cynthia? I heard Quintana arrested her. That guy's got his head up his ass."

"I wish I agreed," Mandy said. "But I can't come up with a better suspect for him."

Tim and Vince had quizzical looks on their faces, and Mandy really didn't want to have to explain the whole situation to the two Aussies. She was saved by a screech of the microphone followed by John Squire's voice booming in the room, "Quiet, everyone, please. It's time to start giving out some of these awards."

A round of applause broke out, accompanied by a few whistles, as people focused their gazes on the front of the room. John and his wife, Carol, stood there behind a table laden with trophies and brand-new fishing gear still in cellophane packages. Mandy used the break in conversation to take a couple of bites of her barbecue and slaw. When Rob draped his arm over her shoulders, she smiled at her injured hero. Maybe she could apply some of her own brand of tender loving care after the ceremony.

He smiled back at her as if his thoughts were along the same lines.

Her growling stomach interrupted her reverie so she scooped another forkful of the succulently sauced beef into her mouth and chewed appreciatively. She realized she was starving and hadn't eaten all day, what with her worrying about Cynthia.

She ate and clapped at the appropriate times as John went through the process of handing out some of the donated gear for the biggest fish caught in each species, the most fish caught each day, and so on. Of course, the donors of the prizes, fishing shops, outfitter services, suppliers, and so on, had to be profusely thanked and acknowledged.

The tension in the room grew as John awarded the third, and then the second-place team and individual cash prizes for the tournament. The clapping and hollering grew louder for each announcement. Then John signaled for quiet before the first-place announcements. He used the pregnant pause to thank all of his volunteers and ask them to stand for applause. Almost half of the people in the room stood up, including Rob.

Mandy smiled up at her battered champion and whistled her appreciation.

Once all of the volunteers were seated and the room was quiet again, John said, "Okay, I'm sure everyone is anxiously waiting to hear who won the big cash prizes for the first place awards. The team that scored first place really racked up the fish count on the wading day, pulling in a total of forty-six trout between them."

He paused for the crowd to acknowledge this, and Mandy saw Jesse Lopez and his partner high-fiving each other. She leaned over to Rob. "Looks like Jesse and his partner think John's talking about them. Is that Jesse's brother?"

"Yes," Rob said. "When Jesse apologized, he told me he thought their scores were good enough to win. His brother's wife is expecting again, so they could really use the money."

"But where this first-place team really excelled was on the float-fishing day," John continued. "Most of the other teams' scores were lower on that day, compared to the wading day, probably because one partner or another had to keep stopping to row or steer the raft. This team's score, however, actually went up on the float-fishing day."

Jesse and his brother were grinning at each other like fools now.

"They caught a total of fifty-three trout on the second day, making their grand total ninety-nine. Couldn't you have caught just one more, fellas?"

At this, the crowd laughed.

"Everyone give a warm round of applause to our first-place team, Jesse and Rafael Lopez."

A roar went up as the two men worked their way to the front and shook hands with John and Carol. John handed them a check and a large trophy on a wooden base with a plaque. Rafael hefted the shiny gold cup and held it aloft for all to see. He nodded toward a dark-haired woman sitting off to Mandy's left, who was clapping wildly with tears in her eyes. The woman's pregnancy bulge was large enough that her belly button was poking out, forming a small lump under her straining T-shirt.

That prize money is coming just in time, Mandy thought as she turned back to the front of the room.

John shushed the crowd by waving his arms down. He put a hand on Jesse's shoulder. "So, tell us your secret, Jesse. How'd you two catch so many fish?" He held the microphone under Jesse's mouth.

"Well, not by cheating, that's for sure," Jesse said.

While the crowd groaned, Mandy noticed Ira Porter glowering on the far right side of the room. She decided he shouldn't be too upset. He did walk away with the second-place individual trophy. His rookie teammate, however, kept them out of the money for the team awards.

"Rafael and I have grown up in this valley" Jesse continued, "and we know the contours of the riverbed like we know the bodies of our wives."

The crowd roared with laughter. Rafael's wife lowered her head, her cheeks flaming.

"We fish the Arkansas every chance we get—"

Rafael grabbed the mike. "Yeah, maybe our wives won't complain so much now after we take them out for steak and champagne to celebrate!"

That led to another round of cheers, one from Rafael's wife.

The two men started to walk back to their seats, but John grabbed Jesse's shoulder, holding him back. "Might as well stay up here, Jesse, because you're our first-place individual winner!"

Rafael ran back and wrapped his brother in a bear hug while the crowd clapped and cheered. John handed Jesse another check and large trophy, and the two brothers held the pair of awards up for all to see.

Once the crowd finally quieted down, John said, "Jesse's individual catch for the two tournament days was sixty-three trout, and he caught three of the four species in the river. Not quite a Colorado Grand Slam, but close. So, Jesse, how do you feel?" He held the mike out again.

"Very, very happy," Jesse said. "I only wish Howie Abbott was still alive so I could have beat him fair and square. But I'm sure I would have. My rod was smoking these past two days."

The two men started working their way back to their table, shaking hands and accepting congratulations along the way. Behind them, John made final announcements, reminded everyone to return next year, and asked people to throw away their trash and for a few folks to stay and stack chairs.

When Jesse and Rafael reached their table, Rob stood and shook both their hands. "Good job, guys. Congratulations!"

"Now I feel even worse for breaking your nose," Jesse said, while Rafael moved on to the next table. "A tournament winner should set an example for the young folks and shouldn't be brawling and cursing."

"I'm sure you'll think twice before you do something like that again."

"Yeah, well now that I've got all this dough, I'll be bringing over a case of beer, not just a six-pack."

Mandy started to say something about Rob's hospital bill, but Rob shot her a look, then turned to Jesse. "And while we're celebrating your win with the beer, we can talk about the doctor bill, and how you might help me out there."

Jesse's eyes widened with surprise, but he quickly recovered. "Yeah, sure thing, man." He held up the trophy and took a good look at it again. "You know, it felt good to whup Ira's ass, but I wish Howie was still alive, so I could have beaten him, too. I really wanted to stuff this sucker in his face."

"As you said up there, your rod was smoking," Rob said with a smile, "so you would have beaten him anyway."

Jesse held up a thumb and forefinger an inch apart. "There will always be that little bit of doubt, but I'll try not to let it bother me." He plastered on a big smile. When Rafael pulled on his arm to talk to someone else, Jesse gave Rob and Mandy a little salute, but his smile was already starting to fade.

"Sounds like Jesse's not quite satisfied with his win," Mandy said as she watched him walk away. And if he really felt that way, would he have killed his main competition right before the tournament? Or did he sneak away from his gas station between customers, and this regretful talk is all just for show?

"Well, I'm satisfied," Rob said while draping an arm over her shoulder. "I've picked up cards from four of the out-of-state teams here who are interested in using our fishing-guide services once we train our guides and buy the equipment. Speaking of which, any word from the real estate agent? Did the couple respond to your counteroffer?"

Mandy tensed. "Bridget called with a new offer from them right after Cynthia was arrested and while I was waiting to see her. I told Bridget I couldn't think clearly then, that I needed the weekend to mull it over and I'd get back to her Monday."

After a pregnant pause, Rob said, "And you're still mulling it over."

"I haven't even started to think about it." Mandy suddenly felt totally wiped out from all the events and stress of the day. She leaned against Rob. "What I really need is a good night's sleep, if I can even get to sleep while worrying about Cynthia."

Rob kissed the top of her head. "Okay, I get the message. I'll give you your space tonight and tomorrow. If you want to talk about it, you know where to find me."

While he walked her to her car, Mandy realized that though she hadn't really meant to send the message to Rob to back off and leave her alone, maybe it was for the better. And thank God he wasn't mad about it. She glanced at him. Nope, he wasn't. It was almost creepy. The man understood her better than she understood herself.

———

Mandy spent Saturday on the Arkansas, rowing her cataraft beside Steve's as they patrolled the river. Thankfully, she hadn't had to rescue anyone because her mind was engrossed with the dilemma of getting Cynthia out of jail. She had called Lee Ellis in the morning and set up an appointment that evening to discuss Cynthia's bail fund with the family.

While she and Steve had paddled through Brown's Canyon in the morning, Mandy had run names of potential donors through her head and figured out how to approach each one and for how much money. She didn't need to worry about Rob; he'd already offered money the night before. Mandy practiced her pitches on Steve until he said he'd contribute some money if she'd just stop obsessing about it and focus on her ranger duties instead.

Only a few pods of commercial rafts and a couple of private rafts were in the canyon that morning since the season was winding down and the water level was low. None of the rafters had any difficulties, and Steve only had to give one private boater a stern warning about not leaving trash on the river bank after a lunch stop. They had watched while the guy paddled back to the shore and gathered up his trash to stow in his raft.

It was one of the last warm days of the rafting season. A cold front was due in late that afternoon, bringing with it rain, plunging temperatures, and the unofficial start of fall, though the fall equinox wouldn't occur for a few more days. Mandy had brought her fleece and spray jackets along in case they were still on the Arkansas when the weather blew in. Right now, though, after finally focusing on her surroundings instead of on Cynthia, she was enjoying the brilliant sunshine sparkling on the river and the brilliant yellows of the hillside aspens.

Steve gave voice to her thought, "A perfect late summer afternoon."

Mandy sluiced her oars through the water. "I'm going to miss being out on the river most days."

"Yeah, the end of the month will be here before you know it, and your employment for the year will be over. You've had a great first season, Mandy. I'd like to recommend that AHRA hire you again next year. You still interested?"

Mandy glanced at Steve's earnest face. "Why wouldn't I be?"

"You and Rob have RM Outdoor Adventures to run." He shrugged. "I thought that might take more of your time, especially if Rob's plans for expansion pan out."

"No matter what, I'll make time to be a river ranger next summer. I like the work. I get paid to be on the river. It's exciting…a little too exciting sometimes, though."

Steve cracked a smile. "I won't count the bodies against you."

"I hope not!" Mandy smiled back at him. "And thanks for the recommendation. It's nice to know I didn't screw up too much. And sorry about bugging you this morning with my pleas for bail money."

"I'm glad to help." Steve's brow furrowed. "But what about future expenses? Can Cynthia afford a good lawyer?"

Mandy sighed. "I doubt it. I'm hoping to convince her to ask her mom for help, even though they're on the outs."

"An even more important question is whether Cynthia really needs a good lawyer. How solid is Quintana's case?"

"He's got physical evidence, her thumbprint on the murder weapon. That's pretty damning. And she has motive, but I don't want to go into it."

"I've heard rumors. Remember, Salida's a small town. The rafting community's even smaller, and we count Cynthia as one of our own. She's served all of us at the Vic. What a bum deal." Steve rested his oars under his knees and peered at Mandy. "Are you convinced she's innocent?"

A lump rose in Mandy's throat. "God, I wish I could say yes, that I'm a hundred percent convinced, but I can't. I want her to be innocent. I really can't picture her using that hatchet on her own uncle."

Steve looked off into the distance. "Nor can I." He pointed. "Hey, there's your uncle's place. I'm starving and could use a break. Why don't we stop and hike up to it? There are picnic tables in the backyard, right?"

"Right. Good idea. I haven't checked on the place yet this week, with all the stuff that's been going on. Thanks for suggesting we stop."

They beached their rafts and tied them to some willow bushes, then hiked up the hill and across the road to her uncle's abode that had also housed his small whitewater rafting business. On the way, Steve said, "I heard you put the house up for sale."

"Yeah, but I'm still not convinced I want to part with it."

"Why not?"

"It's the last home I shared with Uncle Bill. I've got a lot of good memories of happy times here."

Steve nodded and stopped to gaze at the quiet house. "Reminds me of something your uncle told me once. He said the river was his real home, that he always just thought of this as a place to run his business and lay his head at night until you came to live with him." Steve looked at her. "Bill said you made it a second home for him. Until you moved out, that is."

Tears sprang to Mandy's eyes, and all she could do was nod in response.

Sensing her need for some private time, Steve went around to the back to sit at one of the weathered picnic tables there and eat a late lunch.

Mandy used her key to go inside and look around. Since a lot of the furniture had been removed, the old wood floors and walls echoed with her footsteps. She looked over the customer check-in counter into Uncle Bill's office, but without the desk and chair, she couldn't really form a picture of him sitting there anymore with the phone to his ear. It was the same in the other mostly empty rooms. While she had memories still of what had gone on in those rooms, she didn't feel her uncle's presence in any of them. It just felt cold and foreign, like the abandoned building it was.

After locking up, she walked back down to the river and sat on the bank to eat her PBJ sandwich in the sun. A breeze caressed her face and a sense of calm oozed into her tense muscles. Here, outdoors, was always where she and Uncle Bill had belonged, where they found comfort, fulfillment, and their livelihoods. And wasn't outside where she had felt his presence since he'd died? Not once, when she'd been in his house after he died, had she ever heard his voice, felt his touch. But she had sometimes on the river, especially where she'd cast his ashes.

She put the last quarter of her sandwich on the plastic bag in the grass beside her and hugged her knees to watch the current flow by. Suddenly a Western bluebird swooped down and snatched a beakful of bread with jam, carrying it into an alder bush by the bank. Mandy could no longer see the bird among the foliage, but she could hear its soft kew calls and chatter as it savored the sweet treat it had snatched. Probably fattening itself up before it flew down to Mexico for the winter.

"Got a real sweet tooth, huh," Mandy said to the bird.

Just like Uncle Bill.

Mandy stuffed the rest of her sandwich in the bag and got to her feet. She headed back up the hill toward Steve and the house, the house that she now knew what to do with.

SEVENTEEN

Don't tell fish stories where the people know you; but particularly,
don't tell them where they know the fish.
—MARK TWAIN

MANDY WALKED UP TO the Ellis front door with some trepidation Saturday evening. The last time she'd seen the family was when Brenda had yelled at her for picking on a grieving parent and called Mandy despicable. Not a good start for asking the family to donate money to Cynthia's bail fund.

Lee opened the door to her knock and led her back to the living room, where Craig lay on the sofa watching a sitcom on TV. Brenda sat in her La-Z-Boy rocker, jerking the chair swiftly back and forth with one foot. Her knitting needles clacked in rhythm with the chair.

When Craig saw Mandy, he turned the TV off, sat up and, with a wave of his hand, indicated she should take a seat next to him.

Brenda looked up, frowned and resumed her work on the gray and blue yarn Mandy had seen the last time she'd been to the house.

Mandy decided she'd better start groveling. She perched on the edge of the sofa, faced Brenda, and began with her rehearsed speech. "I owe all of you an apology for the way I behaved Thursday morning. I was worried about Cynthia, but that was no excuse for being rude to you. I'm very sorry."

Brenda harrumphed, while Lee settled into his chair next to hers.

He glanced at his wife, then said to Mandy, "Apology accepted. We've all been under a lot of stress lately, and your concern is understandable." As if anxious to change the subject, he quickly added, "Are you planning to come to Faith's funeral service tomorrow?"

"Yes, I'm taking off work for it."

"We're having a lunch reception afterward at the house. We thought it would be more comfortable for Faith's friends to come here instead of having the reception at the church. You're invited."

"Thank you. I'd like to come. " Then as another peace offering, she asked, "Can I bring anything?"

Lee looked at Brenda.

Brenda blinked, as if suddenly realizing she was expected to answer this question. "A dessert, I guess." She dropped her gaze back down to her knitting, obviously avoiding looking at Mandy.

"Sure, I'd be happy to." An uncomfortable silence filled the room. Mandy smoothed her jeans that didn't need smoothing while trying to think of something else to say or a way to bring up Cynthia's bail fund.

Thankfully Craig filled the gap. "We visited Cynthia in jail this afternoon."

Mandy turned to him. "How was she?"

"Depressed. She seemed resigned to staying there for a long time."

"Not if I have anything to say about it," Mandy said. "I'm collecting donations to bail her out on Monday, once the judge sets the amount. Even if it's high, all we need is about five percent to give as collateral to a bail bondsman."

Lee leaned forward, making his leather chair creak. "That's if the judge sets bail. Sometimes they don't in murder cases."

"Crap, I hadn't thought of that." Mandy's hands clenched. "That means she could be in jail for months before they finally schedule her trial. She could lose her job, and if she can't pay rent, her apartment. No, they've got to let her out on bail!"

"What if she's convicted, Mandy?" Craig said quietly. "She'd be in prison for years."

Brenda flinched and dropped a stitch. She clenched her teeth while she picked apart the yarn to fix her mistake.

"Do you think she did it, Craig?" Mandy studied his face. When he raised his brows and shrugged his shoulders in the universal gesture for "who knows," Mandy pressed harder. "Do you really think she could drive an ax through her uncle's throat?"

Brenda gasped.

Mandy looked at the woman, who'd given up on her knitting and sat with her fist in front of her mouth, her face reddening. "I'm sorry, Brenda. I shouldn't have brought up how your brother died. But I just can't see Cynthia committing such a violent act."

"Who's to say what violence someone could be capable of," Lee said philosophically, "if you or someone you love is threatened?"

"But you already said you'd never do such a thing, even to protect Faith," Mandy replied. "Why do you believe Cynthia could?"

Lee shrugged. "It's hard for me to understand what she feels, having been a victim of Howie's …" He glanced at his wife. "You know. But regardless of whether or not she did it, Cynthia is family. We'll contribute to the bail fund, and do everything else we can to make sure she gets a good defense. Right, Brenda?"

Brenda nodded, her hands kneading the yarn in her lap, ruining the neat stitches she'd just put in. Finally she spoke. "I wish the sheriff's office had found someone else to arrest."

"Don't we all!" Mandy jumped to her feet. "There certainly were enough people who had a reason to hate him or were at the campsite. But everyone has alibis that Quintana hasn't been able to crack yet."

She ticked them off on her fingertips. "Jesse Lopez was working at his gas station. Ira Porter was visiting his mother in Colorado Springs. Newt Nowak was collecting cans at Hecla Junction. And Arnold Crawford just walked into the Quintana's office to vouch for you two men."

"Yeah, we heard," Lee said. "Sounds like Arnold will be in the doghouse with his wife for quite a while. I'm glad he finally showed up to vouch for Craig and me, though."

"And I was cleaning house and cooking a chicken dinner," Brenda added softly.

Lee reached over to pat her shoulder. "No one's accusing you, dear. The house looked great and it was a good dinner."

"Yeah, that was the best chicken you've ever made," Craig said. "It was really juicy."

Lee smiled. "Or we were just really hungry after a day of fishing."

Mandy stood with her hands on her hips watching the three of them. Their alibis sounded just a little too pat, a little too convenient, especially with Lee and Craig's good friend appearing all of a sudden to say he'd been fishing with them. He was a gambler, probably with debts. Maybe Lee had paid him off to vouch for them.

Lee had already insisted that he would never have killed Howie, but Craig hadn't said anything one way or the other. And Mandy knew he had a temper. When Mandy caught his eye, his gaze slid from hers, as if unable to stand up under too much scrutiny. And Brenda's gaze flitted around the room like a nervous bird trapped indoors and looking for a way out. Maybe she knew something, something she wasn't telling. Something about Craig, perhaps?

Mandy focused on Brenda, the one she thought most likely to crack. "So who else could have killed your brother, Brenda? Who else besides a family member?"

Brenda shook her head violently. "I don't know," she wailed. "I don't know. I don't know. Just tell them to go away and leave us alone. Leave *me* alone! Howie's dead, and Faith's dead, and nothing anyone does is going to change that." Tears started running down her cheeks. She dropped her face in her hands and sobbed, her shoulders shaking.

Lee reached over to clasp her hand, then looked at Mandy. "Why does it have to be someone who knew Howie? Why not a vagrant, or a psycho just traveling through town who stopped by the campground? Has Quintana thought of that?"

"There's no evidence that anyone was there other than Howie, Ira, and Newt," Mandy said, "besides a family from Texas with small children."

Brenda's face shot up, her eyes wild. "Yes, yes, it was a madman, a serial killer. That's who they should be chasing. Not Cynthia. Not us." She stood and grabbed Mandy's arm, her hand a claw that dug in deep. "You tell that Detective Quintana to let Cynthia out of jail. Tell him a crazy person killed Howie."

Mandy glanced at the painful red marks on her arm under Brenda's quivering fingers, then at Lee and Craig, who stared at Brenda in alarm. The chances seemed slim that a crazy serial killer murdered her brother, but the chances seemed great that grief was driving this woman over the edge of sanity.

―――――

Lucky jumped on Mandy when she opened the gate to her yard, smearing mud on her jeans. A short rain shower had blown through while she was at the Ellis home. She absently bent down to hug and pet the damp dog while visions of Cynthia spending another lonely night in jail swirled in her head. The musty and somehow comforting smell of wet fur brought her back to the moment. She stood.

"C'mon, Lucky, let's towel you off." She glanced at her muddy jeans. "And me, too."

She walked around to the back porch, left her water sandals there, and grabbed an old beach towel off a hook inside the door that she kept there for just this purpose. After toweling off the dog and herself, she filled Lucky's food and water bowls. Then she changed into a pair of old sweatpants cut off at the knees and an oversized FIBArk T-shirt. She'd just opened the refrigerator door to see what she could make herself for dinner when the front doorbell rang.

When she opened it, Rob stood there with his swollen bruised nose, a six-pack of Pacifico, and a brown paper bag that steamed with a delicious aroma. He waved the bag under her nose. "You eaten yet? I brought moo shu pork and egg foo young."

Her mouth watering, she pulled him into the house and stood on her toes to kiss him. "I love you. You know that, don't you?"

She turned to go into the kitchen then realized he wasn't following her. When she looked over her shoulder at him, he was standing stock still with a bemused expression on his face. "What's wrong?"

"That's the first time you've said you love me," he said. "If I'd known all I needed to do was bring Chinese food over, I would have done it a long time ago."

Her statement had just slipped out, but Mandy realized as she watched him approach that yes, she loved this man. She loved him deeply, had for a while and had never admitted it to herself or to him.

She grinned as he put the food on the kitchen table and pulled her into his arms. "It's not the food. It's you, Rob, and how you always seem to know exactly what I need."

"And I know you need this." He thoroughly kissed her, then drew back to gaze at her. After a moment's hesitation, he reached up to caress her cheek with his thumb. "Did you really mean it, then, when you said you loved me?"

Mandy put her hand over his, kissed his thumb, and looked steadily into his eyes. For once, Rob needed reassurance from her, and she could give it to him. "It slipped out, and I should have picked a better moment to tell you, a more serious one. But I meant it, Rob. I love you."

A little sigh escaped his lips. "I love you, too, *mi querida*." He hugged her tight, held her for a long moment, then pulled back. "Now let's eat. I'm starving."

Mandy grabbed plates and silverware while Rob emptied the bag. They plowed into the food and beer until they sat back with full bellies, Lucky at their feet contentedly munching on half of Mandy's fortune cookie.

Her fortune had read, "Something you lost will soon turn up." She had a niggling feeling that she had overlooked some important detail in the case of Howie Abbott's murder, something that might save Cynthia. She desperately hoped that the fortune was true and that the answer would turn up soon. To get her mind working on the puzzle again, she told Rob about her visit with the Ellis family.

After she finished, he took a thoughtful drink of beer. "So, you're thinking Craig might have found out about Howie lusting after his sister and taken an ax to his uncle?"

"Think about it, Rob. That murder was obviously a crime of passion, one done in extreme anger. And what could cause more anger than finding out your sister was being sexually abused by her uncle?"

Rob spread a hand wide. "Finding out that your daughter was?"

"True, but Lee has already said he wouldn't have killed Howie, that he would have let the law put Howie away, in prison where he belonged. His statement rang true to me."

"You sure?"

Mandy exhaled. "No, just a feeling in my gut. And unlike his father, Craig has never outright denied killing his uncle, at least to me. He even said after Howie's funeral that if Howie hadn't already been killed, he'd take great pleasure in doing it himself. And you know, his mother seemed to be hiding something tonight, some secret. Made me think she knows Craig did it."

"So how do you prove it?"

"There's the rub. Unless Craig confesses, I don't see how I can. Arnold Crawford provided him with a strong alibi and there's no physical evidence linking him to the crime scene. Unlike Cynthia."

Rob rinsed his beer can at the sink, then crushed it and dropped it in Mandy's metal recycling bag. "I don't see Craig being callous enough to let Cynthia go to prison in his place."

"Maybe he's hoping she'll get off, that the evidence won't be enough to convict her." Mandy stood and began clearing the table. "He could be thinking that they'll get a good lawyer to convince the jury of Lee and Brenda's wild theory, that some unknown serial killer or psycho vagrant could have done it instead."

Rob nodded. "The lawyer might plant enough doubt that someone on the jury wouldn't vote to convict Cynthia. Or he could go for the sympathy ploy, claiming she went temporarily insane because her uncle raped her in the past, and she thought he would do the same to Faith."

"I'm not willing to take that chance, though. Sure, Cynthia had plenty of motive, with Howie abusing her and going after her cousin. But after visiting the Ellises tonight, I suspect one of them killed Howie, most likely Craig. I just need to find a way to prove it." Mandy clenched her fist.

Rob came up behind her and started massaging her shoulders, releasing waves of tension that she didn't know she was holding in. "Faith's funeral is tomorrow, right? You'll get another chance to observe the Ellises then. You won't solve anything tonight, though."

Mandy sighed. "You're right, and there's something else important I need to tell you tonight."

"More important than saying you love me?" Rob leaned over her shoulder and smiled at her.

Mandy tilted her head back to kiss him then dropped her chin so his wondrous fingers could resume their work on her rigid neck muscles. "No, not more important than that. And keep on rubbing, lover boy. What I have to tell you is that I made a decision this morning."

She told him about stopping at her Uncle Bill's house with Steve. "When that bluebird stole a bite of my sandwich on the river bank then chattered at me, I took it as a sign from Uncle Bill. A sign that that's where he would be for me, on the river, whenever I needed him. Not at the house."

She turned to face Rob and put her arms around his waist. "So, I'm ready to sell it now. I'm going to call Bridget on Monday and accept the counteroffer."

Rob's gaze searched her face. "And you're really comfortable with this? It's not because you're feeling pressured by me, is it?"

Mandy shook her head. "I feel at peace. I spread Uncle Bill's ashes on the Arkansas River. Whenever I need to talk to him, that's where I'll go. Sure, I have lots of fond memories about things that happened in that house, but it's just a building. It doesn't hold his spirit anymore. And I don't need to hold onto it anymore."

Rob hugged her tightly, his chin resting on top of her head. "I'm glad, *mi querida*. And *not* just about getting the money we need for RM Outdoor Adventures. I'm very happy you can still feel Bill's presence and talk to him when you need to."

Mandy smiled against Rob's chest. "Now, if he could only talk to Howie Abbott's spirit, then let me know who killed him."

———

In the middle of the night, Mandy was suddenly awake. She lay there for a moment, listening, trying to hear the echo of a sound, of what might have startled her from her slumber. Rob lay snoring gently beside her, his swollen nose still giving him breathing problems. And Lucky lay on his pillow next to the bed, his doggie's snuffles a quiet accompaniment to Rob's more sonorous wheezes.

As her eyes adjusted to the dim light, she could make out vague shapes of furniture, her dresser and chair, the doorway to the bathroom. But nothing seemed out of place, nothing stirred, except the chests of her fellow sleepers. So, it must have been a dream. Mandy shut her eyes, eased her breathing to drift back into a relaxed state, and tried to remember where she'd been in slumber land.

An image of something swishing through the air flashed through her brain, then a wet thwock as it hit flesh. A cry of agony, and a wet gush of red puddled on the ground. Then the whole scene repeated, as if on instant replay. The "something" was an ax, and the flesh was Howie Abbott's neck.

The next time the scene replayed, Mandy swallowed back her revulsion and tried to pull her mind's camera back, to see who was holding the ax. The look of fierce rage on the wielder's face distorted it enough that Mandy was unsure who she saw. But the scene didn't replay again.

Wide awake now, she picked apart the alibis of the suspects until a crack opened in one. She rolled over and smiled. She could check out her hunch tomorrow before Faith's funeral.

EIGHTEEN

Good things come to those who bait.
—AUTHOR UNKNOWN

MANDY THREW ON HER clothes for Faith's funeral, her trusty black skirt and a matching black twin sweater set she'd bought before stopping by the Ellis home the evening before. She finally had a decent outfit to wear to the funerals she seemed to be attending more frequently these days. Rob had left earlier that morning to open RM Outdoor Adventures and run the shuttle for the morning raft trip. After that, he was going to meet her at the church—the same Baptist church where Faith's uncle's service had been conducted.

Mandy was rushing because she had an important hunch to follow-up on before she went to the service. And she needed to do it that day, a Sunday, the same day of the week when Howie was killed. After Rob had left, she'd used her laptop computer to search for Lee Ellis's name on the Internet, hoping to find a news photo of the family in relation to the articles about Howie's and Faith's deaths. She finally lucked out with one of the whole family taken at a charity event a couple of months ago, and she printed it out on her small, slow printer.

The research had taken longer than she thought, and she would have to move quickly to get her errand done before the service started. Clutching the photo, she settled Lucky in the yard with a rawhide bone and headed for the Safeway grocery store downtown. It wasn't the closest grocery store to the Ellis home, which was the Wal-Mart. However, that Wal-Mart didn't have a fresh deli counter like the Safeway did.

At the Safeway, Mandy went to the deli counter and introduced herself to a white-haired woman behind it, stretching the truth a bit. "Hi, I'm Mandy Tanner. I'm a ranger with the AHRA, and I'm helping the sheriff's office with a joint investigation. Were you working here on Sunday two weeks ago?"

When the woman said yes, Mandy asked, "Was anyone else also behind the counter that day? I'd like to talk to everyone who might have waited on a customer then."

"Kathy was here, too." She waved over a young woman with dark hair who had been ladling potato salad into plastic containers.

Kathy came over and gave Mandy a friendly smile. "How can I help you?"

Mandy introduced herself again and held out the photo of the Ellis family to the two deli workers. "Do you recognize any of these people?"

The white-haired woman pointed to Brenda. "Her. She shops here every Wednesday morning. Buys sliced ham and Swiss cheese religiously, for sandwiches for her husband and son. We shoot the breeze a little most times she comes." She turned to Kathy. "You don't work on Wednesdays, do you?"

Kathy peered at the photo. "No, but I recognize her, too."

"Was she here Sunday two weeks ago perhaps?" Mandy asked.

"The day that fisherman was killed?" Kathy gave a shiver. "I read about it in the paper the next day and tried to remember what I was doing about the time he was killed. You ever do that?"

Mandy and the white-haired woman nodded.

Kathy snapped her fingers. "So I went back over all the people I waited on, and she was one of them. I especially remember her because she came in all flustered and acting weird." She turned to the white-haired woman. "You were in the back, making macaroni salad."

With her heart beating faster, Mandy asked, "What time did she come in and what did she want?"

"It was late afternoon, around five. She said she needed a rotisserie chicken right away, and some mashed potatoes, green bean casserole, and rolls. When I said that sounds like a great dinner, she told me she hadn't had time to fix a homemade dinner and was in a rush to get something in the oven before her men came home off the river. I remember her because she seemed so desperate and looked kind of wild-eyed. Almost made me think her husband was going to blow up at her, maybe even hit her or something if she didn't have a meal waiting for him."

The older woman tsked. "It's a shame how some men mistreat their wives still, in this day and age."

Kathy looked at Mandy. "Why do you need to know this? Did something happen to this poor woman?"

Mandy shook her head. "Sorry, I can't tell you anything yet, but a Detective Quintana may be by later to ask you to verify what you just told me. Thanks."

She rushed out of the store, almost shaking with excitement. Her theory was confirmed, as unbelievable as it seemed. Brenda hadn't cooked the Sunday dinner herself. And she probably dashed through some cleaning chores to make it look like she'd been working hard at home all afternoon. It didn't take long to run a vacuum over the carpet, especially if you were rushing, and she could have just tossed the towels in the dryer with a scented dryer sheet to make it seem like they'd been freshly laundered. Mandy had pulled that trick once or twice when her brother had come to visit and she hadn't had time to wash towels.

While Mandy drove to the church, her heart rate increased as her suspicion solidified. Brenda was about the same size as Cynthia, in fact had about twenty pounds on her. She could have hefted the camping ax. And if she'd found out that Howie was abusing her daughter, that was motive enough, even though he was her own brother. Maybe even especially so.

The horrific certainty landed with a thud in the pit of Mandy's stomach. Brenda had been acting very strange lately. Sure, her brother and daughter had both recently been killed, but more than just grief seemed to be driving her to distraction. Maybe guilt had been worming its way into her psyche, especially since Cynthia had been arrested.

Mandy drummed her fingers on the steering wheel. *Now, we just need some solid proof. Something more than blasting a hole through her alibi.*

She arrived late to the funeral service, which had already started when she slipped into a pew next to Rob, sweat beading on her brow from her dash from the car to the church. He raised his eyebrows at her, but she just shook her head. She heard nothing of the eulogy as her mind raced over the clues they'd found at Howie's campsite and how any of them might be tied to Brenda. After the last hymn, she could barely contain herself while she filed out with the rest of the mourners, searching the crowd for Quintana.

"What's with you?" Rob asked, when they got outside.

"I can't tell you yet, but I just found out something that I've got to tell Detective Quintana. Do you see him?"

Rob pointed toward the edge of the crowd milling around the base of the steps. "There."

Mandy spotted Quintana scanning the crowd with a concentrated expression on his face, as if he was memorizing everyone in attendance. She pushed her way through knots of people as politely and quickly as she could until she reached him.

Almost out of breath, she leaned in and whispered, "I found out something about Howie Abbott's case. I've got to tell you—in private."

Quintana took one glance at her face and straightened. "We'll talk in my cruiser. I can drive you to the Ellis house for the reception." Then he looked at Rob, who had followed Mandy. "That okay with you, Rob?"

With a curious expression on his face, Rob nodded. "Sure. Mandy and I came in separate cars anyway."

Mandy gave Rob a quick peck on his cheek. "See you there. Maybe you can bring me back here to get my car later." She took off at a trot beside Quintana for his cruiser.

Once the two of them were inside, Mandy excitedly filled him in on what she'd learned from the Safeway deli clerks.

Quintana gave out a long, low whistle. "Well, what do you know? It was a woman in the family, but not Cynthia. And that makes me wonder…"

"What?"

"If Howie abused his own sister when they were younger. Maybe that's when it all started."

"Oh my God!" Then Mandy thought for a moment. "But if that was the case, why would Brenda encourage Faith to hang out with her brother? Wouldn't she try to keep her away from him?"

Quintana nodded. "Either way, Faith must have told her mother sometime before she died about Howie's abuse. That blows my theory about Faith's death out of the water."

"What do you mean?" Mandy asked.

"I was thinking the girl committed suicide after her uncle's abuse because she couldn't get the support she needed from her parents. Maybe even that Brenda knew about her brother's behavior and chose to turn a blind eye."

"Craig said his dad even accused her of that."

"But it doesn't ring true if she's the one who killed him. And with an ax. Striking that kind of blow takes a lot of anger."

Mandy replayed her dream from the night before. It had been Brenda's face she had seen, twisted with rage as she rained the fatal blow down on Howie's neck. "Yeah, it's like she'd just found out and couldn't stomach the sick thought that her brother had forced himself on her daughter."

Quintana turned the ignition key to start the car. "I'll definitely follow-up with the deli clerk, but in the meantime, we need to go to the reception at the Ellis home. It's a way to get in without a warrant and maybe pick up some more information. We've blown Brenda's alibi apart, but that's not enough to make a strong case against her. I need physical evidence, something like Cynthia's thumbprint on the ax handle."

"Brenda must have worn gloves of some sort, since you didn't find any of her fingerprints."

"Right." Quintana merged his cruiser into the line of cars leaving the church. "Though I'm going to ask the fingerprint technician to review those small partials on both the hatchet and spray can again, see if he can make a case for matching any of them against Brenda's. He'd stopped working on them when we found Cynthia's thumbprint and thought we had the killer." He gave Mandy a rueful smile.

She folded her arms across her chest. "And threw her in jail. If you'd matched one of the partials on the hatchet to Brenda, would you still have done that?"

He thought for a moment, tapping his fingers on the steering wheel. "Probably. Since Brenda's alibi seemed solid, and since it was family gear, it made sense for her prints to be on it."

"The same could be said of Cynthia!"

"I know. But the spray can is a different story. If one of Brenda's prints had been matched on that, I would have had to rethink everything." He sighed. "I'm not perfect, Mandy."

She uncrossed her arms. "I'm not saying you have to be. I just wish Cynthia hadn't had to go through all that."

"Me, too. Anyway, after I talk to that deli clerk, I should be able to get a search warrant to check out Brenda's shoes and clothing for blood spatters, like I did with Cynthia's."

Mandy turned in her seat to stare at Quintana. "I didn't hear about that. Did you find anything?"

Quintana shook his head. "And that made me worried that I didn't have a strong enough case against Cynthia. Of course, a smart killer would have disposed of or washed all of their clothing, even cleaned their car upholstery."

"But maybe not an emotional one," Mandy replied. "Or one who had to rush to the grocery store to set up a good alibi story. Of course, Brenda's had two weeks to take care of that by now. Are you thinking we should look for a stain while we're there?"

"No," Quintana said firmly. "I don't want to tip our hand until I get a warrant and can thoroughly search without any of the Ellis family interfering. I'm more interested in observing Brenda's behavior today. If I can't find any physical evidence with a search warrant, I'll need to figure out how to get a confession out of her."

He glanced at Mandy before turning into the neighborhood where the Ellises lived. "Do you think you can act normal at this reception? Not let on that you know anything and treat Brenda the same way you've been treating her?"

Mandy knew this was a serious question that required a well-thought-out answer. She didn't want to mess up Quintana's investigation. Could she hide her conviction that Brenda had killed her own brother? Could she grasp a murderer's hand and offer her condolences over the death of her daughter? Mandy mentally rehearsed doing just that in her mind. Maybe if Rob was with her, and she made the interaction quick.

She took a deep breath to try to calm her nerves. "Yes, I think I can."

Quintana parked his cruiser behind some other cars about a block away from the Ellis home. He turned to peer at Mandy. "And you can keep all of this from everyone, including Rob?"

"He already knows something's up. But if I say I can't tell him what, he won't press me."

"Good." Quintana opened his car door. "Let's see what we can find out. Stay alert. You may find that navigating the wicked eddies swirling around this family will be a lot harder than any Class V rapid you've run on the river."

———

Rob was waiting for Mandy at the end of the Ellis driveway. When he took her hand, she realized it was damp with nervous sweat.

"You okay?" he asked as they walked up to the open front door behind Quintana.

Mandy knew Quintana was listening. "Just stay with me while I offer condolences," she said to Rob. "I'm feeling nervous about that."

Then Mandy stopped dead in her tracks, jerking Rob to a halt. "Oh crap!"

"What?"

"I told Brenda that I'd bring a dessert and I forgot all about it."

Rob glanced at Brenda. Dressed in a dark navy skirted suit, she stood between Craig and Lee just inside the front door to greet the mourners. "I don't think she's going to notice."

Mandy looked at Brenda's gray face, with its dark shadows under glassy eyes, and realized Rob was right. Too many other things were going through the woman's head. She was shaking hands and accepting hugs like an automaton. Lee shot a worried glance at his wife and put a hand on the small of her back to give her a reassuring rub before accepting a man's handshake.

Mandy went through the motions with Lee, Brenda, and Craig as quickly as she could. Thankfully when she shook Brenda's hand and murmured, "my sympathies," Brenda didn't respond with a hug. She just pursed her lips, nodded, and dabbed at her glistening eyes with a crumpled tissue she held in her left hand.

After entering the crowded living room, Mandy exhaled deeply and realized she'd been holding her breath.

Rob peered at her. "Can you tell me what's going on, what you had to tell Quintana? It's obviously got you spooked. And frankly, it's got me worried about you."

Mandy shook her head. "I can't say anything." She gave his hand a squeeze. "And I'll be okay, now that that ritual is over with." Her stomach growled. "Let's go get some lunch."

She pulled Rob toward the buffet set up in the dining room. They loaded up paper plates with small sandwiches and munchies from the assortment of potluck donations on the table. Mandy noted thankfully that there seemed to be plenty of desserts, with platters piled high with cookies and brownies, so she didn't feel too bad about forgetting her contribution.

After they grabbed some cans of soda from a cooler, she led Rob outside to the backyard, where the younger crowd was hanging out. She figured she would be less likely to run into any of the Ellises there, other than Craig. Yes, Quintana had asked her to stay alert, but she figured it was more important to hide what she knew and she didn't trust herself around Brenda yet.

The yard was filled mostly with long-legged, gawky high schoolers uncomfortable in their formal clothes. A couple of young men wore brand-new dress shirts with fresh-from-the-package creases. Likely friends of Faith's, the teens perched on an assortment of lawn chairs and decorative boulders, or sat on the grass. They squinted in the bright sunlight, and the girls held their long hair to keep the breeze from blowing it in their faces. They picked at their plates and talked quietly among themselves.

Mandy found a couple of empty lawn chairs next to two young men engaged in a heated, low-voiced argument and took the seat farthest from them. Rob plopped in the other chair and plowed into his food. He soon joined the debate two teens next to him were having over whether the Denver Broncos had it in them to make it to the playoffs that football season. Mandy was content to eat quietly and observe the others in the yard.

Craig came out and made the rounds of the knots of teens, asking if they needed anything and giving them a chance to relay remembrances of Faith to him. He listened quietly and somberly and thanked everyone for their stories. When he neared Mandy, she said, "We're fine. Thanks, Craig," he continued on to a couple of rafting guides Mandy recognized who were standing near the back fence. She figured they must have worked for Lee that summer and had come to pay their respects.

After finishing her lunch, she realized she needed to use the restroom and went inside. She dumped her trash in a large trashcan and looked with dismay at the line of fidgeting women outside the powder room.

An older woman passed by her and said, "Brenda told me to tell folks to use the upstairs bathroom if this one's full. Follow me." She turned and waved her arm over her shoulder.

Mandy gladly followed, along with two other deserters from the line. Since she was last in line after they reached the hall bathroom, Mandy decided to slip into Lee and Brenda's bedroom to comb her wind-tousled hair in front of the dresser mirror. Her gaze passed over a ring tray with a few of Brenda's rings looped over the central spike. That reminded her that the sheriff's office had never found Howie Abbott's pinkie ring. She peered at the rings on the spike, but no luck, no ring resembled the description of it.

Then she saw the open door to the master bathroom in the mirror, and decided she might as well use that one. While washing her hands, she noticed that the toilet kept flushing and tsked. Just like her own toilet. The chain probably had a kink in it. She flipped down the seat lid, removed the tank lid, and placed it on top of the seat lid. Then she peered inside to see what the problem was.

A plastic bag that had been taped to the back of the tank had come loose on one side. The loose corner was tangled in the chain. Inside the clear bag was another one, and inside that lay a folded piece of baby blue writing paper and a man's ring, gold with a brown stone.

Mandy carefully untangled the bag from the chain, then loosened the tape holding it to the tank and held it up. She shook the bag gently to roll the ring from one side to another and read, "Salida High School," and a year, 1979.

This must be Howie's pinkie ring!

While staring at the bag, Mandy debated what she should do next. Open it and see what was written on the paper? No, bad idea. That would be crossing the line from stumbling onto something to illegal search.

Return the bag to the now full tank, find Quintana and tell him about it? No, the bag was torn from her efforts and the paper inside would get wet from the now-full tank.

Take the bag to him? No, she'd be removing evidence from where she found it. She decided to hide the bag in the medicine cabinet, then go get him.

She put the now-quiet toilet back together and opened the medicine cabinet door.

At the same time, the bathroom door creaked open, startling Mandy. She dropped the bag and it fell into the sink with a clink.

Brenda stood in the doorway, gripping the doorknob. The sun streaming through the bedroom window backlit her, creating a halo of light around her. Looking like an avenging angel with wide, white eyes in a shadowed, glowering face, she pointed a quivering finger at Mandy.

"What the hell are you doing in here?"

NINETEEN

Many men go fishing all of their lives
without knowing that it is not fish they are after.
—HENRY DAVID THOREAU

HEART POUNDING, MANDY STAMMERED, "The t-toilet, it kept flushing—"

Brenda advanced and slapped her. Hard.

The slap threw Mandy off balance. She fell back onto the toilet seat lid, putting a hand to her burning cheek.

Brenda slapped Mandy's other cheek, then stood over her, slapping Mandy with the furious speed of a madwoman. She hollered, "Bitch, you evil bitch!"

"Stop, Brenda," Mandy yelled. She tried to stand while blocking Brenda's arms, but the effort put her off balance. She fell, landing on her butt in a corner between the tub and wall.

Brenda started kicking her.

Mandy curled up to protect herself. "Stop it!"

A kick to her stomach released all her air with an "oof" and left her gasping. That was followed by stabbing pain, and more pains from more blows.

Mandy realized rage had full control of Brenda. Mandy had to act and act now or this woman was going to kill her, just as rage had driven her to kill her own brother.

She uncurled and reached out, exposing her vulnerable mid-section. When a well-aimed kick came in, she grabbed Brenda's ankle with both hands and yanked. Hard.

Brenda fell back through the door to the bedroom, landing on the floor with a thump, but she continued to flail with her legs against Mandy.

Mandy blocked and parried, trying to grab a leg so she could wrench Brenda away.

Suddenly space opened between them. Hands were on Brenda, pulling her away and to her feet. Men's voices yelled, "Stop, stop!"

Mandy looked up to see Lee Ellis and Detective Quintana in the bedroom on either side of Brenda, clutching her arms. Her legs were still windmilling toward Mandy, thankfully out of reach.

Panting, Mandy rolled to her hands and knees. Rob squeezed past Brenda and her captors and lifted Mandy to the toilet seat lid. She moaned and shut her eyes against a sharp pain in her left side.

"Where are you hurt?" Rob asked, his hands running gently down her legs and arms.

"My ribs," Mandy gasped, opening her eyes. "I think she broke one."

"What's going on here?" Craig asked over his father's shoulder.

That seemed to trigger something in Brenda, and she finally stopped kicking. She collapsed against Lee's side and started sobbing into his shoulder.

Quintana let her go, and Lee took her into his arms. He lowered her to the bed and sat next to her there. He patted her back while staring at Mandy. Quintana and Craig stared at her, too, as did Rob. Obviously, they all expected her to answer Craig's question, because Brenda sure wasn't going to.

Mandy took a deep breath, which sent another stabbing pain through her left side. "Ow, ow." She clutched her side, but waved away Rob's hand. She took another experimental breath, shallower this time, and found the pain was bearable.

"She, she found me with that." Mandy pointed at the crumpled bag lying in the sink. She stopped to rest, catch her breath, slow her racing heartbeat from the adrenaline still coursing through her bloodstream. "The bag was caught in the toilet chain. It has Howie's pinkie ring inside. And a note."

"What?" Lee's eyes went wide with surprise.

When someone gasped, Mandy realized more people were standing in the bedroom and out in the hallway. A teenage face peeked over Quintana's shoulder.

Craig turned toward the others and shouted, "Give us some privacy here!"

Quintana turned, too. "I'm with the sheriff's office, and I'll handle this." He advanced toward the onlookers with arms wide. "Go on. Get out of here. Move downstairs."

People mumbled and stirred, then footsteps thumped down the stairs. Quintana and Craig herded the last few out of the bedroom and watched them go down the stairs.

Quintana shut the bedroom door and frowned at Mandy. He pursed his lips, obviously peeved at her. "Were you searching in here?"

Mandy's cheeks flushed. She straightened, which sent another bolt of pain through her and made her wince. "No, I wasn't. I swear. I used the toilet, and it kept flushing. So I looked in the tank, thinking I'd unkink the chain."

Craig stepped into the bathroom and snatched the bag out of the sink before Quintana could get a hand on his arm. He moved into the bedroom while opening the bag and pulling out the note. He unfolded it and scanned it. "Oh my God!"

"Read it to me," Lee said.

Craig took a deep breath, glanced at his parents, then read.

Mom and Dad,

When you find this, I'll be long gone. I'll have finally escaped the hell hole I've been living in for the past weeks. Uncle Howie won't be able to paw me anymore with his grubby hands—and worse. I can't believe you let him do this to me, even told me to hang out with him! You won't help me. And nobody else will believe me. I can't stand to live in fear another day.

Goodbye,
Faith

Aghast, Mandy stared at Craig, blood rushing to her head. Was this a farewell note from someone who was running away from home or a suicide note?

"When did you find this?" Craig asked his mother. "And why did you keep it from us?"

Brenda slowly raised her head from Lee's shoulder and looked at him then her son, defeat and utter surrender making both her expression and her body droop.

Lee stared at his wife. "Brenda?"

She heaved a great sigh. "I found it the Sunday morning after Faith disappeared. On the kitchen table when I went down to make coffee. That's what made me run upstairs and check her bed, only to find it hadn't been slept in. Then I woke you both up, remember?"

Lee and Craig nodded.

"I was shocked by what she said about Howie, and that she thought we condoned it. I thought she might have made it all up. I didn't want you to see her ugly lies, so I stuffed the note in my pocket." Brenda closed her eyes and rubbed her forehead.

"While you two went out to search for her and I called her friends and the neighbors," Brenda continued, "that note was burning a hole in my pocket. I kept remembering little clues about Howie's and her behavior. I was horrified that I didn't see what was happening, but finally I had to admit it to myself. I knew my little girl was telling the truth, and she'd been afraid to come to us with it. God, I feel so guilty." The last words came out in a choked voice and tears ran down her face.

Lee stroked her arm. "It wasn't your fault."

"But I pushed her at Howie. By asking him to teach her fly fishing and show her the river, I set her up to be abused by him. And she thought I condoned it, Lee!"

"Howie probably lied to her, twisted the truth all around so it seemed that way to Faith," Lee said quietly. "So after you read the note, you confronted Howie?"

Quintana held up a hand. "Hold it right there. Brenda, you know I'm an officer of the law. You sure you want to answer that question?"

"I can't hold in the lie any longer. It's driving me crazy," Brenda said to him, then looked at Lee. "I started out toward the Vallie Bridge campground planning to confront Howie. But when I saw him lying there snoring on his sleeping bag, the same bag that we found out later he raped Faith in, I lost it."

She clutched Lee's hand. "He was a monster, Lee, a monster who was preying on our daughter. He wasn't my brother anymore, and I wasn't his sister. But I was still Faith's mother, and I had to protect her."

"I didn't know that she was already dead," she wailed and buried her face in Lee's shoulder again.

Craig stared at his mother, horror stiffening his hands into claws. "*You* killed him? You killed Uncle Howie?"

Brenda lifted her head. "Somehow I found the strength to pick up that ax and swing it into his neck, where it stuck. Then when he rose up with a roar like he was going to come after me, I got scared. I saw the bear spray and sprayed him with it. That made him fall back down."

"What about the ring?" Lee asked.

"I stumbled away a few steps, then sat down and watched him die. I was glad at first, because I'd killed the beast who was mauling our daughter. But after he died, the rage just flowed right out of me, and I was staring at my brother again. The brother I'd just killed. I sat there and cried and cried.

"Finally a squirrel made a noise, and I was afraid again. Afraid that someone would see what I'd done and lock me up before I could help Faith heal. I had to get out of there. I stood up and walked over to Howie to have one last look, and that's when I saw his ring. It reminded me of our good years, when we were both children, so I took it."

She looked at Mandy for the first time since she'd started talking. "I thought I was safe. That no jury would convict poor Cynthia. If they had, I would have come forward. Believe me, I wouldn't have let her go to prison. She's blameless in this whole mess. If I was in her shoes, I probably would have done the same thing. Buried the memories of what that monster did. But you, you ruined everything. You and your meddling."

Quintana gave a nod of satisfaction and walked forward to face Brenda. "I'm going to have to take you into custody now for the murder of your brother." He began the slow recital of her Miranda rights while Lee and Craig stared at the floor, shoulders slumped.

After getting Brenda's acknowledgement that she understood her rights, he turned to Craig. "I'll need to take the note and ring with me."

Craig folded the note, returned it to the bag, and silently handed the bag to Quintana, who put it in his suit coat pocket.

With Lee's help, Quintana lifted Brenda from the chair. At the same time, Rob helped Mandy to her feet so she could hobble out of the master bathroom.

As Quintana escorted Brenda out of the bedroom, with Lee assisting at her other elbow, Mandy asked him. "Do you think the note was a suicide note? Did Faith kill herself?"

His reply was solemn. "We may never know."

———

Rob drove Mandy to the emergency room to get an x-ray of her ribs. When the emergency room doctor came in the examining room with the x-ray film, he stopped dead. "You two again? Next time, get a padded room."

Mandy looked at Rob's swollen nose and started laughing. She quickly grabbed her sore side. "Very funny, Doc."

The doctor grinned. "You've got to admit this looks suspicious."

"We didn't do this to each other," Rob said. "Other people decided to use us as punching bags."

When the doctor raised an eyebrow, Mandy said, "It's a long story—two long stories. Maybe once we're healed we'll buy you a beer and tell you."

"I'll look forward to it. In the meantime, look at this." The doctor held up the x-ray film and pointed out a hairline crack in one rib on her left side. "It looks like it might be incomplete, that the crack doesn't go all the way through the bone. Unfortunately, there isn't much I can do about it, other than tell you to take over-the-counter painkillers for the pain, up to twice the recommended dose, if needed. And take it easy for at least six weeks to give it time to heal."

Mandy dreaded not being able to work. "What about paddling? I'm a river ranger and part-owner of a rafting business."

The doctor raised an eyebrow. "The only thing I suggest you paddle in the next few weeks is a pen, at a desk."

"Shit." The only good thing was that the rafting season was winding down. There was paperwork both at AHRA and at RM Outdoor Adventures that she could catch up on, but that didn't mean she wanted to do it. "Do I need to wear an ACE bandage?"

"We don't recommend compression wraps for broken ribs anymore because they can keep you from taking deep breaths, which can increase the risk of pneumonia. So, even though they'll hurt, I want you to make an effort to take a few deep breaths every day." He peered at her until she promised to do so.

After they came out into the reception area, Rob said, "We make quite a pair, don't we, with my broken nose and your cracked rib." He went to give her a hug, then modified it into a gentle caress. "We'll get through it, *mi querida*, by taking care of each other."

They drove to the pharmacy to pick up some more painkillers. On the way, Mandy popped a couple of Advil and washed them down with a swig from a water bottle. Then Rob dropped her off by her car at the church.

"You're sure you can drive?" he asked. "I can take you home."

Mandy waved him off. "I'm fine. You've got to get going and run that afternoon shuttle."

"I'll come by your house after." Rob gave a wave and drove off.

As Mandy eased herself into the driver's seat of her Subaru, her cell phone rang.

It was Quintana. "After I booked Brenda, I filled out all the paperwork to release your friend Cynthia. She's being checked out of the jail now. I thought you'd like to know."

"Thanks," Mandy said. "I'll go over there now. She'll need a ride home. Can you get a message to her that I'm coming?"

After Quintana promised he would, he cleared his throat. "You know, I'm sure, about the legal term, 'fruit of the poisonous tree.'"

Mandy was aghast. "You mean the ring can't be used as evidence, even though I found it by accident?"

"No, that was what saved us. If you had been deliberately searching without a warrant and found it, we couldn't have used it, or the note, or Brenda's confession. None of it."

So maybe she hadn't screwed up. "But now we can."

"Yes. However, the DA may ask you to testify under oath about finding the bag in the toilet by accident. Can you do that?"

Did Quintana not believe her? Did he think she was snooping in Brenda's bathroom? Mandy's cheeks flamed with anger and embarrassment. "Of course I can. It's the truth."

Quintana's voice softened. "Just making sure. I realize you haven't been trained in all the legal ramifications of investigating cases. We have another piece of physical evidence, too, to back up what you found. The technician just matched two of the small partials on the pepper spray can found at the campsite to Brenda's fingerprints."

"Ah ha! Too bad that didn't happen before you put Cynthia in jail, and before Brenda beat me up."

"I know, I know. Look, I'll treat you both to brunch at Laughing Ladies, and I'll apologize to Cynthia then."

"The apology will be the most important part for Cynthia, but I'm sure we'll both enjoy the brunch, too, so I'll hold you to it."

"Good. Anyway, our case is now solid enough that I hope Brenda's lawyer will advise her to plead guilty and save us all the cost of a trial. The DA will probably allow the plea to be downgraded to second-degree murder or manslaughter, given Brenda's state of mind."

"You know, even though she broke one of my ribs," Mandy replied. "I can't help feeling sorry for her. The real villain in all this was Howie. It's too bad Brenda has to go to prison at all."

"Not all cases end happily," Quintana said. "I hope this doesn't discourage you from applying to be a river ranger again next year. You're still learning, but your instincts are good. I wouldn't mind working with you again on a case."

After Mandy thanked him and hung up, she took a deep breath. *Ouch.* She'd forgotten about her rib. She held her side until the pain diminished, and that gave her time to process what Quintana had said. He seemed to believe her, he actually complimented her, and he wanted to work with her again. Her mood lightening, she drove to the Chaffee County Detentions Center.

Before she could pull into a parking spot, she spied Cynthia standing outside waiting for her and holding a large bag labeled "Personal Effects." Mandy pulled up in front of Cynthia and waited while she tossed her bag in the back seat and got in the passenger seat.

"Thanks for picking me up, Mandy."

When Cynthia reached for her to give her a hug, Mandy yelled, "Don't!" That and her involuntary cringe brought on a rib pain and she winced.

Cynthia stopped with her arms in mid-air and looked confused.

"I've got a cracked rib," Mandy said, "It's related to why you're being released. Did they tell you?"

Cynthia's eyes got even wider, and she dropped her arms. "They only said they had new evidence that led them to arrest Brenda instead. What's with these guys? I can't believe she would kill her own brother."

"Let me explain." Mandy turned off her car engine and described everything that had happened at the reception at the Ellis home. By the time she finished, Cynthia had tears in her eyes.

"Oh God," Cynthia said while laying a hand on Mandy's arm. "I hope you won't take this the wrong way, because she hurt you, but I feel so sorry for Aunt Brenda."

Mandy nodded. "I understand. I feel the same way, really, and maybe that's why it took me so long to fight back."

"That poor woman lost her daughter, was driven to murder, and is now going to probably spend the rest of her life in prison. And it's all my fault."

Mandy's jaw dropped. "What? How can this possibly be your fault?"

"Don't you see? If I'd told any of the Ellises about how Uncle Howie had abused me, then they would have protected Faith. She wouldn't have committed suicide, and Brenda wouldn't have been driven to kill him."

Mandy shifted in her seat to face Cynthia, sucking in her breath against the pain. She grabbed Cynthia's hands in hers. "Girlfriend, you listen to me and you listen hard. None of this, none of it, is your fault. It's Howie's fault. You are a victim here, as much as Faith is, as much as Brenda is."

When Cynthia shook her head, Mandy tightened her grip. "Didn't you hear me tell you what Brenda said? She said you were blameless in this whole mess. That she probably would have done the same thing. And at Howie's funeral, Craig told me that he was going to apologize to you for what he said, that it was cruel and Howie's abuse of you and Faith was his fault and his alone."

Cynthia heaved out a great sigh as if she wasn't convinced yet, so Mandy plowed on. "In fact, I bet Lee and Craig are beating themselves up as much as you are, or more. I mean, they were living in the same house with Faith and couldn't read the signs, didn't figure out how depressed she was. And you know what the guilt did to Brenda. You can't claim responsibility for this mess, Cynthia. You're just not that powerful. And if you say you are, I'll make it my job to knock you down off that pedestal."

That drew a grin out of Cynthia.

Relieved, Mandy let go of Cynthia's hands. "If you don't believe me, maybe you should talk to a counselor. I'm sure they'd agree with everything I'm saying."

Cynthia stared out the windshield. "Maybe I *should* get some counseling. If there's one thing I learned from this, it's that I still have some unresolved issues from Uncle Howie's abuse."

"But first," Mandy said as she turned the ignition key. "We are going to get blind stinking drunk to celebrate your release from jail."

"No, first I'm going to take a long, hot shower." Cynthia smiled at Mandy. "Then we'll get blind stinking drunk."

"Now you're talking." Mandy put the car in gear.

"Speaking of talking," Cynthia said with a sly quirk to her lips, "did I ever tell you the one about two blondes living in Oklahoma sitting on a bench talking?"

Mandy didn't care if she'd heard the blonde joke before or not. She was just glad that Cynthia was willing to share one with her again. She stepped on the accelerator. "No, I haven't heard that one."

"Well," Cynthia said while fastening her seat belt. "The one blonde says to the other, 'Which do you think is farther away... Florida or the moon?' and the other blonde turns to her friend and says 'Hellooooooo, can you see Florida?'"

Mandy slapped the steering wheel and laughed and laughed with her best friend, even though it hurt as they drove off into the brilliant sunlight of a perfect blue-sky Colorado afternoon.

TWENTY

When you fish for love, bait with your heart, not your brain.
—MARK TWAIN

LATER THAT EVENING, ROB and Mandy were in his car, leaving Cynthia's apartment, where a flotilla of rafting guides, river rangers, and Victoria Tavern's regulars had gathered for an impromptu celebration. The party had spilled out onto her deck and the yard, but the retired couple who owned the property hadn't minded and had joined in the festivities.

Mandy sat in the passenger seat with her head back and eyes closed while Rob drove. She hummed to herself, enjoying the glow of happiness she felt. She hadn't gotten blind stinking drunk, but she was mostly pain-free, with the combination of Advil and three beers. Life was good.

When the car stopped, she opened her eyes and looked around with surprise. They weren't at either her place or Rob's, but were parked next to the downtown Salida Riverside Park. Through the open car window, she could hear a soft wind rustling the cotton-woods draped over the darkened walkways.

She looked at Rob. "What are we doing here?"

He opened his car door. "It's such a nice night, I thought we'd talk a walk along the river." While she processed that, he came around the car, opened her door, and held out a hand to her.

Moving gingerly so as not to stress her cracked rib, Mandy slid out of the seat and into Rob's arms. He nuzzled her nose, then released her to lock the car. He led her by the hand into the cool archways under the huge trees. In the gaps between branches overhead, bright stars in the clear night sky winked at them conspiratorially.

Still trying to puzzle out why Rob had chosen to visit the park at night, something he'd never shown an inclination to do before, Mandy let the peaceful scene work its magic on her. Her steps slowed along with his and she breathed in the fresh breeze. Thankfully, she wore her AHRA fleece jacket, so she was comfortably warm. Especially her hand, which was encased in Rob's strong, yet gentle fingers.

He turned onto the pathway beside the river, and they moved downstream with the gurgling water until Rob stopped and draped an arm over her shoulder. Mandy nestled her head against his chest while they both looked out across the undulating liquid silver glistening in the moonlight, then up at the Milky Way streaked across the sky.

"You're right, Rob," she said. "This is a beautiful night to take a walk along the river."

"Along our future," he replied. "This is where we both belong, Mandy, where we should live out the rest of our lives."

"Yes." What else could she say to words that were so true?

Rob took her hand again and led her to a picnic table up on the lawn. He sat her down on the bench seat facing the river. Expecting him to sit beside her, Mandy was surprised when he bent down on one knee in front of her.

What's he doing?

Rob took her hand and waited until she focused her gaze on his face and realized how serious he was.

"Mandy." The word came out hoarse, draped with emotion, and he cleared his throat. "I love the river, and I love this place, but most of all, I love you. More than anything, more than life itself."

He pulled a small box out of his pocket and thumbed open the lid. Inside nestled a gold ring with a small, brilliant diamond.

Mandy's heart thudded as she stared at him. She knew what was coming next. *Oh my God.*

His tremulous smile was full of hope, mixed with a dash of fear. "Will you marry me, *mi querida*?"

THE END

ACKNOWLEDGMENTS

I want to thank those who selflessly shared their expertise with me
so this book could be as authentic as possible. My go-to-expert
for the whole Rocky Mountain Outdoor Adventures series, Stew
Pappenfort, Senior Park Ranger of the Arkansas Headwaters Recreation Area (AHRA), answered many questions and reviewed the
manuscript to make sure I portrayed river rangers and river rescue
situations correctly. John Knight, Director of The America Cup Fly
Fishing Tournament held every fall in Colorado, graciously let me
tromp alongside rivers with him for a day and pepper him with
questions while he judged the 2009 tournament. His wife Jodi
also was helpful in providing behind-the-scenes details about how
such tournaments are run. The characters John and Carol Squire
in the book were developed to honor this hard-working and dedi-
cated couple.

Ned Parker, owner of Breckenridge Outfitters, and Adam Gros-
kin, one of his fly-fishing guides and a very patient teacher, provided valuable information about fly fishing in Colorado. It wasn't
Adam's fault that all I managed to hook during my lesson was
my thumb! Peter Sheetz, a member of the U.S. Youth Fly Fishing Team, let me pick his brain about potential ways a competitor
could cheat in a tournament and how the sport of competitive fly
fishing is organized. Christina Herndon, former Deputy Coroner
of El Paso County, provided forensic information such as how im-
mersion in a river would affect dead bodies over time.

Any errors in fact or procedure are due to my exaggeration
or misunderstanding of these experts' patient instruction. One
deliberate twist of fact that I made was to place the Vallie Bridge
campground inside Chaffee County, so my river ranger character,

Mandy Tanner, could continue to work with character Detective Victor Quintana of the Chaffee County Sheriff's Office.

I read many reference books on the sport of fly fishing, but two that were especially helpful were *The Orvis Fly-Fishing Guide* by Tom Rosenbauer and *The Complete Angling Guide for the Summit County Area* by Michael D. Shook.

Finally I must thank those who help me in my writing career. My literary agent, Sandra Bond, works tirelessly for me, and I rely heavily on her literary contract expertise. Terri Bischoff, Acquisition Editor at Midnight Ink, and Connie Hill, Senior Editor, made sure the book's prose was the best it could be. Thanks to Lisa Novak for the brilliant cover art! Thanks also to all of the staff at Midnight Ink who contributed to the production and marketing of the book, especially Marissa Pederson, Publicist. And a huge shout-out to my critique group, Vic Cruikshank, Maria Faulconer, Barbara Nickless, M. B. Partlow, and Robert Spiller, for their extremely helpful suggestions along the way.

If you enjoyed reading Wicked Eddies, read on for an excerpt from

Cataract Canyon

ONE

*"Those who dwell among the beauties and mysteries of the earth
are never alone or weary of life."*
—RACHEL CARSON

"I COULD KILL HIM."

With hands on her hips, Mandy Tanner surveyed the pile of gear
heaped in the back room of the outfitter's building. The rafts, oars
and paddles, sleeping bags, mats, and tents were all there, as were
the kitchen supplies, water jugs, coolers, portable toilet, first aid kit,
handheld radio transceiver, and myriad other supplies and equipment needed for a multi-day rafting trip. But Gonzo, her provi-
sioner, had missed one vital piece of equipment—one of two camping lanterns needed to light their campsites in the evenings.

Mandy swallowed to tamp down the anger and frustration that
were threatening to clog her throat. Could they make do with one

lantern? No, dammit. They had to have two, and preferably three, the extra one for backup.

Mandy's fiancé and business partner, Rob Juarez, gave a shrug. "Gonzo will find one."

How could Rob be so nonchalant? She glared at his infuriatingly calm and handsome face. "The clients are due to start arriving any minute. He's supposed to be here to meet and greet them instead of running around Moab trying to beg a lantern off another outfitter. With so many of them closed for the season, it'll be tough finding one."

Contrary to her better judgment, Mandy had assigned Gonzo Gordon, their best rafting guide, to provision this expedition, their first outside of Colorado. She would have preferred to do the job herself. But Rob had suggested it to show their support of and trust in Gonzo, who was making good progress in his alcohol rehabilitation program. And Gonzo had assured her—multiple times—that he could handle being the 'Quartermaster,' as he had dubbed himself.

"'No problemo,' he kept telling me," Mandy said between clenched teeth as she stared at the equipment pile, "and now look where we are."

Rob put a firm hand on each of her shoulders and turned her to face him. His puppy-dog brown eyes crinkled with worry as his gaze searched her face. "Yes. Look where we are. We are in Moab, Utah, ready to embark on our first combo rafting and climbing trip. We have twelve paying clients and all the gear we need except for one lousy lantern. What's got *mi querida* wound up so tight?"

As he waited for an explanation, he massaged her tight shoulders, easing the tension out of them. "Take a deep breath."

Mandy did, inhaling Rob's familiar aroma of leather, soap, and the grassy outdoors, and blew the breath out slowly. This was no way to start out. She needed to be perky for the clients to make sure they felt excited and confident about taking the five-day, hundred-mile trip down the Colorado River. They would travel down the placid waters of Meander Canyon, the whitewater rapids of Cataract Canyon, and the finger of Lake Powell that had drowned lower Cataract Canyon, before taking out at Hite Marina. She couldn't let her own worries cloud the clients' perceptions of the upcoming adventure.

"You're right. I'm sorry. I've been too distracted to manage the preparations for this trip as well as I should have. I haven't had time to double-check everything like I usually do. It's not Gonzo's fault. It's mine for not going over the manifest with him."

"This is the way it's going to be as our business grows, Mandy," Rob responded with frustrating reasonableness. "You'll have to trust our employees to do their jobs. You can't do everything. And what's been distracting you?" He grinned lasciviously. "The handsome hunk you're going to marry in a few months?"

Mandy finally smiled. She playfully slapped the standing waves tattoo on one of his muscular biceps. "Sure, I can't keep my hands off of you. But the problem is the handsome hunk's mother, who has to talk to me every single, bleeding day about the wedding plans."

"Ah ha." He gave a knowing nod of his square bronzed chin. "The truth comes out."

Mandy's parents had perished in a car accident the summer before her senior year of high school. So after Rob's mother finished gushing over the news of their engagement, she offered to help Mandy plan the wedding.

"At first I was glad to have her help, because I know a lot more about planning a rafting trip," Mandy swept an arm toward the pile of supplies, "than a wedding. But, my God, all the details are driving me mad. The colors, the cake flavors, the bridesmaid dresses, the meanings of the damn flowers—"

Rob stopped her with a kiss, which deepened into a long, savoring smooch that warmed her to her toes. He pulled back but kept his arms around her, his hands caressing her back. "Mama is so excited. She hasn't planned a wedding before."

"But your sister was married." Before divorcing her abusive husband.

"I must have never told you that they eloped," Rob said with a frown. "They robbed Mama of what she views as a mother's God-given right. She sees our wedding as a way to make up for that."

"I guess that explains some of her mania..."

"And you know Catholic, Hispanic mamas live for weddings," Rob added with a laugh. "Mama's the star of her neighborhood in Pueblo. The other ladies gather around her every Sunday after church to hear about the plans. She's in the spotlight and loving every minute."

Mandy rolled her eyes. "Maybe *we* should elope!"

"No way, José. And don't ever joke about that to Mama. She'd have a heart attack." His brow furrowed. "You know Mama's going to be a big part of our lives after we're married. Are you going to be able to get along with her?"

Mandy hoped so, but she wasn't going to show any doubts to Rob. "It's just the wedding that's making us both crazy now. I think your mom's great, Rob. We won't have any problems after we're married."

She gave a little laugh and changed the subject. "I wonder how she's getting along with Lucky right now." Rob's mom had volunteered to let Mandy's golden retriever stay with her during the trip.

Rob grinned. "She loves dogs. You may have a problem making her give Lucky up when we get back."

Kendra Lee, their second-best rafting guide, walked in the room. She stopped and put a hand on a jutted-out hip, her eyes twinkling and a smile splitting her cocoa-colored face. "The first clients have arrived. Can you keep your hands off each other long enough to check them in?"

Rob released Mandy and yanked her blonde ponytail. "Got your happy face on?"

Mandy flashed him a bright, perky smile. "Yes, now that I've realized your mom won't be able to reach me for five whole days. In a way I'm glad there's no cell phone service on the river and we can only radio out from a few locations. I'm sure your mom doesn't like it, but I'm really looking forward to a break in wedding planning."

Rob glanced at the radio transceivers. "Since the radio is really just for emergencies, hopefully we won't have to make *any* calls on it."

———

Mandy stepped into the front room of the building with Rob, leaving Kendra in the back room to deal with packing the food. They were borrowing the building of a Moab-based outfitter that had closed up shop in the middle of September. Mandy and Rob's own business, RM Outdoor Adventures, was based in Salida, Colorado. The 'RM' stood for both 'Rocky Mountains' and 'Rob and Mandy.' Along with renting the other outfitter's building to check in clients and gear, they were able to run their trip under the company's Utah rafting license because they had hired their expert climbing guide to come along.

Like most of those who worked in the adventure travel field, Mandy and Rob juggled multiple jobs. Besides their joint business, Mandy worked as a seasonal river ranger on the Arkansas River in the summer and as a ski patroller at Monarch Mountain in the winter. Rob stitched together a patchwork of construction and carpentry jobs during the off-seasons. And he was extending their out-fitting business into the shoulder spring and fall seasons by adding fly-fishing, horseback riding, and other trips that were not dependent on Colorado's summer snow melt that kept its whitewater rivers gushing.

This climbing and rafting trip was one of those experiments. It was taking place during early October when most of the outfitters had already shuttered their doors. Mandy flashed Rob a crossed-fingers-for-good-luck sign behind her back as the two of them stepped up to the counter. Hopefully the experiment would work.

Two women stood at the other side of the counter. They both had tightly curled hair, though the younger one's was a lighter brown and longer than the older one's, skimming her shoulders. Their similar heart-shaped faces and features showed they were related. Probably mother and daughter, Mandy surmised. The older woman's leathery skin and smattering of wrinkles and sun spots indicated she was a middle-aged outdoorswoman. Contrary to expectation, the daughter wore a loose T-shirt, and the mother's V-necked stretch top clung to her curves and showed some cleavage.

"Hello, ladies." Rob held out a hand. "I presume you're here for our Cataract Canyon rafting and climbing trip."

The older woman shook his hand and eyed him up and down. "I must say I'm looking forward to the scenery." She shot an amused grin at her daughter, who rolled her eyes.

Mandy bristled, but Rob just smiled and said, "I'm Rob Juarez and this is my partner and fiancée, Mandy Tanner. We'll be your lead guides on the trip."

As Mandy shook the women's hands, she thought, *thank goodness he likes using that word fiancée so much.* She bet he couldn't wait until they were married and he started calling her his wife. Her independent streak had not quite reconciled itself to that term, but she had to admit that she savored the thought of staking her own claim on Rob by calling him her husband.

The women introduced themselves as Elsa Norton, the mother, and Tina Norton, the daughter. Mandy remembered that Tina, a college junior majoring in elementary education at the University of Wyoming, had booked the trip. She had been a little worried about missing classes for it.

"I remember taking your call," Mandy said to Tina. "Were your professors okay with you taking this trip?"

Tina nodded. "It worked out great. I'm only missing three classes and a lab, and I can make the lab up after I get back on Friday."

"As a professor at the university myself," Elsa added, "I was ready to jump in and make some calls for Tina if I had to. Missing one or two classes is nothing compared to the experiences this trip will allow her to share with her future students."

Rob cocked his head as he slid release forms into two clipboards. "What do you teach?"

"Geology," Elsa replied.

"You'll find plenty of interesting formations in the canyonlands." Mandy checked the trip roster. "We have three of you signed up. Where's—?"

"Three?" Elsa raised an eyebrow at Tina.

Tina fidgeted, glanced at the clock on the wall, then back at her mother. "I told you I wanted this to be a family trip, since I'll be busy student-teaching soon and I don't know when we'll have the time later on."

"Family? Who else did you invite? Your cousin Kathy?"

"No." Tina rubbed her hands on her jeans, took a deep breath, and faced her mother. "Dad."

Elsa's eyes bugged out. "Your father? You invited Paul on this trip? When were you going to tell me?"

Mandy turned to Rob, and a meaningful glance flashed between them. *Trouble.*

Tina's chin quivered. "I kept trying to bring it up, but I could never find the right time. I figured it would all work out once he appeared." She burrowed her head down into her shoulders like a frightened turtle.

Elsa finally seemed to realize that Rob and Mandy were watching the argument. She turned to them. "Tina's father and I have been divorced for a year. For good reason." She glared at Tina. "How could you do this to me? To him? Do you know how miserable the two of us will be?"

Mandy nudged Rob and pointed at the trip roster, which also listed tent assignments. They had allocated two 4-man tents and five 2-man tents to the trip, thinking the two families would occupy the larger tents. The Nortons were one of those families.

A man walked into the room. He was of medium-height and medium-build with graying mousey-brown hair and bifocal glasses. He blinked as his eyes adjusted to the lack of sunshine. Mandy was struck with the thought that mousey was an appropriate description for the whole man—his nondescript clothing, pallid skin, a withdrawn demeanor, and thin-fingered hands all fit. All he lacked were twitching long whiskers on his clean-shaven cheeks.

Then a smile lit up his face. "Tina!" He held out his arms.

"Dad!" Tina ran into his embrace.

Elsa Norton crossed her arms, murder in her gaze.

Paul Norton glanced at his ex-wife, then at Tina. "When did you tell her I was coming?"

Tina cringed. "Just now."

"Cripes." Paul looked up at the ceiling, then squared his shoulders and walked toward the counter, Tina tucked under one shoulder.

He stopped in front of Elsa. "I'm sorry. I thought you knew and were okay with this."

"No, I'm not okay with this," Elsa said between clenched teeth. "But I can't back out now. I've already taken the leave and arranged for a sub. And I'm sure these good people aren't going to give me a refund at this late date." She swept a hand in Mandy's and Rob's direction.

Paul touched her shoulder, but when she flinched, he quickly removed his hand. "For Tina's sake, we can make this work. We've already done enough arguing for a lifetime. Let's just try to have a fun vacation."

Elsa glanced at Tina, who looked hopefully from her father to her mother. Elsa exhaled, unclenched her arms, and held up her hands. "For Tina's sake, I'll try to be civil, but I'm not sharing a raft with you—or a tent either." She raised an eyebrow at Mandy.

Mandy took her cue. "We'll put you and your daughter in a 2-man tent and Mister Norton in another 2-man tent." How she was going to reshuffle the other tent assignments, she had no idea.

Elsa nodded. "Good."

"It's probably best for me to be in my own tent, anyway," Paul said, "because I snore like the dickens."

"Does he!" Elsa rolled her eyes. "I had to wear earplugs to bed when we were married."

Paul's assumption he would have a tent to himself was a leap. The trip instructions had explicitly said that all tents would be shared because of the tight space on the rafts. But Mandy decided to wait until she had juggled tent assignments before she said anything to him. Maybe she really could put him by himself and spare some some other guy a bunch of sleepless nights.

Paul sniffed. "The snoring's probably related to my allergies. So, I should pitch my tent away from the others each night."

"We'll keep that in mind when we arrange the campsites," Rob said glibly.

As Rob went over the release forms and packing lists with the Nortons, Mandy scanned the roster and tried to think. Besides the Nortons, there was the six-person Anderson family, parents and three grown children—one of whom was married, and three women from different parts of California. She had allocated a 4-man and a 2-man tent to the Anderson family and had assigned 2-man tents to herself and Rob and Gonzo and the climbing guide. She would now have to put Kendra and the three women clients in what would have been the Norton family's 4-man tent. Could the four strangers all get along?

Mandy and Rob said their goodbyes to the Nortons after inviting them to join them for a pre-trip meet-and-greet dinner at Milt's Stop & Eat. The local burger and shakes joint had been recommended to them by the owner of the building they were using. He had told Rob that it set a 'tone of informality' for clients and helped them to start shedding their business-suit personalities prior to getting on the river.

Just as Mandy was going to fill Rob in on the tent shuffle, three women walked in, giggling and chatting with each other. They all looked to be in their thirties and were a variety of races—white, Hispanic, and black. They stepped up to the counter, and after a few more snippets of chattering, turned as a group and looked expectantly at Rob and Mandy.

"Hi, gals," Rob said. "Here to check in for the Cataract Canyon rafting and climbing trip?"

© NEIL GROUNDWATER

Beth Groundwater was an avid "river rat" in the 1980s, running whitewater rivers in the eastern United States in an open-boat canoe. She has enjoyed reacquainting herself with that subculture and its updated boating equipment while researching the RM Adventures mystery series. Beth lives in Colorado and enjoys its many outdoor activities, including skiing and whitewater rafting. She loves to speak to book clubs about her books. To find out more, please visit Beth's website at bethgroundwater.com and her blog at bethgroundwater.blogspot.com.